"Time to turn you to scrap, you shithead!!"

Academy City's strongest Level Five **Accelerator**

"Prayer will reach.
It will save people.
I'm a nun, and that's
how I've spread the
teachings!"

Nun managing the Index of
Prohibited Books **Index**

"Oh my. Were the mortal sinners busy licking one another's wounds?"

Member of Roman Orthodox secret organization God's Right Seat **Vento of the Front**

"Ah!...
ah...says
Misaka...
says..."

Sisters
serial
number
20001
Last
Order

"......"

Girl created
from AIM
diffusion fields
Hyouka Kazakiri

"...I won't let you. What do you take people's friends for?!"

Academy City Level Zero
Touma Kamijou

"That was so cool!!
Now that you're
showing your true
colors, I think I'm in
love, Accelerator!!"

Academy City scientist and Hound
Dogs leader **Amata Kihara**

A Certain Magical Index

VOLUME 13

KAZUMA KAMACHI

ILLUSTRATION BY: KIYOTAKA HAIMURA

NEW YORK

A CERTAIN MAGICAL INDEX, Volume 13
KAZUMA KAMACHI

Translation by Andrew Prowse
Cover art by Kiyotaka Haimura

TOARU MAJYUTSU NO INDEX
©KAZUMA KAMACHI 2007
All rights reserved.
Edited by ASCII MEDIA WORKS
First published in Japan in 2007 by KADOKAWA CORPORATION, Tokyo.
English translation rights arranged with KADOKAWA CORPORATION, Tokyo,
through Tuttle-Mori Agency, Inc., Tokyo.

English translation © 2017 by Yen Press, LLC

Yen On
1290 Avenue of the Americas
New York, NY 10104

Visit us at yenpress.com
facebook.com/yenpress
twitter.com/yenpress
yenpress.tumblr.com
instagram.com/yenpress

First Yen On Edition: November 2017

Yen On is an imprint of Yen Press, LLC.
The Yen On name and logo are trademarks of Yen Press, LLC.

Library of Congress Cataloging-in-Publication Data

Names: Kamachi, Kazuma, author. | Haimura, Kiyotaka, 1973– illustrator. | Prowse, Andrew (Andrew R.), translator. | Hinton, Yoshito, translator.
Title: A certain magical index / Kazuma Kamachi ; illustration by Kiyotaka Haimura.
Other titles: To aru majyutsu no kinsho mokuroku. (Light novel). English
Description: First Yen On edition. | New York : Yen On, 2014–
Identifiers: LCCN 2014031047 (print) | ISBN 9780316339124 (v. 1 : pbk.) |
 ISBN 9780316259422 (v. 2 : pbk.) | ISBN 9780316340540 (v. 3 : pbk.) |
 ISBN 9780316340564 (v. 4 : pbk.) | ISBN 9780316340595 (v. 5 : pbk.) |
 ISBN 9780316340601 (v. 6 : pbk.) | ISBN 9780316272230 (v. 7 : pbk.) |
 ISBN 9780316359924 (v. 8 : pbk.) | ISBN 9780316359962 (v. 9 : pbk.) |
 ISBN 9780316359986 (v. 10: pbk.) | ISBN 9780316360005 (v. 11: pbk.) |
 ISBN 9780316360029 (v. 12: pbk.) | ISBN 9780316442671 (v. 13: pbk.)
Subjects: | CYAC: Magic—Fiction. | Ability—Fiction. | Nuns—Fiction. | Japan—Fiction. | Science fiction. | BISAC: FICTION / Fantasy / General. | FICTION / Science Fiction / Adventure.
Classification: LCC PZ7.1.K215 Ce 2014 | DDC [Fic]—dc23
LC record available at https://lccn.loc.gov/2014031047

ISBNs: 978-0-316-44267-1 (paperback)
 978-0-316-44268-8 (ebook)

1 3 5 7 9 10 8 6 4 2

LSC-C

Printed in the United States of America

CHAPTER 6

A City Stricken by Cold Rain

Battle_Preparation.

1

September 30, 6:33 PM.

One of the God's Right Seat, Vento of the Front, has physically broken through Academy City's Gate 3.

An attack of unknown origin begins at the same time, which harms Anti-Skill and Judgment, tasked with maintaining public order.

With security short of hands, Vento kills three members of the General Board.

The same day, 7:02 PM.

In order to stop Vento, the Academy City General Board's chairperson, Aleister, decides to use the incomplete Imaginary Number School District, the Five Elements Society.

In the rainy night streets, the Hound Dogs, led by Amata Kihara, mobilize.

Their goal is the retrieval of Serial Number 20001, Last Order.

Judging Accelerator to be a threat, Amata Kihara personally launches an assault on him and succeeds.

His attack almost perfectly neutralizes the one called Academy City's strongest Level Five.

However, this is where the Hound Dogs make one small mistake.

"Help..."

They let one girl slip out of their clutches.
And...

"I'm begging you, save him! pleads Misaka pleads Misaka!!"

...her voice reaches the ears of a certain young man.

2

"What are you doing over there?"
The downpour was growing stronger.
Amid the pouring raindrops that resounded through the dark night streets, a girl's voice cut across the ground, filling the ears of the Hound Dogs, Amata Kihara, and Accelerator, who lay on the soaked road.
Her white habit stood out against the black of night.
Index.
She was a slender girl, and even bulky clothing couldn't conceal her small build. Her individual features, like her waist-length silver hair and her large eyes of shimmering green, gave off the impression of a delicate work of art, one that might break if you touched it. She even held a small calico in her arms.
This is the worst..., thought Accelerator as he lay there.
"Sticking out like a sore thumb" didn't begin to cover it. This wasn't the opportunity he needed—it was another difficulty. She wouldn't stand a chance against delinquents in a back alley, much less against Hound Dogs with her dainty arms.
In fact, Kihara was frowning, too.
He hadn't given an ounce of analysis or consideration to new forces appearing. The look on his face was like he'd just seen a baby

bird waddle up to the pitcher's mound in the middle of a baseball game, and that was all.

If he gave the order, the nun would be mincemeat in seconds. Their submachine guns had enough punch to riddle a car door full of holes. Anyone could tell how it would affect such soft human skin and muscle.

What path should I choose? Abandon her? Save her? Or maybe... use this...?

Accelerator thought of the electrode choker around his neck.

He should still be able to use his ability.

Unfortunately, the wounds carved all over his body refused to let him move.

"What should we do, sir?" whispered one of the men in black into Kihara's ear while they formed a perimeter.

Amata Kihara heaved a pained sigh. "What do you mean, 'what'?" Then he simply said, "We have to get rid of her."

Shit!! Accelerator swore to himself.

This "Index" person had witnessed the Hound Dogs in action. Not only that—the organization was an unofficial spy group whose very existence was a secret. That obviously meant they had to keep people quiet. Even if she ran away now, they'd chase her to the ends of the earth. She probably wouldn't last three days.

Doesn't matter if I stay quiet. They're still gonna kill me. Let's get on with this, you bastards!!

The thought of Amata Kihara in tears, rather than saving Index, returned the explosive power back to Accelerator's mind.

I don't give a shit about that sister, but I'm not gonna be happy getting beaten up like this. It's your turn to grind your teeth, Kiharaaa!!

The switch for the electrode choker on his neck had been on since a while ago.

His ability would activate at a simple command.

To do that, he checked everyone's positioning.

Three black minivans were parked around him at a radius of less than ten meters. About twenty of the Hound Dogs stood around, all in black. The biggest problem, Amata Kihara, was directly next to him, but he was essentially impossible to attack. Accelerator's defensive "reflection" couldn't ward off Kihara's blows, and if he tried to change wind vectors to make a burst of air, the man would use his special sound wave to mess the vectors up and neutralize the attempt.

And…

Index was standing outside the ring of minivans, about fifteen meters away.

Wiping 'em out will have to wait.

Still facedown on the road, he touched the wet asphalt with his fingertips.

He checked how it felt through his fingers.

There's only one thing I need to do now. Get out of here to somewhere safe. And take that sister with me!!

His red pupils dilated and contracted.

His ability activated.

"Whooaaahhhhh!!" he screamed, pushing down with the toes of one foot, still on the ground, launching himself as hard as he could. As he did, he changed vectors. His body exploded off the asphalt like a rocket, set on a collision course with the rear sliding door of one black minivan.

The metal door came off its rails like a wrecking ball had hit it and flew farther into the vehicle. His body came to a stop in the backseat.

"?!"

Before the black-suit waiting in the driver's seat could react, Accelerator reached for the door he'd blown inward and tore off the metal fixture that let it slide. Gripping the iron scrap stick, notched and sharpened, about five centimeters wide and twenty long, he shoved it straight through the middle of the driver's seat.

Squelch. The response he got was less a sound and more a tactile sensation.

"I—— Agh!!" The man, now nailed to the driver's seat, tried to groan but barely got anything out.

Accelerator spoke to him. "Drive."

Then, without mercy…

…he told him the simple truth.

"You'll die in thirty minutes. If you don't get to a hospital right now, it'll be too late."

The man could probably tell from the immense pain that he couldn't treat his wounds with only a first aid kit. And besides, he must have known firsthand how Amata Kihara treated injured subordinates who got in his way.

The driver managed a yelp and made his decision quickly. With a high-pitched engine roar, the black minivan took off as if in a bout of hysterics. The black-suits in the road scattered, jumping out of the way to either side.

Kihara yelled something, his face bitter, while they broke through the perimeter. He knew the men behind them were now leveling their guns at him, one after another.

Looking over the driver's shoulder out the front windshield, Accelerator found where Index was.

"A little to the left!!" he shouted, flinging the useless sliding door through the gaping hole in the back and leaning out himself. The sister in white was standing there confused in the middle of the road as the car approached.

"Shit!!"

He reached out of the vehicle with a hand.

Index held a cat in both arms. She'd have to use one of them to grab him, but she might not be able to reach even if he stretched out as far as he could.

He reached for her anyway.

Bang!! came a gunshot.

The bullet scraped his face, but Accelerator ignored it and grabbed Index's arm. Then he altered vectors and reeled her inside the vehicle, slamming her into it.

"W-waaah!!" Index let out an out-of-place squeal.

Accelerator positioned himself so he'd be hidden behind the driver's seat. He also tapped the sharp metal weapon stuck in the seat with a fingertip.

"Urgh?!" The man in the driver's seat lurched.

Then, so Index wouldn't hear, Accelerator whispered into the man's ear. "...Don't make noise. Just go straight. We're both out of time, right?"

"Wh-where to today, sir...?"

"I know a good doctor," answered Accelerator, not sounding very interested. "No normal doctor's gonna fix this. If you wanna see him, you'd better work hard, Mr. Driver."

3

"Ahh, ahh, ahh, ahh..."

Amata Kihara let out a series of frustrated groans as he watched the black minivan get smaller and smaller in the distance.

He held out his right hand. "Ahh, ahh, ahh, ahh! Bring it here! You know the thing—bring it!!"

It was an utterly unreasonable way to make a request, but his subordinates responded obediently. With swift motions, one took a portable anti-tank missile launcher out of the remaining minivan and handed it to Kihara.

He was still lazily yelling at them to be quick about it and punched the man who brought it. Then he rapidly assembled and prepped the weapon, unlocking its safety with the precision and agility of a professional typist.

No hesitation clouded his movements. In fact, the Hound Dogs were the ones who had lost some presence of mind.

"Wh-what about the driver, sir?!"

"Who the fuck cares?! Deserters get killed on the spot! So long, little doggy, I won't ever forget you for at least two seconds!!"

Clack! Kihara hoisted the weapon, one meter long and thirty centimeters thick, onto his shoulder and stared down the sight on its side.

He took aim. He put his finger on the tracking missile's trigger.

The minivan had traveled a few dozen meters and was about to turn a corner in the road. Kihara smiled. He'd make it. That thing could take the turn perfectly, and the missile would still follow the car diagonally and strike the wall of the building on the corner, showering the minivan with a storm of concrete fragments that would flip it over.

Accelerator probably wouldn't die, but he'd certainly lose his means of escape. Then Kihara would just have to cook him real nice, along with the other two injured people.

You're soft, Accelerator! Using a car is like telling the whole world you can't do your delicate wind control anymore!!

"See ya, shithead! Time to burn that white skin of yours to a crisp!!"

With a crazed grin, Amata Kihara almost pulled the trigger.

But…

"?"

The scope aim suddenly went all yellow.

Thinking something in the distance was blocking his view, he took his eye from the scope to see a strange woman standing just ten or so meters away from him.

Cold raindrops slapped the road. No other vehicles or pedestrians were on the main street. In the midst of the traffic lights and pure white glimmers from building windows reflected on the wet road surface, she stood there alone.

He hadn't noticed her until now.

All the piercings on her face made her come off as asymmetrical. She had on heavy makeup to stress her eyes. With a face like that, she clearly didn't care what other people thought of it. She wore a one-piece dress mainly in yellow, but it seemed somehow old, aged. Like she was right out of the European Middle Ages.

None of that mattered to Kihara. More importantly, this idiot woman had distracted him, and now the minivan had disappeared around the bend.

"…" All trace of emotion vanished from his face.

With what could have been called an absentminded expression, he casually pulled the trigger.

The anti-tank missile launched.

The spray of smoke shot in a straight line, driving right into the middle of the obstructing woman's chest. Before he could see her face distort, the shell exploded, throwing a shock wave and a blast of heat around the point of contact.

Slam!! A roar shook the asphalt. It blew away the entire layer of rainwater sitting on the wide road surface and rattled signboards of nearby buildings. Leaves were knocked off their branches from trees lining the roadside and danced through the air.

Because of their close proximity to the blast, the black-suits near Kihara were flung away.

Red flames and black smoke hung like cotton candy, blocking his view.

However…

After a mere five seconds…

Shwooo!! A violent wind blew it all away.

The flames and smoke vanished without a trace, thanks to a new storm, brewing at the center of the explosion. In the middle of the scorching, breaking, scattering asphalt was the woman, still standing as she had been before. Neither her clothing nor a single strand of hair showed signs of damage or burns.

"Nice city," said the woman in yellow suddenly.

She didn't bother to look at Amata Kihara.

"I thought the 'corrosion' would be progressing more quickly, but that's not the case. Isn't it against the rules to have most of the people here be teachers and students? Guess it's only natural the speed of my corrosion would slow down against people like them. Still…" The woman, pierced in many places, looked at Kihara. "Unlike them, you all seem exceptionally guiltier."

Kihara decided to finally open his mouth. "Who are you?"

"A business rival. In murder." The woman turned to look at the street corner where the minivan had vanished. "My target was in

there, too. Doesn't really matter who does the killing, but I don't feel like letting someone else take the credit."

Kihara sighed. The situation was absurd. "Kill her."

The instant he gave the order, the entire team of men readied their weapons.

But...

"You don't want to do that."

...none of them could pull the trigger.

Right before they went to fire, every Hound Dog groaned and fell to the ground—without any resistance. The attack was so smooth it seemed like even the woman would think something was off.

Some fell on the rain-soaked road, of course, and others collapsed directly on top of the remains of the minivan Accelerator had destroyed. And yet none of them so much as twitched. The battle group was completely neutralized.

What the hell just happened? Kihara tapped on the missile launcher's barrel thoughtfully.

Nobody present would have known, but the woman, at least, seemed quite confident in this power of hers. Her face remained steady despite being one step away from getting riddled with holes.

Then she made a bored expression. "Didn't hesitate at all to tell them to kill me, eh? *You long to murder, but you have no hostility.* You don't think of your enemies as enemies. You don't even possess guilt in the first place. Maybe for you, killing is like pulling weeds. First time, this time—it doesn't matter. Your personality is truly rotten. Almost as much as mine, in fact."

Kihara didn't engage her.

Instead, he turned to one of the black-clad men nearby and waved his hand in annoyance. "Split the team in two." He tossed away the expended anti-tank missile launcher. "Round up the ten most useless bastards and have them hold her off. I'll be moving to the 'villa.' Got it?"

It was a vague order, but his subordinates knew they'd suddenly find bullets inside their bodies if they didn't obey. Besides, it was a fact that Kihara was the only one who could get rid of Accelerator.

The suspicious woman, Amata Kihara, and Accelerator—they tried to gauge who was the most terrifying and decided the woman would be the least trouble, despite being creepy.

After delivering his orders, Kihara immediately boarded a minivan.

The woman spoke behind him. "You have no enmity, do you?"

"If you want some of that from me, get a little stronger."

That's all Kihara said before punching the back of the driver's head, making him drive off.

Only the woman and Kihara's stool pigeons were left behind.

"...Well, I would love to know who that was, but I'm sure he'll kick the bucket before I can ask. Lord knows I'm not cut out for information gathering. And I can't kill too many here, either."

The woman cracked her neck and stuck out her tongue. A chain fell out of her mouth with a jingle.

"Anyway...He really underestimated me. I wonder if the lot of you can be useful."

4

Touma Kamijou and Last Order stood still.

Neither had an umbrella. Both Kamijou, wearing a red T-shirt under his long black jacket with a stand-up collar, and Last Order, wearing a men's button-down over a blue dress, were soaking wet. The electronic goggles on her forehead were drenched, too, but they were military-grade, so maybe it wasn't actually a problem.

The small girl had led him to a big corner in the road not too far from the underground mall's exit. Because trains and buses had stopped around the time when the few remaining still-open schools locked up, no one else could be seen on the darkened street.

At least, normal people, ones who stood on two legs.

"..."

Several people were on the ground, collapsed.

Each person was dressed all in black, sinking into puddles as the streaks of rain grew stronger underneath the night sky. The streetlights reflected off their synthetic combat gear, and a thin layer of rain coated their sinister submachine guns. With their heads covered by helmets and highly elastic masks, they were clearly not ordinary people.

He heard a crackling noise—the popping sound of a fire.

Just a few meters from where the men were lying was a crumpled, crushed minivan. That was the firewood. The vehicle had broken through the guardrail and stopped in the middle of the sidewalk—that's how he wanted to describe it. In fact, the minivan had lost so much of its original form it almost looked like it had exploded. No other cars were nearby. Maybe that meant it belonged to the fallen people here.

Last Order pointed to one of them.

Face white, she said, "These people attacked him, says Misaka says Misaka, telling the truth." She repeated, "It's true!"

Kamijou looked at the men on the ground again. *They're...not Anti-Skill?*

Their consistent black combat uniforms almost fooled him, but upon closer inspection...he sensed a difference between their equipment and normal Anti-Skill gear. They definitely didn't seem like they were from some kind of military, but he wasn't knowledgeable enough to figure out everything like model numbers at a glance, so he couldn't be sure.

But if they're not Anti-Skill, then who are they? These guys might have stuff even more advanced, and a bunch of them came attacking...? Plus, the assailants in question were the ones flopped on the ground.

Kamijou grasped the situation. He looked at Last Order. "The one who was attacked here—it was someone you knew, right?"

"That's right, answers Misaka answers Misaka."

"Does this mean he turned the tables on them...?"

"Maybe not, says Misaka says Misaka, shaking her head. He's impatient and has a short temper, so I can't imagine he would stop after only doing this much, considering everything they did to him, says Misaka says Misaka, giving a simple guess."

What the hell is this guy like, anyway? Kamijou quipped to himself. But...

"..."

Espers weren't invincible.

He didn't know what sort of ability Last Order's friend had, but barring something irregular like the Level Five Railgun, he shouldn't have been able to turn the tables on a trained group wielding firearms. It didn't mean much coming from a Level Zero like Kamijou, but espers were still essentially students. Their powers were only strong enough to work in school, and nobody could object to that idea.

Drop one in a battlefield like this and they'd be helpless. If they were quick on their feet then maybe they could manage...but without the time to even think in the first place, that wouldn't do them any good, either. Regular students couldn't steel their resolves like that and fight.

Most would die.

Anyway, I've gotta report this...

It wasn't clear whether Last Order's acquaintance had been caught or had escaped. Regardless, it didn't change the fact that the situation demanded haste. Thinking it best to be upfront and ask for Anti-Skill's help, Kamijou pulled his cell phone out of his pocket.

However...

"...?" Right before he pressed the button, he looked back up.

...Wait...Why hasn't anyone reported this...?

He examined the situation in front of him. A minivan, crushed and broken. An open fire, which had been burning for a short while but whose great light still showed no signs of dying down. With all this happening, *someone* must have heard. Even from afar, they could have seen a fire breaking out. He'd think he wouldn't need to use his phone, and that normally, someone would have already reported this. But there weren't even any curious onlookers.

"..."

Kamijou looked around.

The city, its lights off. The incredibly quiet scene. The lack of an uproar.

What if…?

What if it wasn't that no one made a commotion, but that they *couldn't*?

What if all the people inside those buildings had collapsed like those Anti-Skill officers had earlier?

What if…?

Was it an attack by humans? Or an unintended phenomenon?

Not even that was clear. The emergency situation was perfectly keeping itself secret.

The scariest thing wasn't the silence—it was the fact that by the time Kamijou noticed the problem, Academy City's functions had already shut down, like termites chewing their way through a log.

It was almost like nodding off in the middle of a final exam, then waking up when the examiner announced there were only ten minutes left. And with that blank sheet of paper before his eyes, the boy broke out into a full, greasy sweat.

What the hell is going on in this city?

As he stood there, unable to move, he saw something else stir.

Last Order was crouched by one of the fallen men, tampering with his equipment. Suddenly, her eyes darted upward as though she realized something, and she urgently ran to Kamijou.

Then, grabbing his hand with her cold, rain-soaked one, she started to pull him after her. She looked like a kid trying to drag her parent to the toy section of a department store. "Quick, says Misaka says Misaka, urging caution!" Her voice, though, was bizarrely tense. "They're here, reports Misaka reports Misaka as she goes to hide in an alley!"

Pulled along by Last Order, Kamijou hid himself behind a car parked on the road nearby with a frown, wondering who "they" were.

There was a giant puddle around the car, making him wonder if leaves had gotten stuck in a nearby gutter. One step in and he was wet up to his socks.

He didn't have time to complain, though.

The low sound of an engine rumbling became audible.

A strange black minivan approached with its headlights off.

The soft sound of its exhaust like stealthy footsteps, it parked by the downed men wearing black. The rear sliding door opened, and a handful of people with similar gear poured out. Close to ten, at a glance. With those numbers, Kamijou couldn't win even if they were unarmed.

On top of that...

"...Damn," he muttered. "Where'd they get so many guns, anyway?"

The newcomers all had their own submachine gun hanging from a shoulder strap. They also seemed like they were equipped with pistols, grenades, and everything else.

They didn't feel like Anti-Skill officers protecting the peace of Academy City.

Didn't look too friendly, either.

In fact, Kamijou could feel the tension from where he stood—if they spotted him and Last Order hiding, he was pretty sure they'd open fire immediately.

He spared a glance toward his right hand.

The power residing within, Imagine Breaker, could easily stop even the Level Five Railgun. On the other hand, bullets were totally unrelated to supernatural abilities. His ability wouldn't accomplish anything against mundane firearms.

The men in black hefted their (probable) colleagues from the road and threw them violently into the minivan. Aside from that work going on, there was some other activity—a man with a clear cylindrical vessel on his back, which was about the size of three full-size soda bottles tied together end to end. On the bottom, there was a nozzle, and the man held it like a flamethrower.

"It's the Purge, says Misaka says Misaka, calling it by its nickname."

"What's that?"

"An acid spray...It disperses a special, weak acid that starts destroying things like fingerprints and the DNA information in bloodstains, says Misaka says Misaka, consulting info in the manual for destroying evidence."

"..." *That's bad*, he thought.

Their group thought that covering things up was important enough to bring out such major equipment. If guys like that were somehow, by chance, spotted, it didn't take much imagination to see what they'd do.

In conclusion…

If it goes that far, I'm pretty sure I won't be able to run away.

He gulped.

A soft *splash* rang in his ears.

"…"

Kamijou looked at his feet.

It was a big pond of water, possibly from a clogged gutter. And his foot, steeped in it, was trembling. The trembling had created small ripples in the surface, passed through the car shielding them…and to the other side.

But there was no way they'd notice something so small.

Pouring raindrops were hitting the puddle, too. Even if you looked really hard, you couldn't see what the puddle was like in the dark. *Which means I'm fine*, he thought, almost praying to himself.

Fwip.

The nearby men in black all turned to look in his direction.

5

They drove about ten minutes after that.

Ten minutes in a car was a "decent" distance, or so Accelerator thought. But it was still only "decent." Though not probable, if Kihara's team were openly tracing his escape route using a satellite or something, they'd catch up very quickly.

The man sitting in the driver's seat in front of Accelerator, impaled through the back and trembling, spoke in a low, hoarse voice.

"(…A-are we still driving? Ha-ha, you have to be joking. I'm actually gonna die at this—)"

"(…Shut up. You don't stop until I tell you to, got it?)" Accelerator whispered back, fingering the metal weapon piercing the driver's seat. The man's body lurched, and a moan echoed through the vehicle.

Index, hearing something, looked up a little. "What's wrong?"

"Nothing. Right?" said Accelerator, leaning on the driver's seat and hiding the weapon he held. "Still, though…," he muttered in spite of himself.

This minivan didn't have a sliding door. It was suspicious, practically screaming "I'm a stolen vehicle, I'm sorry." One would think driving it through the streets would cause a situation with Anti-Skill, but there didn't seem to be any of them around. If things went well, contacting Yomikawa might save the effort, but to Accelerator that felt rather anticlimactic.

Don't tell me this silence *is another part of the play that shithead thought up…*

Right now, Accelerator had his electrode choker back in normal mode. It was purely to save battery power. In the first place, it couldn't last more than fifteen minutes after activating ability usage mode. He had already used up quite a bit of time during his fight with Kihara, and performing normal activities still drained it, little by little.

Considering how much he had left, he couldn't fight more than seven minutes at full power.

He wasn't even using the bare minimum of "reflection" right now, of course. He needed to save the battery to fight Kihara and his Hounds. But if they shot a missile or something at the minivan before Accelerator noticed, it would be over.

That was why he was scrutinizing the nighttime streets as they streamed by the missing door, but…

"Oh, I found *The Ugly Duckling*!"

…right next to Accelerator, a sister all in white, whose worldview didn't exactly conform to his, was rummaging around in the stolen minivan's backseat.

Its original owner probably had a child—Index pulled out a children's picture book made with hard, thick pages. The calico sitting on her lap, its hunting instincts perhaps provoked by the sight of the deformed duck on the cover, was trying to edge away, gauging the distance.

What's wrong with this bookworm? Never seen someone's eyes light up like that for a book... "Really not caring about this, are you? Anyway, why the hell were you over there, anyway?"

"Huh? I came to return what I borrowed." Index reached her hand into her habit sleeve and fished around. "Look, a cutting-edge daily necessity! You can't leave something so important with me forever! I'm sure you were worried, but don't be, because it'll all be okay now!!"

"Are you a moron?! Why would I want these disposable and crumpled-up used tissues?! You giving them back is what's making me worried!!"

"Wait, really?" said Index, once again pushing the plastic packet of tissues toward him with her small hands.

It didn't look like this would end until he accepted. Growing exasperated, he snatched them away from Index, then thrust them into his pants pocket with a lack of seriousness.

"By the way, are your wounds all right?"

"Huh?"

"You know, your wounds. You were collapsed earlier—"

"They're nothing. And if you bring it up one more time, I might go wild again."

Index was completely unaware of the driver beginning to quake. As though reassured by Accelerator's back talk, she redirected her attention to the book in her hands.

"Hmm, hmm. So this is how you can translate it into Japanese." She must have already known what the fairy tale was about, because she rapidly flipped through the pages, stopping on only the last one to read it. "And the ugly duckling, whom all the others called no good, was actually a super-hot swan. The end...What do they mean by 'super-hot'?"

"They mean a life-form that's the exact opposite of you."

"Huh." Index shut the book. "...The story was about how the swan was always going to win, ever since it was born."

"That's not what *The Ugly Duckling* is about."

"Then what's it about? There are countless ways to interpret fairy tales, so it's hard for me to figure them out."

"What? Uh, yeah, what was it? According to that stupid brat, 'the swan wanted to be friends with the ducks, but then after it was shown the truth that it would never really be part of them, it was truly happy.'" Accelerator spat. He couldn't handle brats—terribly uncute opinions flew out of their mouths too frequently.

He started hearing more annoying moans from the driver's seat, so he jostled the steel bar stuck in the seat a little to shut him up.

Index still didn't seem to notice. She looked up from her book and asked, "By 'brat,' do you mean the lost child you were searching for?"

"Yeah. Actually, I'm *still* looking for her."

"You got separated again?"

Accelerator paused. "Yeah, that's right," he confirmed. "I've gotta look for her after this. It's annoying, but I don't think she can make it back on her own. Which means we need to say good-bye for now."

"I can help." Index's reply was immediate—never for a moment taking her gaze off Accelerator's red eyes. "I can tell you're worried, too. If Touma was the one here, I think he'd say the same thing."

"Hmph." He looked away in mild anger and spoke to the driver. "Pull over."

Obeying Accelerator, who literally held his life in his hand, the man pulled the car over to the shoulder.

Accelerator looked at Index. "Help me out."

"Okay. What should I do?"

"There's a huge hospital nearby. About five to ten minutes of walking. Go there and find a doctor with a face like a frog. When you see him…" Accelerator paused, then rubbed his neck. "Tell him to get a Misaka network connection electrode battery. He'll know what you mean. The battery's really important. Without that I can't look for the brat. Once you have one, run back here fast. Got it?"

"Got it. A 'Misaka network connection electrode battery.'" She repeated it perfectly. Of course, she probably didn't know what that meant. But before Accelerator had time to consider that she was surprisingly smart, Index had taken the cat and exited onto the rainy street without hesitation.

"Wait for me."

"Huh?"

"You have to wait here for me until I get back, okay?"

"…Right," answered Accelerator. "Just get going already."

Index turned back a few times but eventually ran away, feet splashing through puddles as she went. Her slight back vanished into the dark.

"Piece of shit," he spat, sitting back into his seat.

The hospital wouldn't have a spare. The electrode collar he wore was a prototype to begin with. The battery was special, too, not a mass-produced one. If it were, he'd have packed his pockets full of batteries.

It was a simple lie.

Everything, save for the part about going to find the frog-faced doctor.

That girl would be in danger no matter where she went, but being alone would be the worst. If he wanted to raise her probability of survival even a little, she needed to reach a place with people around. Accelerator was still uneasy sending her to the frog-faced doctor, but it was better than doing nothing.

The thing about to start, in simple terms, was a battle over Last Order between him and Amata Kihara, along with his Hound Dogs. Accelerator already lacked combat potential with only seven minutes of full-power fighting remaining—taking on the burden of that Index girl against such strong opponents would be absurd. That's why he'd sent her away. Returning an obstacle to somewhere it wouldn't be an obstacle.

That was all.

That was all this needed to be.

"…" Accelerator exhaled and switched gears. "Start the car."

"You're…not gonna let me go ye— *Agh?!*"

"Live or die. Your choice."

After he nudged the steel rod stuck through the seat, the automobile quietly drove off.

Another five-minute car ride later, Accelerator had him stop in front of a small park. They were apparently at the edge of School District 7. A transportation sign was right next to the park, indicating District 5.

Grabbing a big bag in the rear section at his feet, Accelerator placed it on the seat beside him. It was probably spare equipment for the Hound Dogs. The synthetic leather bag, which resembled a body bag, was over an entire meter long.

Upon opening the zipper and looking inside, he found a pile of murder weapons. A small pistol that could fit inside a palm, a submachine gun you could probably hide in an encyclopedia case, and the one as long as a mop—an indoor suppression shotgun, perhaps. Also in the bag were claylike explosives, fuses, radios, and masks.

For now, he was after one thing.

Something to use as a cane.

His usual T-shaped crutch had slipped away from him when he was fighting with Kihara. When not in ability usage mode, he needed one to support his body. Whatever he decided to do, he had to secure a crutch first.

He glanced around at the bag's contents. "I guess the shotgun will do," he said, picking a weapon almost at random.

It was a semiautomatic shotgun made of shiny black metal. Along the whole underside of the barrel, from below the muzzle up to ten centimeters away from the trigger, were magazines aligned sideways. It looked to have about thirty shots in total. Accelerator faintly recalled certain submachine guns having a similar loading mechanism.

Just the main part of the shotgun was close to a meter long, and it was made so you could extend or retract the stock according to preference. What seemed like a scope was fixed to the top, but he looked through to find it wasn't for magnification; he hit a switch and saw a red light down the middle of it. It seemed to be a dot sight.

He vaguely remembered it being an aim-assist tool to help precision, though it depended on what the user liked.

Why the hell would they put a targeting thing on a shotgun if it just sprays bullets everywhere?

He gave the sight a light hit, frustrated, but that wasn't the problem. If he held the shotgun by the grip and put the stock under his arm, he could maybe just barely use it as a crutch. *My weight's gonna end up bending the barrel, but this thing isn't for shooting anyway. As long as it can help me walk, that's enough.*

As Accelerator considered it, the driver spoke.

"It's useless…"

The voice was hoarse. As though he'd gone days without water, his stamina was all dried up.

"…If you'd met him in person, you'd know. Kihara is absolute. A person like you who's lost his touch and drunk on peace can't do anything against him with some improvised crap."

"…*You want me to snap this?*"

"Th-that might be nice."

The man's response was unexpected.

"I don't want to die. But…I know how terrifying Kihara is. And I wish I didn't. I…I won't live to see another sunrise. He doesn't know the meaning of moderation. I don't mean mercy—I mean *moderation*. I'm a goner. *I…I might not even get to die.* Kihara, he's…he's the kind who would aim to break a Guinness World Record or make the Three World Incidents into the Four World Incidents, and he wouldn't even care…"

"You're complaining too much," interrupted Accelerator shortly. "Quit fussing." He clenched the steel weapon sticking through the seat with his five fingers. "You know what, this is a huge pain. Kill you? That's too vague. I'm gonna use this to churn up your insides! I'll make you vomit chunks of blood and whatever you had for lunch today, you pile of shit!!"

"*H-hiiieeee!!*"

Just by shouting in the man's ear, he'd easily broken the man's bluff. It had all been nonsense from a man with no familiarity with "death." That was all his words were worth.

The driver cried out, his eyeballs darting all over. "Shit, damn it!! Give me a break! I don't want to die here!! You're both demons, the two of you! I don't want anything more to do with this!! I'm gonna go home, take a shower, have some beer, and watch the show I recorded!"

The only thing left in its wake was a series of unseemly hopes.

This was what happened when people stuck their necks into a dispute between giants without knowing their place.

Accelerator softly spoke to the Hound Dog in the driver's seat, who was quaking. "You don't want to die, right?"

"N-no."

"You want to live?"

"Yes!! So fucking what?! Of course I want to live! Wanting to die is no way to live! I want to live free and proud!! I'm an idiot, aren't I?! I'm the stupidest one here, aren't I?! What am I saying?! It's not even a possibility!!"

The man had been practically forced to the edge of his own grave.

Otherwise, he wouldn't have been speaking so dramatically.

"Soooo, you get it, then, don't you?" said Accelerator, a grin splitting across his face.

The man in the driver's seat saw it from the rearview mirror and gave a yelp.

"You thought you were gonna find a way out of this? You lived in this world, trampled over who knows how many people, and even made an enemy of that shithead Kihara on top of picking a fight with me, and you want to just live a happy life? You're the one I should be calling senile, you dumbass."

"W-waaah…"

"You piece of shit. How many people have you killed?"

"…F-fourteen," he squeezed out.

But when Accelerator heard that, he couldn't help but be a little disappointed.

That's it?

If that was all, he was a far more peaceful person than Accelerator.

And how big of a monster was Accelerator for thinking it made the man a "peaceful person"?

"Choose. Die from blood loss here, or die a hilarious death at Amata Kihara's hands."

"N-no, I don't want to die. Even I want to live!"

"Hah. Then it's the hospital," continued the Level Five, smiling. "You can't die. Not that easily. I won't allow it. You'd kill a hundred times and still thirst for more. You think I'd just let a shithead like you go? I'll make you suffer even longer. You'll keep living just so I can unload all my stress on you."

"Damn it..." Though he was telling the man to get treated, the man clenched his teeth in anger. "I'll be killed. Kihara will follow me to the other side of the world. There's no saving me..."

"The shit doctor I know won't easily abandon a patient even then. Brings a tear to your eye, doesn't it? You'd be able to live maybe another day, right?"

"B-but there's no guarantee."

"I see. But you know, Kihara just might find his heart outside his body in the meantime."

The man fell silent. He must have thought that if Accelerator really did kill Kihara, he might have a chance.

And then he spoke. "It's impossible for anyone to beat Kihara."

"Probably. Myself aside, there's no way you could do it," said Accelerator, rummaging through the synthetic-leather body bag–like case again, looking for something other than the shotgun he could use. Then he found something.

On the surface, it looked like a pistol with a silencer on it, but on its tip was a microphone-like, sponge-shaped sensor. Plus, a little above the grip, where the hammer would be, there was a small LCD monitor, about three inches.

"...That's a scent detector," responded the Hound Dog, catching a glimpse in the rearview mirror. "Normally it's used in the perfume and deodorant industries, but they converted it for military use..."

"It's a mechanized police dog."

It was probably more effective than a dog. If it could convert information from the five senses into data, it could pick out only what it needed from complex, jumbled scents, and save them to memory as well.

Scents fell into several categories, and within each grouping, they shared similar molecular compositions. The design had probably taken that into account, too.

"We always use them to track down targets. Quickly and reliably. I've never seen anyone get away after Kihara gives them the glare…"

"…" Annoyance showed clearly on Accelerator's face.

He had no objections to crushing the Hound Dogs, but the whole "always get surprise attacked" wasn't a pattern he appreciated. He'd rather follow the "surprise attack them first" idea.

"We can't use a car, either. He'll follow the smell of the tires, find this minivan, and then he just has to follow you here and it's over. We keep on pursuing our targets until we stab them through the back. He'll find us, too, soon enough."

As Accelerator listened, he fiddled with the scent detector. "How do you use this thing? Might come in handy for finding the brat."

"…You can't anymore," said the man, smiling a little. It was a pallid, dried-out smile. "The Hound Dogs have a cleansing agent that negates the sensor. It interferes with the molecular composition of scents. You could have used it all you wanted back at the attack site and still not gotten anything…"

According to the man, there were two kinds of this "detergent"—the kind they put on their members' clothing and the kind they sprayed at the scene.

"You got any of that stuff?"

"If I did, I'd have used it a long time ago. I'm with a different branch. They separate those who track people and those who do the record erasing…"

Accelerator sucked his teeth. But merely learning there was an item that could fool the scent detector was good. He tossed the sensor away, then said, "…Nothing else I wanna ask. Don't move from that spot."

The man yelped, feeling an unsettling, writhing atmosphere emanating from the backseat. He'd be killed after all.

Or so he thought, before Accelerator moved toward the car's gaping hole. He was about to leave.

"Wh-where are you going?"

"Eh? Goin' to kill Kihara and save the brat," he answered, annoyed.

The man was amazed. "Why...aren't you giving up? No matter where you run, Kihara will come to murder you with a smile. You don't even have time to prepare for battle. They have all the initiative, not you. And you're still gonna do this?"

"Of course I am."

"...Such a quick answer, but what evidence do you have that it'll work? You've been immersed in this world for how long? Don't you know how bad the odds are?"

"Fuck if I know," spat Accelerator. He put his hand on the doorless exit in the backseat; he was going to call up the frog-faced doctor. "I'm too drunk on peace and lost my touch, remember?"

6

The decision took only a moment.

Once he realized hiding was pointless, Kamijou picked up Last Order's tiny body and jumped out from behind the car they had been using as cover, keeping his upper body bent over her.

The automobile had been illegally parked on the side of the road. Not even five meters stood between them and the entrance to the closest side street.

However—

Grritch!!

A sound like a metal pipe tearing through thin silk rang out.

Several machine guns immediately opened fire.

They shot unbelievably quickly—far too fast to tell how many bullets came flying out per second. The incoming rounds shattered the glass of the car Kamijou and Last Order had been using as a shield a moment ago, twisting the front hood as though a giant had stomped on it and tearing countless holes through the metal-plated doors. The seats burst open, turning the interior into a mess of cotton.

The destruction happened instantaneously, and all the noise had overlapped to create a single explosive sound.

Kamijou kept running toward the entrance to the side street.

Bullets chased along his escape route.

When freedom was right before his eyes, a bullet ricocheted off a concrete wall at eye level. The shooters probably intended to fire once in Kamijou's chosen heading and then riddle him with holes when he stopped to flinch. His neck cringed out of reflex, but he managed just barely to keep his body moving. Small fragments of broken concrete skimmed past his hair.

He dove into the side street almost in a roll, nearly falling face-first onto the wet road.

"You alive, Last Order?!" he shouted. The small girl in his arms nodded several times, not saying anything.

Then he heard metal scraping against metal. It was the men's equipment bumping against one another. He clicked his tongue, then hoisted Last Order again and ran farther down the street.

They needed someplace to hide.

The Imagine Breaker in his right hand was absolutely not cut out for this. It gave him a way to escape from tricky or irregular opponents who used sorcery or supernatural abilities, but against guns, there was no way to use it to his advantage. If he carelessly tried to punch them, he'd meet his end as an old, hole-filled rag.

"Last Order, you control the Sisters, right? Can you use electric powers, too?"

"Yes, but only with enough power to be ranked about Level Three, answers Misaka answers Misaka."

"Can you undo electric locks? I want to duck inside a building from the back door. I don't think this alley is very long. They could be waiting to ambush us when we come out the other side."

"Okay," came the reply.

Kamijou stopped at a nearby door and put Last Order down next to him.

"Hn!" Last Order took a cell phone out of her button-down shirt's breast pocket and turned it off. Apparently, they ruined espers' focus when they were using electric-type abilities. She then held her small palm up to the card slit next to the door and closed her eyes.

Clack-clack-clack-clack echoed more metal sounds from the men in black.

Kamijou couldn't gauge their distance—were they near or far? The street wasn't a straight line; rather, it was a winding path, so they wouldn't start strafing him as soon as they got to its entrance. Still, he didn't know when they'd catch up, and having to wait for something to happen put unimaginable pressure on him.

Done yet...?

He waited, listening only to the overlapping footfalls.

Damn it, you done yet?

There was no change in Last Order.

Just when he started to worry that the Imagine Breaker might be causing some kind of weird interference, she shouted, "Did it! says Misaka says Misaka, opening her eyes!"

A high-pitched *beep* came.

Kamijou took the metal doorknob and turned it. It was unlocked. He picked up Last Order again and set foot in the building.

There was no light inside.

It looked like the kitchen of a family restaurant. It must have been designed with open flames in mind, so they'd probably made sure to have an emergency exit. Kamijou thought the store might still be open, but all the lights were off, giving it a slightly creepy atmosphere. The green light of the emergency exit sign dimly illuminated cooking utensil outlines.

"What do we do now? asks Misaka asks Misaka."

"Let's see."

Kamijou lowered Last Order to the floor and went for the door in front of him. He wanted to reach somewhere well lit, with people around.

"Those guys have a car. They'll probably catch up to us if we try to run. No trains or buses at this hour, and I don't think a regular taxi driver could outrun them, either."

Last Order looked up at him with worried eyes. He wanted to just give up, but he couldn't make such a disgrace of himself.

"Let's just get somewhere there's a lot of people. They won't want to cause a commotion and draw attention to themselves. That's why they're after us in the first place. Committing mass murder would be counterproductive."

"Can we really save him like this? says Misaka says Misaka, bemoaning her lack of strength."

"Don't know. But if we don't live through this, he's out of the question. If we want to save anyone, we have to stay alive first. I'm sure your buddy wouldn't be very happy if you died."

"…He wouldn't, says Misaka says Misaka, shaking her head."

"Great. Then let's survive."

That was a pretty crazy line coming from me, thought Kamijou with a forced grin, opening the door in front of him.

Beyond it was what seemed to be the main floor where guests usually dined. It was filled with pure white light emanating from fluorescent lamps, plus a radio plugged into the wall playing inappropriately cheerful music. A big-screen TV covering one of the walls had a commercial on it. He could smell the particular greasy odor of packed and sterilized food.

But…

"…*Not here, too,*" Touma Kamijou moaned to himself.

Several guests were present in the restaurant. Some were couples and some were men, probably faculty done with the day's work. Waitresses in cute uniforms were in the narrow paths between tables. An older male employee was at the register.

Every single person present was knocked out cold.

Limp, drained, and without a mark on them.

There were no signs indicating any of the patrons had panicked. Some forks and spoons had fallen to the floor, but that was most likely due to people falling onto the tables. All of them had been incapacitated without even realizing what was going on—that's what the scene looked like.

Just like the Anti-Skill officers near the entrance to the underground mall, some of the customers and employees were simply lying there as if asleep. On the other hand, some on the floor were as motionless as stone statues. In general, they could be separated into several groups.

The state of the kitchen had struck Kamijou as odd, but maybe the same problem had occurred in there as well.

Whatever the case, he and Last Order needed a lot of people around, but this wouldn't cut it. With everyone here unconscious, there would be no witnesses.

What's going on? he wondered, dazed. *A whole bunch of those men in black were like this, too. That means they didn't do this, right? Shit, does that mean we've got more than one problem?!*

"Last Order, we have to get out—"

Last Order interrupted him, abruptly pulling him down to the floor.

Bang!!

The row of windows facing the main road burst into smithereens. It took a few seconds to realize someone had fired a bullet into the store. The missed shot struck the radio, causing the speakers all to go silent. The television cracked and sent sparks flying.

Seeing a rain of small pieces of glass pouring onto the guests collapsed on the tables and floor caused blood to rise to his head. Thankfully, none of the bullets seemed to hit anyone. That wasn't the problem.

Damn it, don't they care if there's normal people around?!

Someone entered the main floor slowly, stepping on the shards of glass.

Kamijou grabbed a nearby fork from the floor. It was such an insubstantial weapon, he wanted to laugh.

As if this all wasn't enough, the electricity suddenly went out. The door Kamijou and Last Order had entered through squealed open.

Three more men adorned in black entered as quietly as cockroaches, joining the first man.

With the pursuers carefully searching out their target from two directions, there were very few blind spots to exploit.

With his dully shining fork in hand, Kamijou leaned back against a support beam.

Then he looked up.

The first bullet, which shot in from the window, had hit the beam, leaving a gaping hole just above him.

It…went through? Some shield this is…!!

All of Kamijou's muscles over-tensed with surprise.

The relaxed footsteps, trying their best not to give themselves away via vibrations, slowly tightened the net around Kamijou and Last Order.

7

Accelerator considered using his handheld but decided to make the short walk to a public phone. Kihara and his Hounds might be using machines that detected his cell number from telephone lines.

He went into the public phone booth, which was a little dirty—it had probably been completely unused for a long time. After pressing the red emergency button, he called for an ambulance. Given who had jurisdiction over this area, he shouldn't have to specify the frog-faced doctor to have the wounded driver get to him anyway.

Then, he inserted a few of his last remaining coins and picked up the receiver again. Being sure to check the address book in his handheld, he entered one number at a time into the public phone.

It was Last Order's mobile phone number.

"…"

But there was no sign of her picking up. As Accelerator stood there in silence, receiver in hand, a message came back basically telling him either her phone was off or she didn't have any signal where she was.

He returned the receiver to its hook.

...Well, guess I should have figured.

If she'd fled into a tight space, she might not have any signal, and perhaps she was wary of the ringtone or vibration going off unexpectedly.

The worst case possible also crossed Accelerator's mind, but he began to do what he needed to. He put another couple of coins into the phone and dialed a different number this time.

The call tone continued ringing for a bit.

After it ended, an elderly female nurse answered. Accelerator demanded she put him through to the frog-faced doctor.

He got ahold of him immediately.

"What could be the issue at this hour, hmm?"

"Got some trouble. Big trouble."

"I've already heard the general situation from Little Misaka, or whatever she called herself. They seem to be exchanging information through their electrical network."

Oh, so they don't have to use phones, huh, thought Accelerator, impressed. Naturally, Accelerator couldn't use the network on his own, since he merely borrowed their power to perform calculations for him. "Then this'll be quick. Tell me what you got. How is the brat doing?"

"She seems to be on the run from a separate Hound Dog group, fleeing with a civilian she happened to meet. I don't believe she's been caught yet...but I'll be honest with you. It's only a matter of time."

Last Order must have looked for help after her separation from Kihara. The only problem was the person she'd found wouldn't have the strength she hoped for.

Accelerator sucked his teeth. "Where is she?"

"She doesn't seem to know herself. Though it appears to be a family restaurant somewhere, hmm?"

He thought for a moment, but that obviously wouldn't be enough to locate her.

Because of that, the frog-faced doctor went on to explain, the Sisters couldn't go out to search for Last Order. Of course, the ten or so of them in Academy City were undergoing physical adjustments, so having them walking out in the rain for a long time would be a problem.

He didn't like it, but for now, he decided to carry out his original job. "Did a stupid nun wearing white arrive over there?"

"We were just figuring out how to deal with her. How does she know about your proxy calculations?"

"None of your business."

"...Is your situation bad enough to need a new battery?"

"It's not like you have any more," spat Accelerator, then continued. "Also, take care of the brat who's whining about the battery. For the next twenty-four hours, someone will try to take her life. Don't let your eyes off her."

"My, my. Isn't this problem better left to Anti-Skill?"

"What the hell are some peace-loving idiot teachers gonna do? This enemy is on a different level. If you don't want any extra corpses in the pile, then you'd better get your head in the game already."

"...I suppose so. To think I'd be protecting someone other than one of my patients, hmm?"

"You'll have another one of them, too. A man stabbed in the back should get over there in a bit. Do what you need to with him and prepare for an attack. How much in the way of combat can you manage?"

"Combat? This is getting quite dangerous, hmm?" Even the frog-faced doctor seemed startled, but Accelerator wouldn't engage him at every step.

He needed all the time he could get.

"...You said you knew the situation from those stupid clones' network, right? You know you can't be talking like that right now. Tell me already. The longer you're confused, the more your survival rate plummets."

"Goodness...You like injuries and hospitals about as much as that other boy, don't you?"

He heard a sigh from the receiver.

After a silent moment, the frog-faced doctor answered him. "We have about ten mass production–type Sisters being fixed up. I believe we also have enough weapons from the experiment for a few people—Metal-eater MXs, which are anti-tank rifles, and F2000R Toy Soldiers."

Accelerator thought for a moment, then shook his head. "They'll run over you. And those stupid clones couldn't do much anyway, even if they were at full strength. Can you evacuate all the staff and patients in the hospital?"

"And leave my post? Do you have any idea how many beds are in here?"

"About three hundred?"

"Seven hundred," said the doctor flatly. "About fifty-two are too dangerous to move—newborns, seriously ill patients, you get the idea. I suppose no patients are in surgery at the moment, but don't you know how absurd it is to move so many people at once, hmm?"

"..."

"If I leave here, what will we do if someone has an emergency? You have your problems going on, after all."

Accelerator didn't try to make pointless excuses or thank him. He didn't have time. "Can you do it?"

"I will," came the reply instantly. The doctor's tone of voice had changed completely, from its usual easygoing tone to something different. "We can use smoke bombs and pretend there was a fire. If they link it to some terrorist act, we'll have enough of a pretense to evacuate everyone. Some of the patients will be dangerous to move, but it's my job to safeguard their lives. I'll manage."

"Are you sure? I mean, I know I was the one who asked..."

"I said I would. Even you don't think this will go over well, hmm? We have several emergency plans to choose from, like assigning them to other hospitals. If we didn't, I wouldn't have consented."

"...Sorry about this."

"I frankly don't appreciate being at the mercy of your squabbles, but whatever kind of patients they are, I will treat them equally. If you tell me to protect a patient brought here, I'll do everything in my power."

An ambulance went by, blaring its siren. The man from the Hound Dogs was probably inside, already on his way to the hospital.

Listening to the siren, the frog-faced doctor spoke up suddenly. "How far do you plan on taking this?"

"Kihara? I'll kill him. And I'll crush the Hound Dogs. And I'll save the brat, unharmed."

"Impossible."

Another immediate answer. His voice seemed too direct, too cool for the frog-faced doctor. Accelerator frowned.

"The situation is restrictive, and you have too many objectives. You'll never be able to accomplish all of them. Tell me, the world you live in—is it easy to wander through detours and stumble into your destination?"

"…When did doctors start giving out bullshit lip service? You don't live in this world. Don't talk like you know its darkness."

"You may be misunderstanding something, so let me say this, hmm?"

The frog-faced doctor didn't back down.

He simply spoke the truth to Accelerator.

"*I've seen a hell even worse than yours.* Don't make light of this job. I think I've seen quite a bit more blood and tears than you have. Though it never led to tragedy. Some call me the Heaven Canceler—some say I bring people back from the world of the dead. It's that simple, the difference between you and I. *Whether you stay there or come back.* That's it."

The doctor paused for a moment.

Then he continued. "From someone more experienced with this 'darkness' than you, this is my advice: Limit yourself to one goal. Kill Kihara? Wipe out the Hound Dogs? Anyone could do that later. There should be only one thing you absolutely have to do right now. Don't you understand that?"

"Life comes first, huh? Should've expected that from a doctor. But getting that brat back unharmed and crushing the Hound Dogs are the same thing. I can't round down here—"

"Not that."

"Eh?"

"Rescue Last Order unharmed? *Why are you still talking about impossibilities?*"

"..." Accelerator's blood. froze. Who, exactly, was he talking to right now?

"I said this already. I've heard about this directly from the Sisters as they exchange information through the Misaka network. I believe I understand your circumstances as well. And I'll say this."

The frog-faced doctor spoke in a slow but powerful voice, almost as though he were a teacher lecturing a poor student.

"You need to face reality. You should have realized you couldn't accomplish something like that when you were crawling on the ground. Understand? You're already losing. Even winning at this point will be difficult, and you're piling up all these lofty hopes... What will come of that? Make a compromise, Accelerator. You can't save Last Order unharmed anymore. No matter how high up the person you strike down, she will be hurt."

He felt like he'd just been stricken in a psychological blind spot.

Had he been relying on this doctor too much without realizing it?

"...Piece of shit. Don't you get it? I don't want to admit that, which is why I'm saying I'm gonna kill Kihara even if I have to crawl through mud to do it."

"You don't understand. If everything went as well as we hoped, I wouldn't even be a doctor in the first place. I'd probably be holed up in a mountain meditating three hundred and sixty-five days a year. Hopes alone can't save people—that's why I became a doctor. I'll be blunt. All your claims are childish selfishness in blatant disregard of reality."

"Then what do you want me to do? Look at that brat, all beaten up because of that shithead Kihara, and smile, say great, and have a happy ending?"

"Yes. That's why doctors exist."

Even his indignance didn't move the frog-faced doctor, whose words continued to flow out in a smooth stream.

"Whether it's a broken arm, torn-off skin, or a pierced heart, if they come to me alive, I will heal them. Watch—I will save your loved one with perfection, doing everything from making sure she survives to repairing her wounds and even caring for her mentally. Doctors can answer those expectations. Don't aim higher than you need to—just focus on saving Last Order's 'life.' That's the most important thing. It's the only thing an inexperienced, unskilled doctor like me can't bring back. Am I wrong? If you think I am, then let's hear it. What's more important than her life?"

No, this doctor wasn't unfeeling.

Not in this situation, where a child's life was about to be taken because of adult convenience.

And...

He was perfectly aware of his own position. He knew panicking or yelling about it wouldn't solve anything—that's why he was intent on fighting as a "doctor."

"Kihara? The Hound Dogs? Finish up with those boring preliminary matches and please, bring Last Order to me quickly so we can start the finals."

After that, Accelerator had the frog-faced doctor tell him where they'd be hiding after temporarily abandoning the hospital. He would be bringing Last Order there if he got her back.

He put the receiver down.

He leaned against the public phone booth's glass door.

...*I can't save her unharmed. No matter how high up the person I strike down, she'll be hurt...*Accelerator took in a breath, then let it out.

The Hound Dogs had scent detectors. They'd obviously use them to search for Last Order. She was already in a tight situation, and now the hands of the devil were reaching for her even faster.

There was no time to waste.

He made up his mind.

"That's just fine with me..."

After accepting everything, he was left with a smile.

A crooked, terrifying, otherworldly smile.

"...If it's to save that brat, I'll kill anyone, saint or sinner."

The Hound Dogs had scent detectors. Amata Kihara and the Hound Dogs would have located her immediately and launched an attack already.

First, he'd intercept that.

He just needed a battlefield. He had no time to waste in a place like this.

INTERLUDE SIX

Motoharu Tsuchimikado ran for the gate connecting Academy City to the outside.

The downpour showed no signs of stopping. It obscured the moonlight, negatively affected sound collection work, and even erased the scents nearby. The drenched scenery seemed to greatly lower the chance of surviving this nighttime battle.

Most of the city's functions are down. Guess we're lucky there're no riots or looting, thought Tsuchimikado, without slowing his sprint but still keeping one eye on his surroundings at all times.

For all intents and purposes, the city's peacekeeping groups Anti-Skill and Judgment had been mostly wiped out. A few of their members could still move, but they could never cover the entire city by themselves. If someone noticed that the city functions were in a state of paralysis, store registers and shelves would be raided and looted in an instant.

The only reason mass panic hadn't set in was that Academy City's last trains and buses were aligned with school closing hours—most people hadn't noticed the abnormality outside—and that most students had suffered the attack of an unknown nature and were now unconscious.

An attack.

More specifically, an attack from the magic side.

Those words frustrated Tsuchimikado.

Of course, since his thoughts were extremely level, his frustration didn't appear as an easily understood wave of emotion.

God's Right Seat, eh? I've heard about them, but to think they'd go this far...

Running through the silenced streets, he actually felt impressed.

Tsuchimikado was an excellent sorcerer. Despite that, even after a magic-based attack of this scale, he was completely clueless about what kind of spell they'd been hit with. He was completely in the dark.

But Aleister can't handle this all himself. Other groups are out there. With the city paralyzed like this, if they set foot inside, the city's done for.

It was certainly odd that no other combat forces had entered with the God's Right Seat member. Still, maybe it was simply a numbers problem. If there were ten thousand members waiting outside, if they entered the city from the start, they'd end up having to fight 2.3 million people. But if the God's Right Seat person weakened the city's forces at the outset, it would drastically decrease losses for an invasion force.

The enemy numbers were unknown.

Their positions outside Academy City were also unknown.

...I guess they're not positioned well enough to march at this very moment, though.

Academy City's total population was 2.3 million. If, say, the Roman Orthodox Church were to send 10 million people here, they wouldn't need to wait on the outskirts like this. They wouldn't need Vento to strike first, either. They'd obviously consider using brute force to take control. (Of course, given the city's supernatural abilities and weaponization, you couldn't calculate some parts of the equation with number of people alone—but it didn't seem like the Roman Orthodox Church was taking that into consideration anyway.)

At the moment, less might have grouped up outside than he feared.

Maybe it was only enough to "mop up" after Vento attacked and silenced the city.

It's probably still too many for one guy to handle.

The total annihilation of the enemy wasn't Motoharu Tsuchimikado's goal.

Preventing the waiting invasion forces from getting inside the city until its vital functions came back online—that was his win condition. Not Aleister's but Tsuchimikado's, one he decided on for himself. He'd have to leave Vento to someone else.

Still, trying to hold off an unknown quantity of enemies until the city came back online at an unknown time was basically suicidal.

Can't use normal police, either. And the others like me have their own things to deal with.

He had nobody to help him.

He had no special weapons or sorcery to help him out of the situation, either.

But…

Maika lives in this city.

He thought of his sister—who had no connection to the world of sorcery and just wanted to be a housekeeper.

That was all he needed to prepare himself for battle.

I will betray everything else, but I'll never betray her.

Through Gate 3, which had lost all its security functions, and outside the city ran Motoharu Tsuchimikado—as a sorcerer standing at the pinnacle of *Onmyoudou.*

He had one goal: protect the world of the one most important to him.

CHAPTER 7

Changing Raindrops to Bloody Red
Revival_of_Destruction.

1

Aiho Yomikawa gripped the steering wheel.

On the outside, it was a cheap-looking domestic sports car, but the engine noise was strangely low. Though not visible, it had been lovingly customized to chase down runners. The vehicle had seven gears, which was a good indication of how insane the modifications were.

She'd been driving around looking for Last Order, who had disappeared this afternoon from her apartment.

…? The roads seem pretty empty…

At its heart, Academy City was a city of students. Only faculty, merchants, and college students could use cars, so the traffic wasn't that sparse compared to a normal day in the metropolis.

Nevertheless, today, there were no cars out. Past her windshield, and her periodically moving wipers, was a road that looked more like an empty runway.

"What's up with this…?" she muttered.

Then, on the car radio, which was shoved into where the audio system would be, a light blinked. She put on her turn signal, slowed down, and parked her car on the shoulder.

She looked down at the radio just as it emitted a low *grrrr* and printed out a postcard-sized paper. It worked the same as the small printers on digital cameras. Anti-Skill HQ used it to send wanted photos and such to all officers on duty.

The picture was rough, as though it had been taken from far away. It was blurry, too, like the camera had been shaking at the time. Still, she could make out a woman in yellow clothing, standing in the midst of numerous downed Anti-Skill officers.

"?"

Yomikawa was perplexed.

Normally, the picture wasn't the only thing printed out—they usually got some kind of textual information about the scene, but nothing else arrived. This didn't tell her what the woman had done. She couldn't even tell whether the woman was suspected in some sort of crime or was someone she was supposed to place under her protection.

Last Order being lost still worried her, but "crimes" took priority over "lost children."

She pressed the switch on her radio. "Yomikawa to HQ. Requesting details on call 334," she called in, hoping to get some confirmation, wondering if it was a communication mishap.

But she got no answer—just a low static buzzing in her ears.

She tried speaking into the radio again several times after that, but she never got a reply.

"..."

Yomikawa switched off the radio.

She sat back in her parked car and grabbed the postcard-sized paper again. In it were Anti-Skill officers unconscious on the ground in the rain and, standing right in the middle of them, a woman in yellow.

This woman..., she thought, running a finger across the figure in the photo. *What the hell is she? I mean, she doesn't seem like someone to protect. It looks like she just got done wrecking my colleagues...*

An eerie sensation ran up her spine. At the same time, she felt anger for her colleagues, who were facedown on the ground.

Well, I'll need to have a polite conversation with her if I happen to see her..., she thought idly.

However, she didn't drive off in her sports car again.

*   *   *

Rumble!!

A sudden shock hit Aiho Yomikawa's brain.

"Agh…?!"

She couldn't even scream.

The strength left her body and she slumped over the steering wheel. It jammed into her chest painfully, but she couldn't do anything about it. Not an ounce of energy remained, from her core to her fingertips.

Her vision quickly began to narrow.

What…is…?

Not understanding, she began to drift into unconsciousness.

The car radio switch was just a few centimeters away from her limply hanging arms. But she couldn't move her hands. She couldn't ask for help. Even breathing was a laborious task.

…This…photo…

Maybe it was a sign from her colleagues to be wary of her. Maybe an Anti-Skill officer, in the same situation as her, had rallied the last of his strength to send it out.

But she wouldn't be putting it to use anytime soon.

…Damn it…

The photo slipped out from between her thumb and index finger and fluttered down.

As it fell, Aiho Yomikawa completely lost consciousness.

A road without cars.

An awfully silent city.

A lack of response from the radio.

…Perhaps the situation had already evolved into something monumental…

2

"Resource Reclamation and Treatment Plant 3?" said one of the men wearing black, looking at a group of buildings towering over a part of School District 5.

The plant was right next to District 7. After using their vehicle to chase Accelerator and others on the run from the Hound Dogs, they'd left their minivan near a park on the other side of the district line.

"We'll have trouble if that's where they ran, Nancy," said the other.

The first grinned in spite of herself. "Who're you calling Nancy?" she murmured. That was her code name, though. Nothing she could do about that.

Nancy was East Asian and indeed a normal Japanese person. Both her hair and eyes were darkly colored, and she had no complex about that whatsoever. If she had her way, her code name would also be in Japanese. Amata Kihara was someone she was pretty sure liked having a flashy nickname on the Internet.

Her whole body was covered in jet-black protective gear and a mask, but they didn't manage to conceal her mature feminine curves. The Hound Dogs didn't care about gender—everyone in the group was human garbage anyway—so there were other women besides Nancy. People of the same gender being around, however, didn't create any strange feelings of solidarity. Generally, everyone in the organization was a disdainful pile of trash, like former Anti-Skill officers who had awoken to the joy of chasing down perpetrators or analytical engineers who liked bringing "forms of torture that didn't leave wounds" to investigations.

She slowly waved the tool in her hand. The device, which looked like a toy gun, was a scent detector. Just above the grip, where the hammer would be on a pistol, was a small LCD monitor of about three inches. A multitude of bar graphs moved up and down without rest, looking like the spectrum analyzer bars on a stereo system screen.

"The target's 'scent' leads into there," said Nancy to her colleague waiting behind her. "Not much doubt about it."

A scent. Police hounds couldn't track scents on rainy days like today, but this managed to solve the problem with a pretty high success rate. Particular scents drifted away most of the time because they mixed with other odors, not because the scents themselves disappeared. These detectors could handle these situations well.

They looked ahead to where the "scent" was.

"Huge building," said one of the people in black, coming up next to her.

It was idle talk, but the man was right. The plant before their eyes was enormous—about two square kilometers. It was used for recycling waste. Academy City didn't use much in the way of resources, and they recycled many different things, from basic paper to soft metals of iron and aluminum and petroleum products like plastic. All "resources" from the four school districts around District 5 were collected at this plant to be processed into a usable state.

The huge plot of land brought to mind a coastal petrochemical industrial complex. And it certainly was an industrial park, with the rows of cylindrical fuel tanks in one part over a hundred meters in diameter and the countless smokestacks thrusting into the sky.

And it was a recycling plant to boot. The ideal place for human trash to be fighting.

"Nancy, what do you think he's after?" asked Rod. "This facility doesn't seem strategically important. But if he was just hiding in there, why bother coming here and having to slip past all the security?"

"Hmph. It might actually be pretty simple," replied Nancy casually, causing Rod to frown. She shook the scent detector in front of him. "Maybe he wants to get to the trash processors so he can erase his scent and get away from this little guy."

"...Then the target knows what we're equipped with?"

"Yeah, since that idiot Orson ran away with him. There was a spare in that van, too."

Acquiring the smell of garbage wouldn't quite fool the detectors. But if he used specific cleaning agents that changed the molecular composition of the scent, then it would be a different story. The Hound Dogs' cover-up team had developed one specifically for their use, but she wouldn't be surprised if a resource treatment plant had a chemical that did the same thing.

A last resort, thought Nancy with a thin smile. "Rod, do you have a map of this place?"

"Already got it from the data banks."

"Send it to everyone. How many employees in there? Patrol routes?"

"We don't have to worry about patrol routes," the man called Rod said simply. "Most of the inside runs on autopilot. There are about fourteen workers, but they do all their jobs on computers in the control center. They even call in outside groups to do mechanical maintenance."

"Great. Saves us the trouble of cleaning up afterward," said Nancy offhandedly, giving the scent detector to her colleague. She began to check the submachine gun hanging from her shoulder.

Rod shook the small terminal with the map on it for them to see. "There's a few ways to get in. We don't have the man power to cover all of them and comb the plant at the same time."

The Hound Dogs were currently split up into a few different places—a diversion against the unknown enemy, a detached force following Last Order, and those on guard duty for Amata Kihara. Because of that, they had only around ten people here.

"We'll just have to herd the target. He should think we've got a lot more people than we actually do. First, attack from point A on the map, and after we completely control his movements, we surprise him at emergency exit C. Throwing a few bombs in there should rock his world, easy. Got it?"

"What if he uses his ability and breaks through? We can't herd him anywhere then."

"It's fine."

Nancy looked at the plant again. The cluster of buildings made her think of a heavy industrial plant, the kind with several layers of thick concrete and metal pipes coiling around.

"If Kihara's right, our target isn't that all-powerful."

3

"Here it is…"

In Resource Reclamation and Treatment Plant 3's control room, Accelerator smiled to himself.

Dozens of computer monitors covered the small room's windowless walls. This was where everything was controlled—from factory work oversight to security mode handling.

The fourteen workers here had no defense against an intruder armed with a shotgun. At the moment, they were scattered about, cowering and trembling, but Accelerator didn't pay them any attention. He was staring at a single monitor. On it was a list of cleaning agents the plant had in stock.

He was searching for one that would have a chemical reaction with his scent on a molecular level, changing it into a wholly different substance.

I found it. And there are a few kinds. I can avoid their detectors with this.

He'd resolved himself to fighting the Hound Dogs and Amata Kihara until the bitter end, but he didn't like always being on the receiving end. He had only seven minutes of full ability usage left. He'd of course use it on Amata Kihara, but the underling Hound Dogs would be a waste. Clearly, holding the initiative in this battle was the better course of action.

Of course, safely rescuing Last Order was most important right now, not fighting Kihara and his thugs. *But if I'm going to look for her, I need to shake off the Hound Dogs' pursuit now. If I grab the brat first, she's more likely to end up hit by a stray bullet!*

He'd have a hell of a hard time if he tried to do anything after saving her. In the first place, his ability was for protecting himself and *only* himself. If he had to use it every time the Hound Dogs showed up, the battery wouldn't last.

From that perspective, too, he had to use this chance to figure out when to fight and when to avoid it.

Guess I'll erase my scent with these cleaners and get out of here. Not much time until Kihara gets his shitty hands on the brat. I can't wander out of my way—I need to get back to the actual point as soon as I can. Now, where in the plant are these washing materials...?

Suddenly, one of the monitors shook with a buzz.

The dozens of monitor screens in the control room were drowned out in white noise and static, one after the other. Just before the last one went down, on the security image of the plant's north entrance 2, he caught a glimpse of a man dressed all in black.

If they had the skill to perfectly take down the security equipment in Resource Reclamation and Treatment Plant 3, they must have known where all the cameras were. Which meant those black-suits were purposely letting him on to where they were, inviting him.

Pieces of shit! How are you here so early?!

The plant was already surrounded.

Accelerator couldn't move without a cane or a crutch, which meant he couldn't move with any significant speed. Even if he used a washing material to escape the scent detectors, he'd probably still have to take on the group in the building.

He couldn't escape from *them*. And…

…I don't plan to. Damn stalkers. I'll crush them, right here, right now.

He looked around, putting his weight on his shotgun, using it as a cane. Then he gave a warning to the workers present, who had genuinely just been caught up in all this.

"There's gonna be a gunfight here soon. More of them might come after it's over, too. Wait twenty minutes after hearing the last gunshot, change out of your work uniforms, and get the hell out."

He got a response, though he wasn't sure if they were nodding or just trembling.

Interesting. What pieces do I have…?

Accelerator reviewed the situation.

He probably couldn't use his ability. The plant's interior was blocked off with thick concrete, decreasing electronic communication accuracy with the outside. Plus, it was home to a resource-recycling center—all the huge motors for things like conveyor belts and mechanical crushers were spraying harsh electromagnetic waves everywhere. They rendered the Misaka network completely unusable, since the system operated by changing the Sisters' brain waves into EM waves to create an electronic information network.

Also, the noises they made were grating.

The sounds would make a huge difference between best timing and worst timing. If Accelerator was in the middle of a normal conversation, it might just disconcert him a bit. But if it happened while he was using a flashy ability, it could cause a big misfiring accident.

Besides, using my power here won't reach Kihara.

He'd never experienced a battle in such a naked state before. Without his ability, he was just a kid who couldn't do any more physical activity than walking with a crutch. The only weapon he had was the shotgun, which he was using for said purpose. It probably had around thirty bullets loaded in all the magazines.

"What now...?"

He mentally groped for a way to intercept the Hound Dogs, who specialized in organized combat, with only what he had. With the black-suits purposely showing themselves on camera weighing more heavily on his mind...

What now?

...Accelerator took his eyes off the monitor and looked around for a paper map. Finding one, he unfolded it. Would he accept their invitation? Would he refuse it? The battle had already begun.

4

Mikoto Misaka was in a convenience store.

She stood in a corner featuring rain gear, stock-still.

"Hmm...Too small," she muttered, examining a cheap plastic umbrella. These sorts of umbrellas were popular because they weren't very bulky, but this one was so small it looked like she'd end up getting wet.

She looked out the store's big windows. It was totally dark out now. Fairly large raindrops pounded against the glass.

Mikoto Misaka had won a bet during the Daihasei Festival and gained the right to make Touma Kamijou do whatever she wanted as a game, but they were interrupted. She was searching for the boy again now, but...

"Why does it have to rain?"

She looked down at the paper bag from the cell phone company that she was holding with her school bag. *I don't want my Croaker and Hoppit straps getting wet.*

As she moaned and groaned over what to do, her cell phone ringtone went off. Exasperated, she pulled out the phone.

It displayed the number of her underclassman Kuroko Shirai.

"Big Sisteeeer!"

"What do you want, Kuroko?"

"I won't be coming back to the dorm because of Judgment work, so could you put in a word with that finicky R.A.? It's after curfew, right?"

"Umm, I'm out at the store right now, too."

"*Gyaaah?!*" came back Shirai with a very unladylike response.

Then another voice came through the speaker, a little farther away than Shirai.

"Huh? Shirai, did you not get through to her?"

It was probably Kazari Uiharu, one of Shirai's colleagues in Judgment, which meant she was probably at their HQ right now.

"How aggravating. Big Sister is out right now, so she can't contact the R.A. I'm not sure what to do. You need to file paperwork to extend your curfew, and the R.A. won't answer her phone. We're bound to have points docked for sure."

"Oh, I see. I wonder why Miss Misaka's breaking the curfew?"

"?!"

Mikoto heard a gasp, followed by a sharp cracking noise. Shirai was probably squeezing the phone with violent force. She asked, "C-could it be...Are you on a night date with that rotten ape of a man?! That jerk, that asshole—what a refined choice of atmosphere, picking a rainy day to have a little fun!!"

"That's not it, you stupid idiot!!" Mikoto shouted on reflex.

Shirai didn't seem to hear. "Guh, I can't leave things like this. Protecting Big Sister's chastity—sounds like a job for Kuroko Shirai!!"

"D-don't say 'chastity' so loudly!"

"Then if I had to put it in more concrete terms—"

"Just don't!!" shouted Mikoto, her face bright red. But Shirai didn't seem to be listening to anything else right now. Words continued to fly out of the phone receiver.

"In any case, I'll come to you, I will come for you for sure, Big Sister where are you right now and I'm using a GPS service so please send me an authentication code over a text mess—"

"You can't do that," came Uiharu's voice, jamming up the Shirai verbal machine gun. "I mean, we're nowhere near finished with this packet of office work or the huge pile of finance documents or that mountain range of instructional files. We're really going to be up all night, you know. I made sure to buy a meal from the store for dinner, so please don't take a single step outside and no taking baths, either."

"*Ugaaaaaaaahhhhhhhhhhhhhhhhhhhh!!*"

"Eek, *gyah*?! Shirai, Miss Shirai!!"

The sounds of struggling could be heard from the phone.

Slowly distancing the cell phone from her ear, Mikoto said in annoyance, "Umm, I'm hanging up, then, okay?"

Instead of the deranged Shirai, Uiharu was the one to answer. "Oh, okay. I'll make sure Shirai stays here, so, umm, I'm rooting for you!!"

"I said I'm not on a date!!" she shouted with all her might, but it didn't seem to go through. As soon as she heard the sounds of violence resume, the call ended with a *beep*.

5

Touma Kamijou and Last Order hid behind the support beam.

The darkened family restaurant was filled with a terrible silence.

Followed by thirty seconds of despair.

He thought his brain would collapse from all the stress. But as he waited behind the pillar, not breathing, he noticed something was off.

No matter how much time passed, the men didn't come nearer.

The people dressed in black who had entered the restaurant must have had a good idea of where they were hiding. They probably also knew the pair had no real weapons. A group fully decked out with firearms and combat armor had no reason to be cautious and wait out an unarmed high school student and a girl.

What's going on?

Part of him said moving would be dangerous…

…but the other part disagreed, saying he'd lose his only chance if he didn't get going now.

"…" Last Order, practically glued to him, grabbed onto his shirt forlornly.

Those small hands helped Kamijou just barely keep his presence of mind.

Another thirty seconds passed after that.

No conspicuous noises.

The rain blowing in from the broken windows alone rang loudly in Kamijou's ears.

He held his breath.

He shut his eyes.

He waited.

And then, there was movement.

"Hello, hello. ♪ Did I frighten you? You don't have to be scared, so come on out, okay?"

But what he heard was a woman's shrill voice.

Kamijou couldn't see her face because the support beam that he hid behind blocked her from his vision.

It was difficult to tell where she was, too.

But…

What? She's clearly acting differently than the guys just before.

The black-suits creeping up on Kamijou and Last Order had been trying to kill them, quickly and without making any noise or saying anything. Essentially, they were taking the easiest possible actions, doing their best to waste as little effort as possible.

But this woman's voice was exactly the opposite.

The simple fact that she'd spoken, giving away her own presence, didn't line up with how the black-suits were acting. She felt like a commando on the other side of the spectrum compared to those shadowlike figures, whom he couldn't tell if they were even people, much less distinguish between male and female ones.

Which means she's…not with the black-suits?

Still, he felt it was dangerous to come out into the open. After all, he didn't know who this person was.

"Ha-ha. You *are* scared," the woman's voice continued with a laugh. "I guess there's no helping it—that was quite the pinch you were in. But, you know, I've got, you know, my own stuff going on, so if you won't listen to what I have to say…"

Then, acting as though their unrest and caution didn't matter, she spoke again, voice indifferent.

"…I'll have to beat you into a shapeless hunk of flesh."

"!!" Kamijou picked up Last Order and immediately crouched and dove out from behind the pillar.

Then, there was a thunderous *slam!!*

An invisible attack sliced horizontally through that very same pillar, striking at about its middle. It snapped at that point, then flew into the wall. The velocity gave it the force of a cannonball, and the wall exploded into chunks.

The entire building shook.

As though the structure's very framework had collapsed, there was a sharp *crash*, and any glass inside the restaurant that had avoided abuse from the black-suits now shattered.

Kamijou, still covering Last Order, quickly scanned the room.

In the middle of the darkened main floor stood a single woman. The streetlights from outside dimly illuminated her silhouette.

She was strange.

Her clothing looked kind of like a dress worn by women in Europe in the Middle Ages. All of her hair was bunched up and covered with a cloth; not even a single strand was visible. On her face, she had piercings in her mouth, nose, and even eyelids—enough of them to throw off the balance of her face. She wore heavy makeup to emphasize her eyes, making her even more intimidating than she already was.

And her hands…

They gripped a giant hammer over a meter long. Sharp barbed wire coiled around it, beginning midway up the grip and climbing to the tip. A safeguard against the handle being grabbed, maybe, or some kind of ritual decoration.

…

It certainly looked painful to get hit with, but with the armed group sporting submachine guns and combat armor, it didn't seem like enough to beat them all. Despite that, somehow, some way, the men in black were lying around the woman's feet.

Not a single one appeared conscious.

This is…

How had she neutralized the black-suits, with their submachine guns, armor, and all that combat discipline, without making a sound?

It's just like…

The lack of information made everything all the uncannier.

Like those Anti-Skill officers all over the place when I got out of the underground mall…

He knew only one thing—she was no ally to Kamijou, either.

…And the black-suits collapsed near the crushed car…!!

"You're…?" asked Kamijou in a low voice, getting off Last Order and standing.

The woman shook the strange hammer at him a little and said quietly, "A member of God's Right Seat—Vento of the Front."

The woman who called herself Vento stuck out her tongue playfully.

"Target found. Anyway, that's that—so let me fucking kill you, Touma Kamijou."

A slender chain attached to her tongue jingled down.

——And on its tip, covered in saliva, was a small cross.

6

The Hound Dogs silently infiltrated Resource Reclamation and Treatment Plant 3, where Accelerator was hiding.

When they entered the plant's concrete interior, the machines were louder than they'd imagined.

Maybe we should've cut power to them, too, Nancy thought for a moment. No, the extra work would have been a waste of time. Accelerator probably couldn't use his ability well right now, but it was best to avoid any situation that could give him any kind of mental leeway.

Nancy had about five colleagues near her.

They were on herding duty, so they had to put on a show, make their target think they had as many people as they could. Nancy's group would pump bullets inside, and when Accelerator ran farther down the passages, the other team would be lying in wait. That was the plan.

They could use the scent detector, which she'd given to a teammate earlier, to roughly track which paths their target chose. And if they searched inside the rooms, too, they'd never miss him.

The only worry now is the firearms.

According to the detector, the target's scent had used the minivan parked on the road and come to this plant. Nobody was in the vehicle now, but there had been a bag full of spare equipment in it. If he'd unzipped that, he could be carrying a weapon now.

No, Accelerator isn't skilled at shooting guns. He's been completely reliant on his ability his whole life. There's no way he's been trained. We should have the upper hand here no matter what, thought Nancy. *Still...*

Maybe it was because most of the mechanical work was automated, but the concrete building wasn't air-conditioned. It was hot and oppressive inside. Cold rain was falling just outside, but the interior air was filled with heat from the giant motors operating nonstop.

As the plant grated on their nerves little by little, they crept through a steel hallway. Even the white fluorescent light felt like it was adding to the heat.

She was tense.

Nancy decided that was why it felt like this. She glanced at her colleagues' black-mask-covered faces, seeing only a little bit of stiffness, awkwardness in their movements.

The plant blocked electrical waves in a number of ways.

Accelerator was apparently getting assistance from communications equipment to use his ability. An ability he almost certainly wouldn't use, in Amata Kihara's opinion, because there was too big a chance of it misfiring.

All the Hound Dog members here, Nancy first and foremost, thought it was a valid assessment. He had too many restrictions to be careless with his ability. The stronger the power, the higher the risks of it having unintended and dangerous effects.

On the other hand, there was still cause for worry: If they cornered him, he might use his ability even if it was risky.

Only Amata Kihara could take down Accelerator when he was serious. The bullets and bombs Nancy used literally wouldn't put a dent in him.

The absolute, ironclad rule is to kill him before he feels like he's been cornered.

That was the reason for the whole herding strategy.

The target was cautious, but he'd relax his attention after progressing deeper into the plant. They'd aim for that moment and the other team would shoot him dead. To succeed, they needed to come out in the open and attract Accelerator's attention, risky though it was. He couldn't use his superpowerful ability, but it was highly likely he had a gun. Someone could end up with a bullet in their head if they were stupid and got too caught up in their little diversion.

Well, of course we're tense. The only thing anyone here is good at, including me, is killing instantly. None of our training was with this kind of situation in mind.

There were different kinds of soldiers.

Soldiers active in jungles didn't need to know about how hostage negotiations worked, and urban snipers didn't need to learn how to live on uninhabited islands. Groups could create more forces with better strengths if they specialized training regimens with specific fields in mind. It eliminated waste and was a more efficient usage of time.

In essence, they were desert combat specialists on a forced march through snowy Arctic mountains.

Can we do this...?

Behind her black mask, Nancy gulped.

...We have to, or we'll die.

Ka-click.

A soft, metallic sound cut off Nancy's thoughts.

"?!"

The group immediately pointed their guns in that direction.

But nobody was there. Nor was there any space to hide. Maintaining her stance, Nancy made eye contact and communicated with the colleague right next to her using her hands.

"(...That didn't come from any machine.)"

"(...I agree. But if someone's here, where would they hide? It doesn't seem like an advantageous position, either.)"

"(...Any chance he threw something that made the noise?)"

"(...If he did, that would mean the target's right nearby.)"

The entire group tensed.

"(...Rod, the scent detector.)"

"(...One minute. Analysis is about to finish.)"

Her pulse quickened. The index finger on the trigger trembled. A thin layer of sweat formed between her skin and her gloves.

A moment later...

*   *   *

Ka-click.
This time, all the lights turned off at once.

It was like the darkness had been timed.
A tactic to spur nervousness using light and sound, psychologically tormenting them.
This is bad, Nancy realized belatedly.
If they pulled the trigger on a prank, someone would get hurt—they were clustered tightly together. They could aim up, but everything around them—walls and ceiling both—was big hunks of metal. Ricocheting volleys would mean trouble for them.
She hadn't given thought to the safety on her gun.
She couldn't stop worrying about if her shaking finger accidentally moved and pulled the trigger. Accelerator seemed to realize they didn't have night-vision gear.
"(…Wait!!)"
Nancy immediately tried to look each of them in the eye—then realized that wouldn't work in the dark.
It would be best to use her voice, but that would alert the "enemy" to their location.
Thump-thump-thump-thump!! Her heartbeat rang ominously in her ears.
The finger on the trigger trembled.
Trigger…gunshot…misfire…Images ran through her head.
And then there was an earsplitting *bang!!*
She thought her heart would stop.
Kuh…ah…!! That's…that's steam exhaust! Just a normal sound!!
She somehow kept her finger from moving, then began to mentally focus her senses to find the target causing all this, when…
"Gah?!"
A low voice suddenly rang out right beside her.
Ga-thunk, came the vibration of a person falling, transmitted through her feet on the floor.
She caught the scent of metal.

Oh...shi—

If she'd been thinking clearly, she'd have known it was just a spanner thrown through the darkness. If she'd seen the trick, she might have regained her calm just from that.

But...

The enemy's goal was to steal away their "calm," one bit at a time.

That bastard...He's not just using his ability but human fear to his advantage...?!

By the time Nancy noticed it, it was too late.

Just as she began to rally her nerves, there in the darkness...

...clunk. Another implement hit her in the shoulder, without much in the way of force.

Her body moved before she could think; she'd panicked more than she thought.

The shaking in her trigger finger crossed the threshold...

...and several gunshots pierced the air, along with the smell of even more metal.

7

The pitch-black restaurant was filled with a bizarre tension.

Touma Kamijou stood face-to-face with the woman who called herself Vento.

Damn it. If it's not one thing, it's another...

If she was from a magic faction, then unlike before, it would be Imagine Breaker's turn onstage. But that didn't mean he could feel relief. If Vento's abilities were the real thing, then she had enough skill to instantly wipe out four people armed with submachine guns without even letting them make a peep. Before any of the Imagine Breaker stuff, there could even be the danger of getting killed instantly.

And...

He hadn't closely inspected the black-suits on the floor, but they weren't wounded or bleeding at all, making them incredibly similar to the "unconscious people" he'd seen so many of up to now. If the two were the same, the one who was paralyzing the functions of all of Academy City was, indeed, this woman right in front of him, Vento.

A woman, come to smash the top of the science side by herself...

By that logic, her danger level wasn't even comparable to the black-suits.

"You know, you don't need to be so tense," insisted Vento, chain jingling as it swayed. "You won't even have time to feel any pain."

Vento casually swung the barbed-wire hammer in her right hand.

A single horizontal blow.

Kamijou thought it had over five meters to go before reaching him...

"!!"

...but then he felt a chill, so he thrust Last Order out from under him and bent down right as something whipped over him. It turned out to be a mass of wind that had swallowed small pieces of something. It chewed through the air, tore through the wall, and swallowed up small pieces of wreckage, turning from transparent to a dull color as it shot from right to left over a wide area.

Ga-bam!! The entire building tilted.

A spell where she swings her hammer around and it launches projectiles...?

Kamijou's ears, pale with fear, heard a sprinkle of falling fragments.

The action didn't spare any thought for the normal guests unconscious around them.

"Stay hidden, Last Order!!" he shouted as she tried to move away from him when he pushed her away. He watched as she relocated behind a rectangular pillar.

What the hell? First the black-suits and now this woman...!! Kamijou ground his teeth in anger, but that wouldn't be enough to stop Vento.

Vento continued, backing up as she swung the hammer a few more times, sometimes vertically and sometimes horizontally. The chain connected to her tongue jingled as it swung back and forth. Each of the hammer's trajectories seemed dangerous to her, like it would scrape the tongue chain. In reality, orange sparks had flown a few times already. Just a few millimeters off and it would have ripped through her tongue, chain, and piercing, but Vento actually seemed relaxed.

Her hammer split through the air.

Boom!! An explosion hit his ears.

A storm of destruction broke out.

The hammer was like a bat, with which she hit heavy iron balls. It launched away tables, overturned the floor, sent the fallen black-suits' limbs flying, and dropped on the limp patrons. Kamijou's mind flew into a rage, but it was all he could do just to deal with the wind weapon flying at him.

Bam!! As soon as it touched his right hand, the air burst and vanished.

Imagine Breaker.

Without this ability, which canceled out all strange powers, his body would have been smashed to bits already.

The masses of air weren't only flying in straight lines. Some curved to the right or left to block his passage, while others came down straight on his head from above when he stopped moving.

"Ha-ha, so that's the famed right hand. You're doing a good job of keeping up!!"

As Vento laughed, she hurled the hammer down vertically. Winds of destruction appeared in its wake.

Vertical!! Kamijou hastily brought his hand over his head.

The wind then came piercing through *horizontally, from right to left.*

"...!!"

A cold sweat broke out on his skin. He immediately bent over backward, his upper body alone hanging down. It roared just past his face, taking off a bit of skin from the tip of his nose.

The wall to his side went *ker-crush!!* and completely broke apart.

The ceiling was already on an angle, and now an even more hazardous tremor occurred.

What? Her hammer and her attack don't match up...?!

Questions came to mind, but Vento wasn't going to answer them.

"Kya-ha-ha-ha-ha-ha-ha-ha!! This is so much fun!!"

The long chain on her tongue moved left and right with her mouth movements.

Hooked on the very end, the cross gleamed with an unnatural light.

It flickered on and off a few times.

Then Vento, making a face like she'd missed something, frowned. "I see, I see." She nodded, seeming very interested as the crashing *bangs* and *booms* marked one violent wind attack after the other. She was being dealt with perfectly. She couldn't close the five-meter gap.

"Killer of illusions, right? Looks like your right hand is outstanding, just like the reports said. *The real attacks I'm weaving in all over the room aren't working at all.*"

Real attacks? wondered Kamijou as he swung his right hand around again.

Hearing that Imagine Breaker was in a report made him think as well. Maybe the Roman Orthodox Church's priority on him had changed.

"Hmm, but I still don't really get it...Let's test this out."

"?"

"Something like this!!" shouted Vento from her core as she swung the hammer she held from in front of her to her side.

With a loud *pop!!* another air club appeared.

It veered heavily away from Kamijou and toward the civilian patrons collapsed over their tables.

"Bastard!!"

He immediately stuck out his right hand and jumped. The tip of his fingers touched the air club just before it collided with an unconscious patron's head, making it explode everywhere. The single attack had had a horrible amount of force behind it.

Anger blossomed within Kamijou's mind and spread to the rest of his body.

Vento watched and narrowed her eyes, seeming interested. "...I see, so that's how it is. That actually doesn't look like the easiest thing to use, huh?"

Scouting out how much I can do? thought Kamijou. Maybe Vento was studying Imagine Breaker's actual effective range.

"I apologize!" He'd blocked all her attacks thus far, but Vento's face showed no panic as she continued talking. "It looks like I can't do it so fast you won't feel the pain. I'll have to kill you with this guy directly. You'll be awake for it, so it'll hurt a ton, but it'll be the shock that kills you. If you still want to be happy, then why not embrace your masochistic side?"

He heard the jangle of clinking metal.

The chain attached to Vento's tongue swayed along with her movements, arcing right and left. She swung her hammer around vertically, grazing it against the chain.

Bggztt! Orange sparks flew.

?! What's she been...?

They were swept away as the air club came in for an attack on a curving trajectory from right to left...

Her hammer and her attack movements aren't matching up—

...as though tracing out the same movement as the chain attached to her tongue.

This pattern again?!

As though being guided by it.

"Could it be...? The cross on that chain!!" he shouted, crushing the wind weapon with his right hand.

Vento laughed in response. "Oh no! I've been found out!"

The long chain on the cross accessory continued arcing right and left without stopping. Each time she swung her hammer so that it skimmed it, an attack made of wind flew off in a route aligned to the shape of the chain.

Damn it! Knowing doesn't make it any easier to defend!!

He was unintentionally reacting to the large shock-wave-creating hammer's trajectory. But the hammer and the chain were actually moving independently. She could swing it down from above, but the chain would arc in a curve—and if he saw it coming straight across, the chain would be hanging vertically.

The "attacking motion" and "direction of the actual attack" didn't align with each other. If she fooled his eyesight even a little, he'd be slow to adjust and she'd cut his body open.

"Shit!!"

"My goodness! It's kind of getting to be a bother. Ugh."

Roar!! A significantly stronger aerial club came at him.

Moreover, it didn't aim directly at him, instead landing on the floor a bit in front of him. The flooring material flashed up, transforming into a flurry of wood splinters, sharp fragments that flew at Kamijou.

"Ghh—ahhhhhhh?!"

They didn't stab one part of him—they hit all over.

Kamijou flew backward before rolling onto the floor.

He shook his head to clear the pain-induced haze in his mind and desperately tried to kick his senses back into action.

Before he knew it, he'd been pushed almost back to where Last Order was.

With a gasp, Kamijou looked up from the floor.

Last Order was supposed to be hiding behind the pillar, but she'd stood up, and now she was about to run over to him.

"Run!!" he screamed.

"Mm-hmm!" Vento laughed with amusement.

Her attacks could easily demolish the entire pillar along with Last Order.

Last Order didn't move. Either she couldn't move or wouldn't move under her own volition—he couldn't tell.

At this rate, her small body would be flattened into a hunk of flesh.

"Damn!!"

Kamijou got off the floor and ran, pushing the still Last Order to the floor. She hit the floor at the same time Vento attacked. The new air weapon mercilessly crashed through the pillar and was erased there by Kamijou's right hand. Nevertheless, a storm of fragments exploded.

It was too dangerous.

He had to get Last Order out of here as soon as he could.

"Go!! Now!!" he shouted. But Last Order, overcome with surprise, shook her head.

She probably didn't want to leave him to die.

"Now!! Call for help, please!!"

So Kamijou gave her a false goal—one that she'd never accomplish in time.

After that, she finally got to her feet, wobbling. The contents of her pockets seemed to have fled when she fell, though. Upon seeing her toylike, pastel-colored, glossy children's cell phone on the floor, she went to reach for it.

"Don't!!" he screamed. Her shoulders gave a jerk, and her little feet began to run. She went through the broken window and out into the road. He could tell as she ran away how panicked and utterly stupefied she was.

Vento aimed her giant hammer wrapped in barbed wire at the petite girl.

But Kamijou came around and stood directly in between her and Last Order. As he did, the building gave a low rumble. A bunch of support beams had been destroyed, and now the ceiling was on the verge of collapsing entirely to one side. The window from which Last Order had escaped was crushed by the falling roof and blocked off.

Vento had let a target go, but her face betrayed no irritation.

In fact, she seemed delighted as she smiled and spoke to him. "Wow, you're a cruel one! Pretty heavy burden you just put on her, having to run away in the darkness with no destination. She might be on the verge of breaking down out of fear."

She flourished the giant hammer. "You both would have been happier if you'd died together instead of your putting her through that, wouldn't you?"

Kamijou, in spite of himself, spat on the floor.

This bastard was the worst.

"...A burden? I won't put that on her."

He clenched his right fist again...

...and aimed it at the gleefully smiling Vento.

"If I go get her, there's no problem. I just won't die."

"Oh, this is fun. ♪ But answer this! Could you say the same thing after I've stuffed your organs into a blender and made a flesh milkshake out of them, hmm?"

She swung her hammer, creating a sharp noise. Her tongue chain jingled and swayed.

"Anyway, you were my target here, and I do so hate it when pagan apes give me trouble. If you aren't going to be a good boy and run away, it'd really help me out if you made yourself easy to hit!!"

Several more wind attacks swept through the family restaurant as her carelessness continued to destroy it.

8

Accelerator held his breath and waited in the lightless plant.

As long as the opening move of his strategy worked, everything rested in his hands.

He had stolen several pieces of equipment from the minivan. One of them was the shotgun he was using as a cane. Another was a small radio—he could use that for his strategy, too.

His clustered enemies were afraid of friendly fire in the dark. They'd scattered, and now they were using their radios to communicate. Accelerator was talking, too, pretending to be an "ally," his voice disguised by static. He was giving them false information, throwing off their coordination. They'd caught on to his disruption early on, but they had no way to figure out which of the voices belonged to allies and which were Accelerator's. Every time they heard another voice, they doubted it a little more.

And if they couldn't use their radios, they wouldn't know where their allies were.

Even if they spotted someone, they were afraid of shooting one of their own (or being shot by one of their own). The shooters would hesitate to aim at their targets. It would interrupt their coordination. Accelerator, on the other hand, could just assume anyone he saw was his enemy. This was a huge advantage for him.

Firearms and group tactics: Those two things were how the Hound Dogs posed a threat. It was safe to say they'd lost both of those already, thanks to his trick.

Using this kind of terror tactic—the kind that didn't involve his ability—was a first for Accelerator, but they fell for it amusingly easily. Fear really was a trait shared by all mankind. In the backstreets and alleys, he had reigned as a symbol of fear without doing anything. He was just putting more focus on that aspect—and it was getting him big results.

They were no longer opponents.

Just fish in a barrel.

All right.

The radios and fear had torn them apart, and now each moved on their own. If he cut loose now, reinforcements would take full minutes to arrive. He didn't have to care about his surroundings.

Waiting quietly in the darkness, Accelerator let his lips pull up into a grin.

Ahead was his prey, singled out from the others, nervously searching for him.

I'll eat my fill now that you're all fattened up, you damn pigs.

About fifteen meters to the target.

The closer you were with a shotgun, the more punch it packed. In that sense, the distance wasn't quite ideal. Nevertheless, Accelerator leaned back against the wall, lifted his cane from the floor, aimed haphazardly, and fired.

Bang!!

With the earsplitting noise came an impact trying to crush his shoulders. As expected, the buckshot scattered before striking the target. But all around them was hard concrete and metallic plating. Several bullets bounced off them like pinballs and crashed into the black-suit from various angles.

A scream.

In the darkness, a human silhouette spun around with fluid

spraying out like in an action movie. After seeing that, Accelerator approached the black-suit, again using the shotgun as a cane.

It looked like he'd hit the arm.

Accelerator put a hand on a nearby wall and pressed the shotgun muzzle to the black-suit's chin from the side.

"This...this is a joke, right?"

The voice was surprisingly high-pitched. Upon closer inspection, he could tell even through the full-black clothing that the person had feminine curves.

"A joke? Let me see...," he said in an offhanded way, knowing it didn't matter.

"Yep, just thought of it."

He pulled the trigger.

There was a sharp blasting noise as the shotgun fired and sent Accelerator, unable to withstand the recoil, falling backward. *Guess I can't shoot this thing with one hand*, he thought. He shook his head and stood back up as the woman in black writhed on the floor.

"Oh, *orgh, bwahhhhhhh*?!"

She clamped her crushed hands over her mouth, but they went strangely far into her face. The bottom section of her jaw had been blown off by the sidelong shotgun blast. If she moved her hands, she would have realized she had only her top row of teeth left.

Accelerator noticed something warm stuck to his cheek. He twisted his mouth and moved his tongue over it, licking it. It tasted like meat.

"Ah-ha!"

A laugh escaped his lips.

He didn't need to devote so much time to an incapacitated woman. He needed to leave immediately. If the other Hound Dogs had heard the gunshots, they'd be on their way. A face-to-face gun-fight wouldn't be in his best interest. The best option was to stay hidden in the dark and take down his prey one at a time. *I should leave*, he thought. *As soon as possible.*

But.

Unsteadily, with his shotgun as his cane, he stood straight up.

This was getting *kind of fun.*

He knew he shouldn't be doing this, but he couldn't hold back this sense of *bursting liberation.*

As his teeth crunched and munched, he moved to stand before the woman whose jaw he'd blown off.

"…Oh, wow. Need a teething ring or what?"

The woman gave a jolt and looked at him, the lower portion of her face gone.

Accelerator couldn't even imagine what sort of face he was making right now.

"How dare you stay alive with that face! Quit fucking around!!"

Anyway, he decided to kick the crawling woman in the gut.

Thump! Thump! Splat!! A series of sharp noises followed. He kicked her five times, ten times, fifteen, twenty, and as he was doing it, her body suddenly disappeared into the dark.

Upon closer examination, he saw a metalworking press machine.

This area was like a cliff, with the machine itself three meters deep and ten square meters around. It looked like metallic items came through on a conveyor belt, fell in, and got compressed. Considering there was already a mountain of empty cans, steel rods, and the like inside, his size estimation might have been too shallow.

Three meters below, the woman squirmed. An unsightly person, both arms wounded and the bottom half of her face blown off.

Even that didn't arouse pity in Accelerator.

He glanced over at the corner of the window where objects entered the machine. The control room manipulated most of the equipment, but a few appeared to be manual. To prove it, there was a big button alongside the machine wall.

The woman must have guessed what Accelerator had just seen.

Looking up at the entrance, she began to plead. "Ahh, *eeh-ahh, ahh-ehh-ehh—*"

"Sorry," interrupted Accelerator.

*   *   *

"Do you have any clue who you pissed off?"

Bang!!
With his palm, he slapped the big switch.
Without an ounce of mercy in his actions.
As the machine began its work, its motor gave off a very dull rumble that echoed through the facility.
"Welp…"
Accelerator wasn't looking there any longer; he gave a long, exhilarated sigh before beginning his prowl anew.
"Wonder where my next prey's wandering around…"
The only thing on his lips was a wide grin stretching across his face.

9

Vento's attacks continued to disassemble the family restaurant, piece by piece.

It didn't take long for her to drive Kamijou into a corner.

He was covered in blood now, leaning against a broken wall. Imagine Breaker could protect him from all the direct attacks, but it couldn't repel fragments of broken flooring or tables.

Eventually, the cramped space would limit his options.

If he was chased to one point, all he could do was keep blocking with his right hand. Vento wasn't attacking very many times, but each attack's trajectory was complex. He had to foresee each one before acting, so his moves always seemed to lag behind.

In terms of pure destructive power, it was not as strong as Mikoto Misaka, the Railgun. Kamijou had been able to deal with the girl because of geographical issues. Whenever he fought with her, he never, ever preferred a confined space. If he didn't have somewhere to move about freely and flee without restriction, he didn't even try to face her.

If he did, he'd be cornered in a heartbeat.

Unfortunately, in this near-destroyed restaurant…

…there are other people lying around unconscious…

Guests and waiters were on the floor and slumped over tables, out cold from the unknown attack. Vento could directly hit them, and if she did too much damage to the building, the whole ceiling could fall and crush everyone.

Kamijou was paying too much attention to his surroundings.

And to Vento's eyes, too, it was all too clear.

"You're such a good person." She chuckled, leveling her giant hammer. "Shouldn't you be worrying about yourself? Look. ♪"

Fyoo!! She swung her weapon frivolously.

The chain attached to her tongue indicated a path that would veer past Kamijou's face. The wind club bent slightly horizontally from him—purposely controlled to be just out of reach of Kamijou's hand.

"!!" He jumped with all his might and hit it just before it collided with a patron.

Next, Vento released a wind club in the other direction.

She was toying with him like receiving practice for volleyball. She launched attacks at one nearby patron after the next, sometimes throwing in a feint and firing one straight at Kamijou. It demanded ludicrous movements from him, and he began to breathe heavily. What stamina he still had was being sapped away very quickly.

"You!!"

"Mm-hm-hmm?" She chuckled. "Why bother getting so passionate now? You know the state Academy City is in, don't you? If I were the type to care about others, I wouldn't have done that in the first place."

"Shit!!"

Was it true? Had she really caused this entire absurd situation just so she could kill him?

He couldn't believe that was true. This was way too involved to just be for killing a mere high school student.

"You don't realize your own worth, do you?" said Vento lightly, her giant hammer mowing through the air again. "*My objective is*

Touma Kamijou. Anything else is a bonus. Even that archive of forbidden books doesn't mean much compared to *you*."

She spoke as if her point was so simple.

"You are, without a doubt, an enemy of the Roman Orthodox Church right now. And we will use any means necessary to kill our enemies. Allow me to make a very bold statement. We will kill you even if we have to annihilate the very nation of Japan." She paused. "Still, *with that right hand*, I don't think I can rely on my usual method. Anyway, it looks like I'll need to kill you directly."

As she spoke, she produced papers as though by magic and waved them at him. They seemed to be some kind of orders, but he couldn't read them in the dark. He doubted they were written in Japanese anyway.

"As you can see, the pope signed this himself. There are two billion people hunting you now."

The hell? Kamijou was astonished.

He was surprised both at hearing the words *Roman Orthodox Church* coming out now and by the ridiculous intent to wipe an entire nation from history to take out a single person.

In the past, Touma Kamijou had been wrapped up in all sorts of incidents. None had centered around him personally since maybe the Aztec sorcerer from August 31.

Seeing the terrified boy, Vento made the papers disappear, again like a magic trick. "Does that sound like a joke? Why don't I wake you up to the fact that it's not?"

Whoosh. She hoisted her hammer again and smiled.

The chain attached to her tongue's tip moved, the cross swaying slightly from side to side.

"What...?"

"I'm about to kill everyone in this restaurant."

Kamijou caught his breath.

Vento smiled at him sweetly and continued. "That seems like it'll make you suffer more. Dumb reason for committing mass murder, isn't it? But I'll do it. Maybe then, even you'll wise up to the present circumstances."

"No!!"

Ignoring the situation, he felt his feet begin to run toward Vento. She smiled and moved away, waving her head. With a jingle of metal on metal, the chain attached to her tongue coiled around Vento in a helix.

If she swung the hammer now, she'd cause a vortex of destruction with her at the center.

"I'll blow you away, you hear me?!" she howled, moving her right hand.

Boom!! The earth rattled.

A metallic smell filled the darkened, ruin-like restaurant.

10

The sound of short breathing rang in the hot, oppressive, dark plant.

Vela, the Hound Dog hiding in the shadows, was a woman nobody could seem to imagine falling to a place like this. She never failed to be cheerful, friendly, and still keep proper distance from others. Mental and physical labor, she handled flawlessly. That's how she was.

She had her own circumstances, too, but if anyone seemed interested in that, she had enough conversational ability to skillfully deflect the topic.

Be that as it may, Vela, who had decently good sense, sought harmony with others even among the gathering of trash known as the Hound Dogs. Her efforts stood out against the constant mocking and scorning everyone else preferred. Still, she wanted to build trust with her "comrades," even if it wasn't much.

Unfortunately…

…The radios are making things worse.

She was incessantly hearing screams and voices begging for support, but Vela reacted to them in a troubled manner. She couldn't tell which were real and which were traps. Keynes had gone off on his own, saying he'd save them—and she hadn't heard from him since. Which meant it would be dangerous to try to reply to this.

She couldn't trust anyone anymore.

Everything she'd spent so much time thinking she was building—it was all coming tumbling down.

"Ugh…"

A groan escaped her lips.

She had to leave the facility for now and go back to square one. Rod had said there might be a trap at the exit, too, but that warning was suspicious. Was that really Rod? She needed to get out even if it meant accepting risk. Even if she had to leave her "comrades" here. They couldn't be wiped out.

This is the worst… Worst day of my life…

Vela started searching for the exit, her steps wobbling and uncertain. She had no will to fight anymore. The tension was too much for her; it continued to gnaw away at her focus and thinking.

Then she noticed something.

The radio…

It had been so noisy before, but at some point, it had changed to a constant buzz of static and nothing else. She'd been keeping silent lest she caused even more chaos, but this was disheartening. Vela pushed the switch and brought her lips to it.

"This is Vela. This is Vela. Requesting sitrep. Over."

No one answered her request.

Beads of sweat broke out on her skin. Were they rejecting her transmission as false, too? Then the worst case possible crossed her mind—that everyone had already fallen prey to Accelerator.

Or is it…?

As she searched for an escape route from that idea, she hit upon another possibility.

Maybe everyone alive retreated outside like I'm trying to do. This plant's walls are thick, and they block most radio waves. If everyone went outside, they'd have a hard time reaching me.

That would mean her "comrades" had abandoned Vela, but that was still better than the alternative—their all dying in this stinking trash processing plant.

That's right. The Hound Dogs would never die this easily. Accelerator's tactics work only in complete darkness. Under the moonlight, we don't need radios to tell who's an ally or not. Getting outside and dealing with him there will be more effective.

Now that she understood, she had to get outside where it was safe, too. Her conclusion led her to move with stronger, firmer steps as she searched for an exit.

There was still hope for her. With everyone together, even Accelerator wasn't scary. And that was exactly why...

...the moment she saw her colleague crushed by a pressing machine...

...her thoughts did a complete 180 and plunged her into immediate terror.

Strictly speaking, she couldn't actually see the "crushed colleague" herself. She saw only a piece of equipment meant for compressing steel products into heaps. There was an area dug down about three meters from the floor. It looked like it was ten meters across.

Inside the press, a thick iron plate was descending.

Despite that, *she could hear moaning from the other side.*

...Nancy!!

She cared about her friends, so she could identify the one moaning just from that slight voice. Meanwhile, with creaks and groans, the thick iron plate continued its slow trek downward.

"Uh, uwaah. Uwaahh, ahh, ah!!"

In a state of near frenzy, she banged on the button on the wall with her palm. With a jolt, the press machine gradually came to a stop.

The moaning continued.

No human body could withstand being compressed by that metal plate. Nancy was probably only alive because there had been a blanket of metal parts on the floor underneath her. Her body had sunk into the mountainous cushion of metal.

But there was still no doubt she was near death.

Maybe dying would be easier.

If she pressed a different button on the wall, the iron plate would rise again. That might be enough to save Nancy.

But…

The button was covered with something sticky. It was black and viscous, like the stuff in a garbage can next to a vending machine. If she wanted to press it, she had to get her hands dirty.

Even if the "dirt" is actually human blood and flesh.

Even if the thing stuck to it is a tiny piece of flesh, crushed skin and bones still in it.

"…Ah, ha?"

She felt the thin thread from which she was hanging snap.

She thought she heard a small *rip*.

"*Ugah?! Gyah!! Gyaaaahhhh!!*"

Vela let loose a scream strong enough to tear her throat and lurched backward. She couldn't take any more of this. She could distinctly *feel* everything she'd created until now coming tumbling down. If a drop of water had fallen onto her skin right now, she was pretty sure she'd die from shock.

With such a situation, her foot tripped over something, and she fell onto her rear end with a slimy sensation.

She looked at her foot—a soft, fist-sized piece of meat clung to it.

It was crushed, but it still clearly looked like a human's lower jaw.

"*Uwaaaaaaaaaaaaaaaahhhhhhhhhhhhhhhhhhhhhhhhhhh!!*"

She flung it away and tried to flee.

But when she ripped her gaze away, she met another colleague. Well, *met* may not have been the proper term. His body was bound by thick wire and boiled in high-temperature steam that had sprayed from a severed pipe—whether or not the word *met* applied here was a mystery.

Vomit and excreta burst forth.

The mask covering her face got in the way, and the contents could not escape. The fluids gurgled out of her mouth and nose—but she didn't appear to be bothered by the discomfort. She didn't have time to be.

"Hee, uah, aaahhhhhh..."

Her voice sounded like it had been spread out very thinly, coming out as a long groan.

Vela looked at the silent radio. This was what it meant.

The silence—it was simple. There was no strategy. There was no recovery, no come-from-behind plan. Every one of her colleagues had probably failed to exit the plant. Each and every one of the Hound Dogs was now incorporated into some creepy park attraction in Resource Reclamation and Treatment Plant 3. They'd been wiped out. The others had probably ended up like she was now—mentally broken, robbed of any ability to make judgments, standing still. And then they'd been toyed with and cooked.

Vela's hands lost their grip. Her radio and submachine gun clattered to the floor. She, too, collapsed to her knees.

Who the hell was she fighting?

Accelerator had never used weapons before—on purpose. He'd never considered the terrain. All he did was advance, his supernatural ability cutting through any obstacles. She had thought, anyway, that the chances to kill him were pretty good depending on their strategy now that his ability was limited.

But everything was different now.

He used weapons. He took advantage of the building. He predicted how they would think, devised the most efficient way to throw them into confusion, and executed his plan. He wasn't just letting his anger drive him to beat them to death—he was hitting them with immense mental damage and even leaving them to try to find ways they wouldn't be killed.

The terrifying thing was the growth rate of his mental capabilities. He was no longer just a child completely reliant on his power. He used everything he could get his hands on to murder. He'd turned into a huge threat already, but the magnitude of that danger would speed along, ever growing—until nobody could handle him, and he destroyed the world.

The sheer astonishment paralyzed Vela's mind. He'd even taken the right to be scared away from her.

He was a demon.

And in their foolishness, the Hound Dogs had helped him break out of his shell.

Click.

A soft footfall rang out directly behind Vela.

Without turning around, her head hanging, she smiled a little.

11

A watery gurgle echoed through the dark restaurant.

Clumps of blood began to drip onto the floor.

As Kamijou was just about to deliver his punch, he faltered at the sight. The blood was definitely fresh. He looked blankly at the point the redness had burst from.

At Vento's mouth, which had just been celebrating triumph a few moments before.

"Urgh…" She bent over, put her hands to her mouth, and produced another gurgling cough. With each breath, more sticky, heavy fluid leaked from her fingers.

"Gah, ah, ah…"

She took a couple of shaky steps back. Her previous calm was gone. It didn't look like an act; it looked like she was actually in pain.

What…?

The sudden bloody outburst had almost frozen Kamijou's thoughts like a bucket of water. *A side effect of her spell? I feel bad for her, but maybe this is my chance.*

He snapped out of it. It pained him to swing a fist at someone suffering, but frankly, he didn't have the luxury to spout niceties. If he didn't take her down while he still could, she could involve even more victims in her half-serious games.

He clenched his teeth, steeled himself, and gripped his right fist.

"G-gwaahhhhh!!"

But before he could move, Vento spun around and swung her

barbed-wire hammer in the wrong direction. It arced along her chain, creating sparks between them. The levity from earlier was gone. She swung like a drunk trying to hit someone—wildly and violently.

With a heavy *crash*, a huge hole opened in the wall. Vento ran for it. She sent a few attacks at the pursuing Kamijou before jumping out of the building and fleeing.

"..." In this situation, he honestly wasn't sure whether he should follow her or not.

What...was that? Vento didn't do anything else, like destroying both Kamijou and the restaurant from outside. She didn't seem like she gave a damn about the patrons, so she must have had her hands full dealing with whatever strange thing was happening to her body, without any room to think about anything else.

In his head, Kamijou slowly organized the new problems that had appeared.

God's Right Seat...

Vento of the Front...

...and the Roman Orthodox Church.

12

Kuroko Shirai and Kazari Uiharu were in Judgment Branch Office 177.

The name sounded grand, but it was really just a room in the middle school Uiharu attended.

Several desks were arranged in a line, but not the plywood-and-metal-pipe kind you usually saw in classrooms. They were more like the kinds found in an office, with work laptops on the desks. A bag of potato chips, its owner evidently not caring about the delicate electronics, was plopped down at one of them.

Kazari Uiharu plunged her hands into the plastic bag and rustled around. "Shiraaai, do you want a Chinese-style rice bowl or a fish meal for dinner?"

"What does it matter?!"

"Huh? Okay, then I'll just take the rice bowl."

"I'm eating that one! Mgh, at this very moment, Big Sister and that rotten ape-man are walking together down the street at night and— *Ugaaaahhhhhh!!*"

The twin-tailed girl Kuroko Shirai pounded the desk with her hands.

Their voices were the only ones in the room. There was a big radio, too, but that had been quiet. In general, Judgment duty ended with the final school closing time, because their main responsibility was settling school quarrels. Still being in the workplace at this hour wasn't part of the regular schedule.

Kazari Uiharu, one of those girls working overtime, took out her cell phone.

"Oh, it's time for the variety show I always watch!"

"Do your job, Uiharu!!"

"Do you have the right to say that, Shirai? By the way, I'm smart enough to watch TV and work at the same time."

Her phone probably had TV on it, but she must have really liked this particular program, because she took the time to switch on the big-screen television in the room.

"Hmph!"

But when a vexed Shirai took the remote control away, she accidentally changed it to a different channel. A completely dull and uninteresting news show appeared. "Ahh! What did you do, Shirai?!" cried Uiharu as they began struggling to gain possession of the remote.

"And now we turn to, hmm…N-news from Academy City."

Startled, Shirai and Uiharu stopped their war and turned toward the TV.

This news broadcast was a national one, based outside of Academy City. Such "outsider" organizations almost never ran news about the city. That was probably part of the reason why the newscaster had fumbled.

"There appears to be an intruder running amok in Academy City. We're hearing that damage inside the city is spreading. Ishisura is at the scene. Ishisura?"

The picture on the screen changed.

It was a rough, super-magnified image; the camera was probably outside Academy City. It showed a blurry figure walking on a rain-pelted road—a woman in yellow clothing.

The woman's gait was unsteady as she moved unconscious people out of the way with her foot, walking down the rainy street. She was sticking out her tongue, and a long chain connected to it was swaying side to side.

Then, before showing the reporter on the scene, the camera rocked and made a clattering noise, and the image was immediately covered in gray static. The newscaster in the studio said the person's name several more times but got no response. It wasn't clear whether the reporter was even there.

The studio immediately came back onscreen.

It was perfect timing—just barely not a broadcasting error.

"Th-that must have been the intruder."

A commentator sitting next to the newscaster answered, voice cool as a cucumber. "Given the state of Academy City's security, it doesn't seem very probable that this is a simple degenerate targeting the students, unlike schools elsewhere."

"Right."

"It could be a terrorist act against so-called science worshippers or a theft of cutting-edge technology. Perhaps it's something like that."

"Which means that the thing most of our viewers are worried about, the safety of the children, could be affected?"

"Of course," the commentator agreed, shaking his head very theatrically. "There are children being caught up in adult problems. It could even be someone worse than a phantom slasher. I say—who was that woman in the image? It is true that slowly, the lives of children are being treated with less importance, but there is no way we can leave someone so absurdly unsuited for our society to their own—"

A series of *thumps* interrupted.

The commentator had suddenly fallen forward, his forehead hitting the table.

"?" Shirai frowned.

She thought it was another theatric display of his, but then the commentator's limp body fell to the side and down beneath the table. She heard the announcer scream. The camera wobbled from side to side, and young people in casual clothes who looked like advertisements came dashing into the studio.

A series of powerful voices shouting orders came from off camera, and the image immediately switched to a commercial. Clearly, they were having some sort of trouble.

Uiharu took her eyes off the young female talent—whose small face was well known—acting impressed at how wonderful a foaming face wash was and turned back to Shirai.

"...Wait, did we get a report about that video they had on? I've been buried in paperwork all day long, so I didn't notice. But if a single person overpowered Anti-Skill, then she must be extremely dangerous. Why do such creepy types keep invading...?"

"Judgment almost never gets called out for stuff out of school...or at night, either. If things were really bad, we'd get a support request from Anti-Skill. Until then, let's get as much of this work done as..."

"..."

Kazari Uiharu didn't answer her.

Shirai saw her body sway back, then fall to the floor with no reaction. She heard a pretty loud *slam*, but she didn't show any signs of movement.

Startled, Shirai ran over to her. "Uiharu!!"

Despite shouting her name in her ear, despite slapping the collapsed Uiharu in the face, there was absolutely no response.

She didn't know what was going on. The television sound came back to her.

The commercial had ended, but the news program hadn't come back on yet. Instead there was the message WE THANK YOU FOR YOUR PATIENCE overlaid on the screen.

13

He'd mostly finished cleaning up the Hound Dogs.

It was still necessary to stay alert for ambushes, since he didn't know their exact numbers, but Accelerator's instincts told him the battle was over.

What he'd just done, from the time he'd sprung his traps to the duration of the intervals of silence, was a program—one that had done all the needed cerebro-physiological calculations to send his victims 100 percent into a state of pure terror.

Not a fear they could overcome with belief and willpower but an emotion beaten into them on a brain impulse level. Nobody would be able to fight properly now. As long as they were human—as long as they weren't completely off their rocker—this attack was inescapable. Crying, wailing, and waving their arms and legs was about the most they could do.

Accelerator popped open the bottle of washing material he'd found in the plant. He poured the clear liquid down his head, emptying it, then tossed the container to the side. *Kihara's gotta do something now. This was all a lucky break in my book, but I hope the shithead panics. Reports will get to him in a few minutes. What should I do before then?*

His objective was rescuing Last Order.

But he didn't know where the girl was right now, since she was still running away—and actually, he didn't even know that for sure. It would be a different story if he could get through to her via cell phone, but that didn't seem like a very viable option. To help her, he should focus his energy on obstructing Kihara and his dogs.

He'd draw all their attention to him. The only way to win was to get them to think this: *We need to do something about Accelerator here before stealing our goal, Last Order.* Of course, the more that came true, the more of a bind it would place Accelerator in…

Doesn't matter what happens. I'll do it.

Using the shotgun as a cane, he headed for the facility's exit.

Interrogating the Hound Dogs for information was an option, but he avoided doing so. He couldn't use his ability in the plant, and with his cane, he couldn't carry an adult outside. The only reason he'd won thus far was because he'd planned ahead. He couldn't be careless now, even if the opposition was seriously wounded. One bullet was enough to kill Accelerator in his current state. If he messed up and they turned the tables on him, there would be no one left to save Last Order.

Accelerator thought about his next objective.

Maybe I'll look in the Hound Dogs' minivan again. Don't think they'll have left a piece of paper telling me where their base is, but I've gotta get a little info on where the other groups are if I want to crush them.

Then he stopped thinking. There were bloodstains on the floor.

He saw the spots of red leading off and frowned slightly. The enemy soldiers had all moved as he'd planned, taken by fear, and he'd finished them off one at a time. This route, though—he didn't remember using it to corner anyone.

Someone was still alive.

" ... "

As far as he could tell from the bloody route left behind, the enemy had been uncertain, his focus wandering. In his state of extreme fear, he was afraid of everything. It looked like Accelerator's mental manipulation had worked.

Or maybe he's just pretending, and leading me in.

He and his cane slowly followed the trail of blood.

It led to a small emergency exit. A green light-up sign was above the metal door. Next to the door was a box on the wall, protected by reinforced glass. It was cracked, and the lever inside had been moved.

Someone had unlocked it and gotten out.

Accelerator leaned against the wall next to the door, then touched the knob by reaching out with one hand. The cane was getting in the way again. If he could use both hands, one of them would already be ready and waiting on his electrode choker. His ability could go off accidentally, but he might still have to use it if it came to that.

He slowly turned the knob.

Without a sound, he pushed the door open.

" ... "

Nothing suspicious here.

At least, it didn't look like there were any bombs planted or anything. After making sure of that, he flung the door open all the way.

The rain had become a downpour and pelted his body. It was a comfortable, stimulating feeling for him, since he'd been lurking inside the hot, oppressive factory this whole time.

But…

"I see…"

He wasn't smiling.

This place he was standing in—it was the second floor. Down the steel emergency staircase was about twenty meters of asphalt, and a wire-netting fence beyond that to mark the property.

He saw a figure squirming up the fence.

The figure's black suit was a dead giveaway—a Hound Dog.

Also, a car was parked right outside the fence. Accelerator had a good idea of the black-suit's destination.

He thought it was Hound Dog reinforcements, but he was wrong.

The car was a patrol car used by real Anti-Skill officers.

Why the hell…? thought Accelerator.

There was something wrong with them showing up here.

This was a battle between darkness and more darkness—it wasn't a place regular folk should be coming to, was it?

"…………………………………………………………………………………………"

A thin, slight breath escaped Accelerator's lips.

He had no words.

The black-suit's wailing reached his ears as he stood there silently.

Despite twenty meters and a downpour separating them, he heard the yelling clear as day.

"Hey! Is anyone in there?! Help…Help me! Help me, now! You're Anti-Skill—you protect people in the city, right?! Then get me to safety already! It's him…He did all this! Ha-ha! Fuck you! I was saved, and now you can't get to me, you demon!!"

Accelerator heard noise.

Wordsmorepatheticthananyhe'dheardbefore,despitesomuchtime spentintheworldofdarkness.

"You hear me? You can struggle all you want, but it's over! I've got Anti-Skill on my side. If you want to kill me, then just try! But if you touch Anti-Skill, they'll put you on the official wanted list!! Now your days with that fucking brat you wanted to protect so badly are all over! You'll be sent right back to a heartless laboratory! I hope you enjoy your life as a lab rat!! Gya-ha-ha-ha-ha-ha!!"

The hand holding the shotgun filled with intense power.

His mind burst.

Everything—the choker's battery, conserving it because only seven minutes remained, not being able to fight Kihara if he used it here—everything went straight out the window.

Accelerator put his hand on his neck.

He didn't hesitate.

I'll make a bloody mess of that shithead even if it kills me.

That was the only thing on his mind right now.

14

Ryouta Saikou and Edao Sugiyama were lucky Anti-Skill officers.

While most of the city's peacekeeping agencies were grinding to a halt, they'd been sleeping. Accidentally, anyway—they hadn't fallen into a dead sleep like the other members. Nobody was answering them on the car radio, but they decided it was malfunctioning. For better or worse, they'd been left out to dry.

For better, in this case.

Because Saikou and Sugiyama had gotten out of the car, from the driver's and passenger's side respectively, and were currently walking over to help the blood-splattered man climbing up the fence.

At that very moment, the first thing they heard was a war cry.

A bestial shout from a person.

Before Saikou and Sugiyama could find the source of the bellow, the second wave hit.

There was a thick metal door.

It spun toward them end over end at an insane speed, then just barely scraped by the skins of the two officers, crashing like a giant buzz-saw blade straight into the patrol car they'd parked.

*   *   *

Gr-graaash!!
Sparks flew everywhere as the car suddenly bent into an L shape.

It was like a cannonball suddenly slammed into the side of the normal, unremarkable car. The back half came up vertically, while the front was crushed like paper and twisted to the side. The immense force didn't even let the car slide that way—the part hit by the "cannonball" spread open like a metal flower.

The metal door that destroyed the automobile didn't slow down. It crashed into the asphalt, shattering it, and finally stopped. The gasoline pipe had been torn through in one swing, and an equally severed cable brushed against it. They started sparking.

That was all it needed. The sideswiped car exploded, spreading flames and smoke.

"Wh-what?!"

Saikou couldn't see anything with so much smoke, and that was all he could shout.

The metal door had flown at them with such incredible speed that he didn't know what had made the car explode. Not being able to see anything caused his sense of urgency to start ballooning.

He couldn't see his colleague, either, even though he was right next to him.

And through the smoke...

"*Gyaah?!* Stop, no!!"

The voice of a man he didn't know rang in his ears. Before Saikou realized it was the man who they were about to take to safety...

"Wait, please, wait, Accelerator! No, please, this isn't...!! Anti-Skill! Wh-wh-wh-wh-where are you?! Help, *eebyah, byahh, gowahhhhhhhhhhhhh*?!"

There was a loud *crunch*, like someone biting into a firm hot dog. Saikou, feeling a threat to his safety, drew his pistol on reflex but couldn't do anything else. The smoke was too thick. He couldn't get a read on anything. If he shot blindly, he could hit Sugiyama or the man they were trying to secure. He couldn't even tell what was happening beyond the veil of smoke, where to fire his gun, or whether the "thing" causing all of it was a person or a beast.

"Stop, stop! Don't move! Step away from that man!!" shouted Saikou anyway, blindly guessing where to point his gun.

He thought he heard a laugh from very close by. Not a very loud one; it sounded accidental, like someone was trying hard not to laugh.

The dull noises continued.

After about ten seconds, the screams stopped.

Saikou was never able to make a move.

Some things in this world should never be seen.

He knew instinctively that the smoke blinding him was a stroke of fortune.

The downpour extinguished the fires from the exploded vehicle. With it, the smoke clouding his vision also subsided at last.

Sugiyama had fallen onto his behind right next to him.

He moved his mouth up and down, but no voice came out. However, his face pale, he was pointing to the ground with a shaking finger.

Saikou looked.

The man they had been about to secure—he wasn't there. He looked all over, but nothing.

The spot Sugiyama pointed at…

…held nothing but a small bloodstain and two torn-off human big toes.

INTERLUDE
SEVEN

Academy City's periphery had many faces to it. The city boasted a surface area equal to one third of Tokyo, so the scenery and characteristics of the periphery changed completely depending on which side it was facing—toward east Tokyo, Kanagawa, Saitama, or Yamanashi.

Motoharu Tsuchimikado was currently running through what seemed like an area between city and forest. Several giant, abandoned factories were buried in the thick coniferous woodland. Fiercely thriving weeds and ivies coiled up their concrete walls, relentlessly incorporating them into nature.

In one of those buildings, Tsuchimikado loudly screeched to a halt.

The place looked like it was formerly a bus maintenance station belonging to a transportation company.

The concrete-walled space was somewhat smaller than a school gymnasium. Its costly equipment had been removed, leaving only useless, rusted hunks of metal. They made it feel deserted, but there were still steel scaffoldings to walk on up where the second and third levels would be. The upper paths were made of wire netting, and they were littered with holes due to rust.

Half the ceiling had caved in, and the rain was mercilessly pouring inside. One entire wall consisted of metal shutters, but those had rusted over and fallen as well.

...*Here it is.* A wooden stake was sticking out of the floor in front of him.

It was massive, too. Fifteen centimeters in diameter and over three meters long. Its tip, pointing straight up, was sharpened like a pencil tip. Pelted by countless raindrops, its surface had water dripping down it like a shower of blood.

It was an article of magic. Was that the Chinese windmill palm he saw in it?

"Now here's a surreal sight."

Tsuchimikado's lips twisted into a smile, and a moment later, more three-meter-long stakes burst out of it, covering its surface all around. They weren't wooden stakes—they were made of stake-like pieces of wood. He danced back, away from their edges, as more of the stakes shot forth from the floor nearby, the path on the second story, and the piles of rusted equipment, all of them striking out directly toward his body.

He continued his backstepping with meandering, snakelike movements, and as though they felt they couldn't catch up, several stakes exploded. With a *bang* and a *boom*, they sent hundreds of fragments flying at him.

Tsuchimikado, sometimes ducking and sometimes hiding behind machinery, let all of them whiz past.

In a matter of seconds, the place had turned into an execution site covered with dozens of stakes.

The giant pencils grew like grass across the entire floor around him.

I get it. They were planning on attacking Academy City like this, too. By skewering everyone who couldn't move. Bastards, he swore, adjusting his positioning slightly and moving his head.

These "stakes" were probably growing in other places beyond the maintenance facility, too.

Purposely guiding me into this trap—no, this is too large-scale for that. It'd make more sense to look at it as something they'd plunge right into the middle of their real objective.

The Chinese windmill palm's primary meaning was "blessing." By using that trait, it would also be possible to grant it the property of slipping by any defenses that would "check" or "repel" it. If Tsuchimikado had carelessly used defensive sorcery, the attack would be recognized as a "blessing," and the stakes would have easily gotten past it and pierced every spot on his body.

He'd be surprised if they'd actually brought thousands of them with them, but...

"Hmph. They're cheatin' their numbers."

The explosive stakes suddenly stopped appearing.

Something sounded slimy.

From the previously empty darkness appeared a figure in white.

It was like looking at the light at the end of a tunnel. The man who had cast the spell cut away the darkness like a removed puzzle piece. Because of his glow, perhaps, twelve shadows appeared at equal positions around his feet in a circle, like an analogue clock.

As though the shadows were themselves the key to triggering the spell, each continued to expand and retract, obeying unheard commands.

"..." Tsuchimikado took a step forward, yet he didn't get any closer.

The man didn't seem to have moved, but somehow, he'd kept his distance. Almost like saying Tsuchimikado could never close the gap between them.

Not good...

To make things worse, he felt more than one presence nearby. Several of them, in fact, both inside and outside this building. In total, they numbered in the dozens. At this rate, other people like them could be fanning out in other spots in Academy City's periphery.

Tsuchimikado spoke quietly to the silent enemies.

"Three to indicate the celestial planes, four for the earth, and twelve for the world. You don't need to prepare all the stakes. By appending meaning to a specific 'number' of them, they gain a single unit of 'vastness,' eh?"

The point was, if he found one of the seven core stakes and broke even one of them, it would forbid the enemy's spell.

Out of all these stakes.

From these mountains of stakes, of which there were already thousands, and likely more to come.

Tsuchimikado grinned. "Nice spell, but...this isn't Crossist. This comes from the theories of the Pythagorean Order in BC-era Greece. Since when did the lot of you start accepting the world before the Son of God was born?"

His words must have incited rage in the man.

The blurry figure roared.

An earsplitting *boom* rang out. Wooden stakes exploded, shaking the entire facility. The rust on the walkways on the second and third floor and the half-collapsed roof fell off and were given "power." New stakes burst from the rusty fragments' surfaces, assailing Tsuchimikado from all angles.

As they stabbed toward him from every which way, the space between them closed up, causing stakes to knock together, each destroying the other with sharp smashing noises.

But Tsuchimikado was already gone.

He was now standing on a steel-built third-story walkway high up in the building.

Cold, inhuman eyes looked up and found him from far below.

The countless stakes completely covering the concrete floor exploded one after another, their shards of flak heading up at Tsuchimikado. He jumped across the walkway, avoiding the rusted-out holes. The path right behind him continued to break, snap, and crumble.

A drop of blood slowly trickled down from the corner of his lip. Not because a magic attack had hit him—but because he'd used magic himself to jump to the third-story walkway.

Tsuchimikado was both an esper and a sorcerer.

And when an esper used sorcery, his body would reject it and be harmed.

Shit. Nothing good will come of dragging this on, he thought, wiping away the blood.

There was no sense of distance with that figure. It was like chasing an afterimage left on his eyes. The more he advanced, the more the figure would retreat, and the more he retreated, the more the figure would approach—a slippery one indeed. Directly striking the figure like this would be impossible—well, maybe not, but at least extremely difficult.

Instead of being particular about that, he should stop the mountains of stakes from working first. After he stole the figure's weapon, he could take his time handling him.

"How unfortunate."

As the rusted walkway cracked, boomed, and smashed apart behind him, Tsuchimikado jumped over its holes, pushing toward a single destination.

"Whenever I see such an intricate spell, I almost don't want to destroy it!!"

In front of him was a single wooden stake, buried in the rest of them.

It was one of the seven—and the weak point controlling them all.

CHAPTER 8

God's Right Seat and the Imaginary Number District
Fuse_KAZAKIRI.

1

"Aiho!!"

At last, Kikyou Yoshikawa found her old friend in the downpour.

All around her in the city this night, it was eerily silent.

Yomikawa was leaning limply on the steering wheel of her domestic sports car, parked on the shoulder strip. It looked like a painful position, with the wheel pushing into her chest, but it didn't even make her flinch. She was unconscious.

When Yoshikawa put her hand on the door, she found it wasn't locked.

As soon as she opened it, Yomikawa's upper body swayed to the side and slid out of the seat.

"!" Yoshikawa managed to get her arms around her and push her back into the driver's seat.

...What happened here? she thought, putting a palm to the woman's mouth to check her breathing and a hand to her neck to check her pulse. She seemed to be alive for the moment, but even so, she showed no signs whatsoever of waking. This didn't seem like regular sleep.

"..." Yoshikawa looked from the car to her surroundings, worried about the rain as well. The car was parked on a main road, but not far away was a back road where a bunch of delinquents hung out.

Maybe they attacked her, she thought—but Yomikawa didn't have a scratch on her. Even coming from another woman, Aiho Yomikawa was a beauty. Plus, she was an Anti-Skill officer. If she'd been attacked, the situation would have been unimaginably bad. The delinquents probably would have also taken pieces of the car and sold them for pocket change.

Which means it was someone else...?

Yoshikawa frowned. If it wasn't a band of ruffians, who on earth had done this to her?

Anyway, hospital...They have an emergency room; it would be quicker than calling an ambulance! she thought, scatterbrained, before hearing a low *brrrr.*

In the car, the small printer attached to the radio was operating. It had spit out a piece of paper the size of a postcard.

"Ngh..." Yoshikawa reached over Yomikawa, who was spread over the driver's sheet, and took the paper.

And then she froze.

It read:

"Report from Ryouta Saikou, Anti-Skill Branch 84, Suzuyama High School.

"Comparison performed with city data banks in accordance with evidence found at the scene of the crime in School District 5.

"Name: Accelerator. Wanted as a suspect in an attempted murder."

On another paper that came out at the same time was the mug shot of a person she knew well.

It couldn't possibly have been anyone else.

2

Accelerator stood in a filthy back alley.

He had returned to School District 7, but that wasn't likely to put him at ease.

In the continuing sounds of rainfall came a heavy, metallic *bang*.

It was the sound of his throwing a Hound Dog member, now an old rag, into a giant dumpster and shutting the lid. Drops of red fluid leaked from the gap between the lid and the container like the drool of a glutton.

Accelerator put his hands on the dumpster, which was about up to his waist, then leaned back on it, finally letting his legs give out and sliding to the ground. He thought he felt an oily puddle seeping into his clothing and skin.

"Ha-ha," he laughed.

He hadn't crushed meat in a while.

It felt like he was gulping down coffee after going without it for a long time. It should have felt good, but he was despondent. It should have excited him, but somehow, it gave him this insurmountable resignation. He'd drunk it for so long, and how delicious it was—but now he was in a strange mental state where he was confused. Had this been all coffee was?

One way or another, he'd found out.

Right now, Accelerator didn't consider it a good thing to kill someone. Actually, it might have been more accurate to say he'd realized it on August 31. Somehow or other, his meeting with Last Order had been that big a turning point for him.

He didn't want to kill people like Last Order. And it was possible for him to feel the same way about others, like Yomikawa and Yoshikawa, who lived in the same world as her. It was wrong for sentimental people who walked in the light to end up victim to those lurking in the dark like Accelerator. To put a stop to that, Accelerator wouldn't quit fighting on his own.

That might seem like what a normal human would think.

But there was a hole in this logic.

For example, if a rotten piece of shit who didn't have the slightest resemblance to Last Order showed up. If someone un-savable tried to take away someone who could be saved. In that case, Accelerator's shackles that asserted "killing is wrong" would come undone.

His fear was someone who lived in the light falling prey to someone who lived in the dark. He hated himself for being part of that world already—he couldn't ever accept another entering that same place.

Therefore, in specific, special circumstances, he wouldn't hesitate to tear someone's flesh apart. Every drop of what he held inside would burst out until he was left with nothing.

Like how he was now.

"..." Accelerator hung his head in the torrential rainfall.

In the end, it hadn't been enough—the turning point on August 31 hadn't fully wiped away those dark, ingrained properties. That wasn't enough. Something—something was missing. There were more pieces to the puzzle for him to go back to being human.

Having thought that far, he smiled—a somehow resigned, relinquishing smile.

Loneliness overwhelmed him.

He'd returned to how he was before meeting Last Order.

"Ha-ha..."

His back against the dumpster, he looked up at the sky.

Raindrops hit his skin. The clouds were thick, and so black he felt his soul darken as he watched them.

Only four minutes left of ability mode..., Accelerator thought, sick of this, reviewing the situation. *Anti-Skill's on my tail, too. My mug shot's probably all over the city by now. Even if I do kill Kihara and rescue the brat, I can't go back.*

His time with Last Order was already at an end. Even if he rescued her unharmed, they couldn't walk the same path. What he needed right now wasn't the effort to accomplish that goal—it was the strength to accept the truth right in front of him. The strength to act only to save her despite what he knew, not caring about that.

He clicked his tongue in frustration. It hadn't been very long, but now that he'd lost it, he felt a hole in his chest.

But that wasn't enough to make his red eyes waver.

I'll admit it. So fucking what?

He grabbed his shotgun from the puddle with one hand.

I'll bring that brat out of the darkness, even if she's the only one.

That should have been my only objective anyway. Let's cut out the flab. I'll do what I need to, and that's making sure the little shit is safe.

He used the weapon as a cane to wobble up to his feet.

Amata Kihara, the Hound Dogs, Anti-Skill, what happened after this was all over—none of it mattered now. He needed only one goal.

That made it easier to think. He felt like he'd thrown away all the weight on his shoulders. Now he could selfishly think he would accomplish any objective, no matter what.

The final chain had been broken. Accelerator, who had regained the title of strongest in exchange for something important, let his cane lead him into the rainy streets.

Everything to crush his next target.

To settle the problem, even if he came out hands drenched with blood.

And he had an idea of where to find the flesh of his prey.

3

"All facilities clear," reported Hound Dogs member Dennis on the radio, giving the information he'd gathered to the team on standby. "Nobody's around."

"I see," came back a curt response from a colleague.

He and the others in his group were in a hospital, currently in the big reception lobby on the first floor. With the huge glass panes on the walls, it was designed to let in a lot of sunlight—but it was night right now, and all the overhead lighting was off. In a word, the pitch-black hospital was *creepy*.

The group of fourteen had orders to dispose of Orson, former member of the Hound Dogs who had deserted in the face of the enemy. In addition, they were to make sure the sister in white who'd witnessed their operation wouldn't talk. They were even instructed that in the worst case, they had permission to plant bombs in the facility and blow up the entire hospital.

Dennis continued his report. "Used smoke bombs located in the third-floor hallway. It doesn't look like they've been gone long."

"The report they gave stated that there was a danger of terrorist activity, and since they're possibly still hiding suspicious items inside, they evacuated all the staff and patients outside the building temporarily," answered his colleague Mike, who was getting said information from his portable computer.

Dennis took his ear away from the radio. "...They noticed us."

"Probably," Mike said dully. "Personally, I feel like it's better that way."

"But wouldn't the hospital have had patients needing large equipment?"

"They probably used hospital vehicles," said Mike offhandedly. "Special ambulances, about thirty meters long. 'Bout the size of a sightseeing bus. Apparently, they can speed to the scene and do basic surgery on the spot."

"I've never heard of that."

"Wouldn't think so. It was a failure—the large size was actually its biggest flaw. It couldn't make tight turns, so it would never get to the scenes in time. It might have worked if it wasn't Japan. Or if they could coordinate somehow with smaller ambulances, like the ships in a fleet."

"You're saying this hospital had some of them?"

"Yeah, probably in the underground parking lot. Nothing surprises me when it comes to this hospital. You could tell me they had ten of the behemoths, and I'd just be like, yep, that makes sense. They must have moved the patients requiring complete bed rest to them and had everyone who could walk evacuate on foot." As Mike spoke, tone facetious, he shut down the portable computer. "It's been a while since we lost contact with the Accelerator suppression team."

"He must have gotten them."

"We'll need to assign some people to chase him, so we can't rest here. We're pulling out. If everyone related to this hospital fled, everywhere that might have been their destination will have been dealt with anyway."

"Kihara won't be happy."

"It doesn't matter how much time we take—he won't be happy anyway if we tell him we didn't find any clues. Difference in priority. We should deal with Accelerator, then wash away the hospital people after that. If we try to cover each mistake with an achievement, it'll soften his anger. We probably won't all be executed.

"Call everyone here," said Mike in a monotonous voice.

In reply, Dennis hit the switch on the radio—but something happened.

Beep-beep-beep, went a cell phone's call sound.

" "
...

" "
...

Dennis and Mike turned to look around.

The source was coming from behind the reception desk. It was precise, like they'd not only predicted where they'd be but called a specific phone as well.

"Any chance it's a trap?"

"I'm not picking up any wires or infrared rays," said Dennis.

Mike, attentive to his surroundings, jumped over the desk. After staring for a moment at the blinking red call light, he took the receiver.

"Oh, you're late."

It wasn't a normal, everyday voice.

Mike frowned. If not for the black mask, others might have taken it as a sour face. A doctor he was used to hearing had spoken the words on the phone. The doctor had saved his life once before.

"Heaven Canceler..."

"One of my pleasures as a doctor is talking to former patients, but I don't really have much time, so I'd like to make this short. Is that fine with you?"

The doctor seemed to have identified him. Apparently, he was one of those people who never forgot a patient's name or voice.

...Where is he watching us from?

He thought they'd gotten rid of all the facility's security before breaking in. Given the frog-face doctor's pinpoint timing with the call to Mike, though, it was better to assume there was another security system running.

"You sound calm. Basic tactic when hiding out is to not take provocative action like this and stay silent. You want to get traced or something?" Mike said.

"I'm not a child—I wouldn't make such a basic mistake, hmm? Besides, sometimes you need to take a few risks to do what needs to be done."

"And what's that?"

"I am an ally to patients. Even if you were the type to involve immobilized bedridden patients in fighting, if it were your life on the line, I'd have to save you. A doctor's words are important, hmm? I'm asking you to please listen to me."

The doctor spoke smoothly. There were still a few thorns in his voice, though.

"Leave Kihara and flee. If you don't, your lives will be in danger."

"Are you serious?"

"Accelerator will kill you."

"That coward?"

"You seem to be misunderstanding something." The doctor wasn't ruffled. "Accelerator is by no means a do-gooder. In black-and-white terms, he's certainly not white. I believe he got a little light, got a bit of white goodness from it—but in general, he's black, evil. Until now he was…a gray so incredibly dark it was almost black, let's say. He's dangerous—one of those unstable people who could fall either way, hmm?"

"…"

"You understand, don't you? He finally got a tiny bit of white, and who was the one who painted over that with black again? It was all of you—so don't expect moderation. Not mercy—it's moderation he'll lack. If he wants to prevent that small light from being buried in the dark, he'll get as much blood on his hands as he needs. You must not meet Accelerator. That's all I can say to my patient. I repeat, you must not meet Accelerator. He's not the child you saw before."

"This is nonsense."

"I see. It's a shame I couldn't get through to you."

The doctor paused, then continued. "By the way, who do you think informed us of the danger?"

"What?" Mike frowned—and a terrible feeling dropped into his chest. *Could it have…been him…?*

That thought snapped him awake. If he was the one to tell them it was dangerous, then of course they predicted the Hound Dogs would come here. Mike was about to gesture to Dennis to get him to redo their guard layout, but the doctor spoke first.

"Don't die. As long as you don't die, I'll save you."

Gyaaaahhhhh!!

A building-shaking scream burst out from the direction of the ceiling.

Series of gunshots broke out in various places on the premises. But each quieted just as surely, as though being picked off one by one.

Something was closing in.

Mike tossed the receiver away. He and Dennis readied their submachine guns. They hid in the shadows, focused on what was past the darkness, trying to get at least a little preemptive information.

And then.

Fear itself appeared before their eyes.

The Hound Dogs team, including Dennis and Mike, were wiped out in about ten minutes.

4

Vento was on a street, standing in the rain.

Shit…

Her movements were slow. Thick blood spilled out of her fingers pressed against her mouth. Sometimes her back would lurch, and a moment later she'd cough up red chunks onto the ground.

...What is this? Am I under attack...? Bastard. Just a little more and I could have killed my target.

An artificial light shone on her as she suffered.

The light was moving.

On the side of a department store hung a spacious screen, which was showing the news. The reporter's urgent voice pounded in her ears. It seemed to be a government broadcast.

"Yes. We're receiving reports from throughout the nation of people suddenly losing consciousness. The police are rushing to identify the cause, but—"

"Gah...ah..."

With the pain and coldness inside her, she couldn't pay attention to that.

But she worked her bloody lips anyway. "...It spread there, too. It's just...hard to aim this attack. If only...we could have taken control of Academy City..."

"We appear to have reports of this damage from abroad as well, not just Japan. It has started to take effect on the schedules of airports, boats, and other transportation services—"

"Ha..." Vento let out a long breath. "*I do hope it didn't spread to the Vatican.*"

Her voice didn't sound all that concerned. The chaos seemed to be continuing on the news, but the program was on a schedule, too. After swapping reporters, the new one began to read from the next sheet.

"Now on to economics. The other day, there was an autumn dessert fair at Parallel Sweets Park in Tokyo, featuring confections from around the world. As they start business—"

"..." Vento's eyeballs rolled over to watch the big screen.

"The estimated number of visitors exceeded two hundred thousand over the week of the park's opening. The park is expected to coordinate with small to medium companies for goods manufacturing, affecting not only the theme park attraction industry but the region's economy as a whole—"

With a *bang* and a shower of sparks, the big screen blew away.

Vento hoisted her hammer onto her shoulder.

She began to walk again down the rain-drenched street.

5

Kamijou dragged the unconscious patrons and employees from the restaurant, which seemed ready to collapse at any second. He didn't want anyone to be flattened into pancakes. Next, he began first aid on the wounded. Only the black-suits were missing limbs. He stopped the blood by tightening a rope on their stumps as a tourniquet. Maybe the sensation hadn't caught up with him yet, because seeing the wounds didn't make him panic—which was actually a scary thing.

Then he called emergency services, but taking into account the city's current status, an ambulance actually getting there had maybe a fifty-fifty chance.

Right. Where's Last Order...?

He looked around, but of course, she wasn't there. He ran through the rain and into a nearby Anti-Skill station, figuring that if she was looking for help, she probably would've gone there. Unfortunately, it was dead quiet inside, with an Anti-Skill officer slumped over a table.

Same situation as the restaurant. Kamijou stopped by a few more stations farther out, but all of them yielded similar results. The stations wouldn't be safe, so where on earth had Last Order run to?

As he searched around, the only thing that happened was time passing.

Then Kamijou noticed something was in his pocket.

It was a cute-looking phone designed for children. Last Order had dropped it in the restaurant when she ran away. Now she couldn't get in touch with anyone.

Those black-suits, and that Roman Orthodox woman calling herself Vento...If both of them are after her, I can't be slow about this anymore.

Vento seemed to be after Kamijou, but that didn't mean she'd smile and be friends with Last Order if she ran into her. The girl may not have been her target, but she didn't seem the type to care about others.

"..."

Kamijou looked at Last Order's phone again. He felt guilty, but he turned it on and looked at her address list.

He didn't know whether Last Order would run away on her own or ask someone she knew for help. But if she asked someone she knew, he might find her if he went to those addresses. Even if he didn't, it would be good to alert those people about the danger. They could tell him where she might have gone, too.

There were extremely few entries in the list.

He didn't even have to scroll down to see them—only four were there. It really had only phone numbers, and not even names for them. They'd been left as the cold default text: "Entry 1," "Entry 2," and so on. Maybe her guardian was just making her hold on to it, and she didn't actually use it at all.

He called each of the numbers, one at a time.

But all he got was the call tone; nobody seemed to pick up. Maybe Vento's strange attack had more far-reaching effects than he thought.

The third number came back silent.

If the last one was the same, he was out of ideas.

Praying, he pushed the button.

He put the phone to his ear.

The monotone call sound began to ring in the hard rainfall.

6

Accelerator glanced around the dark hospital.

He'd rolled the sloppy mess of gasping enemies to the side. None of them had guns that fired the same bullets as the shotgun he was using as a cane, so he couldn't resupply. The option of picking up a different weapon existed, but he avoided doing so. He didn't want them to think he was relying on firearms too much.

That makes two teams I've crushed now, he said to himself, staring out the window, raindrops pelting the glass. *Now even that shithead*

Kihara's gonna have to change up his plan a bit. He'll want to kill me way more than before, and that's the plan—put the stupid brat in a less risky spot.

The situation was seemingly in his favor, but his inferior position hadn't actually changed. He could kill as many regular Hound Dogs as he wanted—it might make Kihara impatient, but it wouldn't scare him. The man had a special martial art he could use to take down Accelerator barehanded.

Plus, he didn't have a clue as to where either Amata Kihara or Last Order were in the city. He couldn't take any decisive action right now. Waiting for the enemy to make a mistake was all he could do.

If they hadn't captured Last Order yet, the tactics he'd been using would be effective. Kihara would change his plan, send more killers after him—and the more he did that, the less would be following Last Order.

But if Kihara had already caught her, Accelerator's efforts would be in vain. He couldn't go rescue her now, since he didn't know where Kihara was, and then there would be no chance whatsoever for Kihara to make a mistake. Last Order was their prize, not Accelerator. He didn't need to keep moving on Accelerator at his own expense.

One of the two, and they're mutually exclusive? This is some serious bull.

Accelerator sucked his teeth in anger and looked down to where one of the Hound Dogs' radios lay. He'd crushed it underfoot in his irritation. Kihara seemed to know he'd gotten his hands on a radio. They hadn't been talking about anything important for a while. He couldn't use it anymore.

But why pick now to go after that brat? He leaned against the wall and thought. *If they want her for research or something, then it's the Sisters he wants after all. But he said himself—they ain't much in the way of a combat force. Kihara's the idiot who developed me, after all. If he really wanted to use espers for the military, I'd think he'd use my DNA map or make an even better one.*

When Kihara was about to kill him outside the underground mall, he'd said something strange. Something along the lines of the

Radio Noise project's goal not being military use, and that if they really wanted to do that, they'd use Accelerator's DNA instead of Railgun's.

The Radio Noise project—and the Level Six shift experiment that followed. His eyes wandered idly...*What have that brat and I been tangled up in all this time?*

He thought he was onto something, but his thoughts didn't continue for long—his cell phone started vibrating.

"..."

Accelerator held his breath, then took the small communication device out of his pocket.

The screen showed Last Order's number.

He thought, *Either it's actually her or the shithead Kihara. Both extremes on the spectrum.*

He pushed the call button.

He pressed the phone to his ear.

"Thank God I finally got through to you!"

The voice wasn't Last Order's—but it wasn't Amata Kihara's, either.

For a moment, he thought one of Kihara's underlings was using her phone. *But wait, this voice...*

He felt like he'd heard it before somewhere, but he couldn't put his finger on it. The waves were bad right now anyway, and there was the sound of violent rain in the background as though the person was outside.

"I've been calling every number in Last Order's cell phone. You're the only one who picked up. You may not know the situation, but I need your help. She's in danger!"

It was entirely possible this was a trap.

Unfortunately, Accelerator's only means of survival was to walk into it.

"What's the situation?" he asked, focusing in order to glean as much information as he could.

The voice on the phone spoke quickly.

A little after the final school closing, he'd met Last Order in the city. She'd asked him to help someone she knew, who was being attacked by a group of unknown origin. When he went there, he found men in black suits collapsed on the ground but not that person. Then, black-suits—probably friends of the ones on the ground—chased them, and Last Order fled before he did. He didn't know if she was safe, nor could he contact her. He couldn't even tell if people were targeting her, so he wanted to get her to safety quickly.

The black-suits' movements and Last Order's location—the Hound Dogs would have an easy time figuring out both.

The possibility of this being a trap was increasing, but at the same time...

That sounds like exactly what the brat would do, doesn't it?

"Hey, you...wouldn't happen to be the 'acquaintance' she mentioned, would you?"

"Probably am."

"Great. You're safe. With what's going on with Last Order, if you see her, take her and hide somewhere."

The discussion was getting off topic, so Accelerator reined it back in. "Where did you last see her?"

"School District 7, near the Fight Street—er, you wouldn't know that name. It's an inside thing. Actually, I wonder if this road has a real name."

There was silence for a short while—maybe he was looking for a street sign or something.

"There it is. It says it's the corner of Route 39 and Konoha Street. There's a Spanish family restaurant called Olla Podrida."

Accelerator had an idea where that was.

That neighborhood was generally lively, but away from the main roads were shadowy alleys out of everyone's sight. A place with lots of connections between the civilian world and the underworld—and plenty of people getting dragged in.

"Which direction did she run?"

"Don't know. I had my hands full just getting her out of the building. I think she'll follow the roads. It's been a while since I saw her, so we honestly can't guess where she is now."

Not true, thought Accelerator.

With final school closing time past and no buses or trains, there were no vehicles for her to ride in the city. Even if she tried to call a taxi, none of the drivers would be polite enough to stop for a soaking-wet brat who clearly didn't have any money.

Last Order had to walk.

To make things worse—though he was the perpetrator—she'd been dropped into water from a high place to get away from Kihara, which had worn her down. Even if she wasn't tired, it was raining cats and dogs out. The person on the phone said it had been a while, but Last Order probably hadn't moved very far—she'd be in a building recovering her stamina.

If the caller was right, Accelerator might manage to save her if he acted now.

Even if it was a trap, it could still lead somewhere.

"All right. I'll pick her up. You get rid of that phone and go right back to being a civilian."

"What are you talking about?! I'm obviously gonna help, too!"

It was actually easier to move by himself, and, well, he didn't want an amateur throwing any wrenches into the situation—but he was being surprisingly persistent. Trap or not, this guy was an idiot.

Fed up, he said, "Right. You go to the big iron bridge in School District 7. We made that our emergency meet-up spot. If she's on the run, she'll go there."

"Got it," came the weirdly enthusiastic response.

Accelerator lied, of course.

"Be careful," the voice said. "Something's going on with Academy City today. Some weirdo infiltrated, and there's Anti-Skill officers and regular people collapsed all over the place."

"What?" Accelerator frowned. This was news to him—both the intruder to the city and many people knocked out.

"The intruder is one thing, but you didn't know about what's going on in the city, either? It looks like Anti-Skill and, uh, these guys in black clothes got hit by something. The guests in the restaurant were all down, too. Nobody directly punched them and knocked them unconscious, either. They were just walking along and then dropped to the ground suddenly. I didn't check everywhere, but doesn't it seem strangely quiet to you?"

"..." *What's going on?* thought Accelerator.

Would Kihara go that far? Even his Hound Dogs had gone down. That made him wonder, but maybe Kihara wouldn't hesitate to discard people like that.

He had a bad feeling about it, but that was for later. Getting Last Order back was his top priority.

"The attacks look pretty indiscriminate, so you be careful, too."

"What a pain..."

The two of them fell silent for a moment after that.

Eventually the voice on the phone spoke.

"Sorry. I really shouldn't have left her by herself."

"...Goes for both of us. I left her alone, too."

He hung up.

After looking at his cell phone for just a bit, he shoved it back in his pocket.

On his shotgun cane, he headed for the hospital exit.

This was the moment of truth.

7

Amata Kihara was in a dark room.

It was an office not currently in use. Most of the equipment used for the job was gone, leaving only a bunch of work desks and chairs. Kihara sat in one of them, relaxing with his feet up on a dusty desk.

All around him stood men clad in combat gear.

Compared to before, there weren't many. Maybe five or six at most.

Still, it didn't erase the relaxation from Kihara's expression.

The higher-ups would send him as many Hound Dogs as he needed. Human trash was lying around everywhere, basically. Others would probably look at Kihara and call him the perfect example of an evil person. But at the very moment they made that criticism in calmness, they were no more than trash who didn't understand human pain.

Erase them all you wanted—they never ran out. He wasn't worried.

"We've lost contact with multiple teams, sir. More than likely…"

He heard the nervous voice of a subordinate.

Kihara shrugged it off, his voice relaxed. "…They fled or died. Either way, *we'll have to harvest their hearts later.*"

Death wasn't enough to punish failure. Kihara always made them pay—even if it meant tearing parts from their dead bodies.

"But which one was responsible?"

"Doesn't really matter. Accelerator's nothing right now. He's so weak it almost breaks my heart when I'm punching him…The problem is that woman."

Kihara, too, had information that Academy City's functions were on the verge of total paralysis.

His own subordinates had come under the exact same attack, too.

Which would mean "that woman" was the one attacking the city now.

…That was an interesting trick she had.

He felt like it wasn't some invisible, physical effect, like nanotechnology or electromagnetic waves. Normally if someone used those sorts of weapons, they'd equip special masks or suits for it. That woman had no defensive measures whatsoever.

Kihara spoke to another subordinate, standing right next to him. "Remember the woman who got in the way right when we were about to fire the missile at Accelerator's minivan? Did you pick up the guys we used as decoys?"

"Yes, sir," said the man in the black suit, gleaning just from that what Kihara was really trying to ask. "We're currently investigating the wounded using the gear we have on hand."

"They all turn out the same?"

"No, sir. By our observations, there are three groups. Some are just unconscious, like they're asleep, but others are petrified like statues."

"What determines how they turned out? Where they fell?"

"Even people down in the same spot fall into different groups, sir. We don't know how quite yet. The biggest group, though…we haven't sent them to a research agency, so we don't know the exact values for this, but it seems like the decoys' bodies have an extreme lack of oxygen. There's been no necrosis to the bodies as far as we can tell, so we believe their brains and organs are still receiving the bare minimum oxygen they need to function."

"...Inducing apparent death through artificial means."

Most animals, not just humans, had a defensive instinct that lowered their level of body functions the more they lacked what they needed to sustain life activities. An animal hibernating in the winter was an easily understood example.

The subordinate continued. "But nothing happened when we supplied them with a fixed amount of oxygen from a tank, so I believe we should consider some kind of 'power' at work...Just who is that woman? Shit. Our plan's success rate is going down because of her, and now Olaf and Lulu are—"

Just as the man's voice was cut off, he crumpled to the floor. The heavy *thud* rang clearly in Kihara's ears, much to his annoyance.

"..."

Kihara, sitting in his chair with his feet up, looked around carefully. Nothing else happened.

They waited for a short while but saw no signs of a second shot.

He thought it was some kind of sniping ability, but if she'd had something like that, she'd have used it to pump Kihara full of holes, too. Not attacking Kihara first, and the timing of his subordinate going down—both bothered him.

Hell...How in the world is she aiming that...?

This abandoned office had windows on one wall, but if she was targeting them through one of them, Kihara would have to be the first one in her sights. Was she using some unique aiming method besides eyesight? Something that would miss its aim, instead hitting his subordinate?

Kihara mulled it over. The unusual phenomenon assaulting the Hound Dogs right now—this string of attacks—could a supernatural ability be enough to pull it off?

Wouldn't be easy.

Going for one or two people was possible. But from earlier reports, many more of his subordinates had gone down. It was hard enough to maintain a fixed oxygen amount in individuals, but if many people in many different places were totally under this phenomenon's control, it would be far beyond what mere skill could accomplish.

Moreover, his subordinates reported there were people with differing symptoms, too.

If you gathered as many espers to attack as there were victims, it'd be possible…but that would take way too many resources. And having one soldier to take out one grunt each wouldn't make any sense, either.

He was the one who had directly developed Accelerator. If a supernatural ability development expert said so, it could basically be accepted as truth. Then what the hell kind of laws could have caused the bizarre occurrences he was seeing?

Powers other than supernatural abilities could be any number of scientific technologies, like nanotech or electromagnetic waves. But in that case, Kihara would have no reason to be okay. And besides, knocking someone unconscious with tech like that was one thing, but was it even possible to control the amount of oxygen in someone's blood?

Neither Academy City–made abilities nor high technology could do that.

But if that was true, then everything pointed to a more occult world.

Could the woman Kihara saw really be someone who used a power other than a supernatural ability?

Something "unscientific"…

Kihara narrowed his eyes. He wouldn't reject that word.

Because he was at the forefront of science, the boundaries of the word *unscientific* were actually very clear to him. Do a few thousand experiments and you'd get a few oddball values that theory alone couldn't calculate. Ever since developing Accelerator, Kihara had been bothered by something vague, something murky. It felt like there were invisible holes somewhere in the perfect world of theory he believed in.

He sucked his teeth in irritation and took his legs off the office desk. "Whatever. We know what we need to do. That Aleister bastard is always strict, so let's get a move on and end this quickly."

Kihara hadn't gotten an explanation on what Aleister's final goal for capturing Last Order was. But they'd been told what they needed to do. All they had to do was carry it out.

"Is the Testament ready?"

"Right here, sir."

A different subordinate than the one who'd collapsed placed a silver attaché case on the desk. The electronic brainwashing devices were usually pretty big, but if you cut out everything but the parts you absolutely needed, you could get it down to this size.

Of course, the more "extra bits" you removed, the less safe the subject would be.

Accelerator...

He watched the man undo the case's locks and click together the device, then suddenly said to himself, "Controls every vector, hmm. What about irregular shit like that?"

"Sir?"

"Nothing," said Kihara.

8

Accelerator came to the corner of Konoha Street and Route 39 in School District 7.

He immediately found the restaurant the "man on the phone" mentioned. The thing was destroyed to the point where concrete iron bars in the structure showed, like a bombed-out war-torn building. Kihara's Hound Dogs were all down, having received very rough first aid. Nobody had tried to conceal them at all.

"..."

Maybe the "man on the phone" wasn't a trap.

If he wasn't, then he was the real deal—letting at least Last Order escape, despite being wrapped up in a disaster like this.

Shit. I have to find her quick. Where the hell did she go?

He hoped she'd left some kind of sign, but she probably hadn't had the time to be that considerate. Even if she had, the rain would have more than likely washed it away.

She should be fleeing according to the evidence erasure manual they used for the experiment by going through the Sisters' network. Just like with Ao Amai on August 31.

Just thinking about the "experiment" made him feel shitty, but that was where her escape route was.

...She'd slip by satellite images and around the security robots' patrol routes.

The "man on the phone" had searched for her in Anti-Skill stations on the main street, but he was probably barking up the wrong tree. If she was basing her route on the evidence erasure manual, she was more likely to be on back roads.

Using the shotgun as a cane, he entered the alley. The hard rain pelted him as he dragged his hard-to-move body through it. On the way, he checked each of the buildings' back entrances, looking for signs that she'd used her electric ability to force any of them open.

No results.

There was more than one road, and she could have hidden in a building somewhere.

He simply had too few clues.

She was fleeing the enemy, so it wasn't her fault, but he had no way to search for her.

"Piece of shit..."

Last Order should be around here. That much was certain. Maybe if Accelerator was the one to leave a sign instead, Last Order would come out. What would that sign be? She didn't have her cell phone anymore. If he couldn't contact her like that, then maybe unlocking his electrode switch and raging around would work.

But then he hit upon a different way. It was a stupid, idiotic method, but the idea hadn't occurred to him until now.

He should just yell her name really loud.

If she knew it was his voice, she would come out.

Unfortunately, walking around calling the name of a child he couldn't find would make him look like a dad searching for his lost kid. He felt like that was at the exact opposite end of the spectrum of his character.

It was laughable, but it was the only way. He clicked his tongue in bitterness and took a deep breath.

But his voice didn't make a sound.

Because he found what he was looking for right then.

In a dirty puddle created by the downpour falling onto the ground, he noticed something. It was a torn scrap of fabric, about the size of a handkerchief. He drew near and examined it closer—finding a men's button-down shirtsleeve. Accelerator recognized the cuff design. It was from the one Last Order wore over her sky-blue camisole.

His mind went blank. The blood started to drain from his face.

This is...

Could it be...?

No...

As though timed, his cell phone vibrated. Accelerator sluggishly took it out of his pocket. An unfamiliar number was on the screen.

No, he thought.

If this was *him*, he'd have no reason to contact him. He wouldn't use such an easy-to-understand method. It was fine. This wasn't what he thought it was, Accelerator told himself.

He pushed the call button.

A really loud voice hit his ear before he could bring the phone up to it.

"Heeey, Accelerator, how ya doooin'? Gya-ha-ha-ha-ha!!"

He heard the phone creak in his hand.

It was so predictable he thought he was about to burst a blood vessel in his brain.

Accelerator's pupils swayed. A vortex of a noisy emotion began to scatter from his center to everything around it. "Heeey, what's the deal, Kiharaaa?"

"Just havin' some fun. In both shogi and chess, you gotta declare you've won before the game ends, right? Whoever made those rules really knew how to have fun. They knew how to get the most out of seeing some shithead, one who had pissed them off for way too long, the moment they were stricken with defeat. Is there any better way to enjoy the true taste of victory?"

"Declare what? You fuckin' serious?"

"Sure, you don't have to believe me. But did you see a piece of the brat's shirt lying around? Figured you'd still be looking for her, *so I left it there on purpose.*"

"…"

"Testament's a crazy thing. Injecting a virus into a human brain? It's fucked up! Ha-ha! I'll make this brat's body tremble in fear!! Hey, man, gimme your address! I'll send you a video in the mail!!"

His blood curdled.

That's why they kidnapped the brat…?!

Kihara was doing almost the same thing Ao Amai had on August 31. He was trying to use a brainwashing machine to directly overwrite Last Order's brain. He didn't know what sort of command he'd add in there, but nobody with any sensitivity could ever do this. It was more profane than rubbing all the semen you could muster into her brain.

"You really don't get it, do you? Not killing the enemy can be real effective. Ever heard of a 'living hell'? *People fool themselves into thinking dying is the scariest thing in the world,* and if you pressure 'em with this, they puncture like a flat tire. Like my guys did. But, see…"

Kihara let out a dry breath, like a teacher disappointed with how incompetent a student was.

"*I know all about it, so it doesn't work on me.* I see right through your cheap act, you little shit. Listen up, 'cause it's time little shits like you got a review lesson. Corpses are meant to be killed. Making them stop breathing is just touching up the face on a statue. Your dead body wouldn't be good enough to hang in a gallery. Who the hell would carve up a rock blindfolded and toss it away? It's not polite to the chunk of meat!"

Accelerator didn't engage him. He began analyzing the current situation.

"So I thought I'd show you a good example. I'll teach you how to make meat real pretty. Just be sure you don't pass out after seein' what's left over of the brat!!"

He continued to laugh loud enough to break the speaker.

Accelerator listened to it for a little bit, then eventually spoke into the phone. "So, uh, what reaction was I supposed to have?"

"Eh?"

"Doubling over laughing is the right one, yeah, Mister Masochist?"

"Hey now. Your ability to judge the situation busted now, too?"

"Are you even trying anymore? If this was just to make me mad, you wouldn't have grabbed the brat. You'd just make her a corpse and send her over to me. Testament? You a fuckin' idiot? How would I even tell what happened to her?" Accelerator laughed. "Those punks hanging around seem to think getting into the world's darkness will grant them freedom, but it's actually the opposite. The further down you go, the stronger the hierarchies are. Right? Mr. Kihara, little puppy slave?"

"Oh, I see. You get your kicks from her screams, don't you?"

"Yeah, could you let me hear them, actually? This is all so simple I'm bored of it. I want to see if she's alive. I mean, you could cut off her nose and send that to me, and that would be fine."

"Is that your order, *sir*? If you act now, I'll send her ears as a bonus."

"Don't try to scare me, you greenhorn. Someone employed you, too, yeah? Wouldn't make sense to use the brat for your personal research. Somebody's getting a kick out of using you. They didn't give you some tear-jerking order like 'bring her back unharmed,' did they? They just wanted the brain and heart to be okay and didn't care about the rest. And now you're too fucking scared to lay a finger on her? What the hell is wrong with you?"

"Got it, got it."

"You're pathetic, *Mr.* Kihara. Who're you playing delivery boy to? Were you all panicked like that before 'cause if you don't make the delivery in thirty minutes someone's gonna be mad at you?"

"You're dead."

Beep. The call ended abruptly.

He suddenly felt like the sounds of the downpour got closer.

Twirling the cell phone in his hand, Accelerator went over the conversation.

With his personality, after I said all that to him, he'd at least have crushed one of the brat's eyeballs while on the phone. But he didn't, so...My, my. Are you telling me he really is just a gofer?

It was a dangerous tactic, but he couldn't compete with Kihara unless he took risks like this.

"...Which means..."

On the other hand, someone important enough to stop Kihara in his tracks.

In light of the gear the Hound Dogs had, the biggest possibility...

No...Academy City itself?

Then it was probably the General Board, who directly oversaw everything. This was no different from the "experiment" with the Sisters. Or maybe this was actually all related.

I don't know where Kihara is. But the General Board is easy. If I investigate them, I might get more info on this "plan" than Kihara has. Hmm? ...Hey, wait, this is crazy. This is ballooning out of control. Are we gonna be okay at this rate? thought Accelerator, laughing and banging on the wall.

He clicked the phone closed and put it in his pocket and screamed.

"Don't fuck with me, you bastaaaaaaaaards!!"

He flicked the electrode choker switch.

His vast calculation abilities returned.

All around him in the narrow alley was concrete wall, everywhere he looked.

It didn't matter.

He obtained his target's exact position from his absolute coordinates. His eyes rolled around to look. He knew of it—because he had been deep in the dark. He knew what stood in that direction.

The enemy is Academy City! And the General Board chairperson is in charge of it!!

A building with no windows.

The shelter of Academy City's General Board chairperson.

"Gah, aaaaaahhhhhhhhhhhhhhhhhhhhhhhhhhhhhhhhhh!!"

Accelerator stuck his hand into one of the nearby concrete walls. By manipulating vectors, his arm sunk into it like tofu. As he screamed loud enough for blood to come up from his throat, he violently swung around the arm inside the wall.

He had total control over every vector.

A thunderous *slam* rang out.

That very moment, the earth, on September 30, had its rotation delayed by five minutes.

His arm had stolen the planet's immense rotational energy and transformed it into a demonic strike through vector manipulation.

He gouged out the concrete wall and hurled it at a terrifying speed. All around him were corners of the alley surrounded by buildings, but the multitude of structures in the way of his "target" came down like scrap paper.

Consideration for his surroundings, worrying about involving civilians—all those concerns had disappeared instantly.

By the time he realized, he'd already thrown it.

Over two kilometers separated him and his "target."

The windowless building.

The world's strongest shelter, called the castle of the Academy City General Board chairperson, Aleister.

The giant structure said to be able to ward off nuclear weapon impacts without a problem.

The wall shot toward it with immense velocity.

A terrible vortex of sound exploded. It was over two kilometers away, but it didn't matter at all. The wall blew through a few buildings—unmanned banks, offices, etc.—and pierced through the gap between buildings on the other side of the road. It tore away electric signboards attached to the sides of high-rise structures as it shot straight toward the target. It was nothing less than a miracle that no human casualties occurred on its path. Accelerator hadn't given an ounce of thought to it.

Gray dust scattered. For a moment, he couldn't see anything.

The dense fog enshrouded him and stayed there for a short while.

Eventually, his vision slowly began to return.

The world spread out before Accelerator.

"…"

And the world hadn't changed at all.

He had used all the power of the strongest esper in Academy City, even sapping the very planet's rotational energy for his attack. All that hadn't even made a dent in the windowless building.

The result was clear.

The wall before him was just too big.

"Kuh, ahhhhhhhhhhhhhhhh!!"

Accelerator crumpled to the ground and slammed his fist into a dirty puddle. No matter how much he power he used, it never reached Aleister. Some unknown technology dispersed any impact—and there was no proof he was even in there at the moment. It could have all been a dummy. It didn't matter. It really, really didn't matter right now.

Last Order had been taken.

It was the worst situation he could think of.

Everything he'd wanted to protect had been torn to shreds, leaving nothing left.

I'll kill him, he thought in silence, clicking the electrode's switch back. The idea of trying to get in touch with Yomikawa or Yoshikawa had fled his mind completely.

I'll kill Amata Kihara. I'll kill him for sure. A hundred deaths aren't enough for that shithead. I'll compress them all down to one time and fucking kill him. Anything less is out of the question.

Using the shotgun as a cane, he wobbled up to his feet.

He focused on the cell phone in his pocket.

Kihara's number was on it now. Even if it was a dummy, it was worth checking out. If he couldn't do so in a normal way, he'd do so in a not-so-normal way. Accelerator had no future, and if Last Order's was being stolen from her, what did he have to hold back for? If the databases at Anti-Skill and Judgment stations didn't work out, he'd gain complete access to the data banks even if he had to destroy the General Board's hideouts one by one. Who cared about twelve important people? He'd crush their faces or their hearts if need be.

He'd bring them into the streets if he had to light a fire to do it and slaughter them all down to the last cell in their bodies.

Muttering in a singsong tone, he began to walk slowly through the alley.

His back disappeared even farther into the darkness.

9

Aleister was in the windowless building.

Despite the scale of the impact, none of the interior furnishings budged. He was floating upside down in a cylinder filled with red liquid in the middle of a wide room, but all that happened inside was the slight quivering of the liquid.

It would seem things are occurring outside.

He didn't focus on the cause.

As though saying something so trivial wasn't worth his time.

Aleister's eyes were on the sky.

By some technology, several square windows were floating in dead space. They changed what they displayed in line with the movements of Aleister's eyeballs and registered command inputs in line with his fingers.

These commands were nothing he had to move his body for; he could compensate by brain-wave detection.

But, heh...I must exercise once in a while.

Aleister, who left most of his bodily functions to a life-support machine, strictly speaking didn't even have to blink his eyes. He was always submerged in a regulated solution, so his eyes didn't need to be moistened. Even moving his fingers was registered as an "event."

It picked out value in that slight movement, analyzed the signals being sent from his nerves to his brain, and just that one motion induced divine inspiration.

He had no internal concept of "training his body."

Electrically contracting his muscles and controlling his organs—it was all nothing but miscellaneous tasks that the machine handled. If you heard he hadn't walked in decades, it might sound unhealthy, but Aleister preserved his own health in a more ideal state than anyone else in the world.

This went for intellectual activities, too.

For Aleister, the brain was nothing more than a single part. It existed in detachment from a soul or life, and there were plenty of replacements. His inspiration was drawn outside his body via cables, brewed in the computer standing there, and returned to Aleister's brain as an individual thought. The life-support machine was his skin, his organs, and his brain. Perhaps the cluster of huge devices was itself alive at this moment. Just like organ transplants taking hold in a patient's body, the metallic heap, which had drawn far too close to being human, was so advanced that one might not be able to figure out whether to call it a machine or a person.

Put an ear to those hard metal clumps and you might have even heard a pulse—and surrounded by them, Aleister smiled comfortably.

Several pieces of data were displayed on the images he stared at.

On the first was a map of the Sisters' worldwide distribution and a graph representing their brain-wave patterns.

On the second was the organic data for *that* which was coming into existence in the city now.

On the third was an image of Vento leaning on a railing and coughing, captured via super-magnification.

And it would seem Kihara has successfully recovered Last Order, the final command. Change is already taking root in the "place" of Academy City during the preparation phase after injecting the target code.

There was a relaxation to Aleister's thoughts. As this was an emergency, the output was far lower than he'd predicted, but this much would be quite enough.

Using the involuntary diffusion fields, the Imaginary Number District, the Five Elements Society has been fully deployed. If one uses magic inside Academy City, no matter who the sorcerer is, they will lose control and self-destruct. Vento of the Front, was it? Even your body is no exception.

His inspiration created thoughts and his thoughts created inspiration, the repetition continuing to create a massive intellectual torrent that would soon change history.

With the current output, it cannot spread over the world, of course. Even the magical pressure is at just barely tolerable levels, but... This isn't everything. I still haven't truly activated the code. With the appearance of Fuse Kazakiri, I will turn the tides of the situation.

A new window appeared in the air.

It displayed Hyouka Kazakiri, confused at the change in the city as she uneasily walked through the rain.

10

Vento stood on an iron bridge.

The bridge spanned a large river. The iron and asphalt construction was single-mindedly dreary. Perhaps because of the downpour, the dark river below had risen, the dirty water making muffled noises.

She coughed a few more times—wet, violent coughs. Heavy blood was leaking between the gaps in the fingers with which she was holding her mouth. She looked at her blood-covered hand. It was trembling fiercely.

What...could this possibly be...?

It was natural that even she wouldn't understand the cause. What happened to her body? How damaging was it? Would it be all right, or was it done for?

...My body...might be specially made...but this has never...happened before. This isn't its fault...

The coarse sounds of coughing continued.

A new color red began to spread on the rain-soaked road.

Stricken by the torrential rain, the makeup on her eyes was running somewhat. The gimp on the cloth covering her hair was disheveled, and frayed hairs were poking out onto her forehead.

Which means it's a new...magic-based attack...? No, that isn't right, either. This...this is Academy City. It can't possibly be a magic-based attack. I don't see any signs...of spells being used. Besides, I would intercept all such things anyway...

"...!!" She shuddered.

The pain began to withdraw from her body.

Her condition hadn't recovered, though.

It was the opposite. Something else had happened that needed more attention.

She felt an oppression. Not merely something pressed against her body. It was squeezing her, every part of her, from her skin's surface to her organs' insides, leaving not a single blood vessel untouched.

It was a "presence."

An unbelievably enormous presence had shaken the very city itself. She felt no hostility from it. It wasn't looking at the weakened Vento. It was more like a panther or lion yawning right in front of her. It may not have been hostile—but a meager human couldn't help but start to sweat and tremble.

She couldn't tell in what direction the presence was.

The unit of scaling was far too different. It was almost like the presence was covering up the entire city. She supposed a person swallowed by a beast attempting to learn the identity from inside it would be pointless. It was so intense, but she couldn't even see its outline. If this was an enemy, it was the worst kind.

On top of that...

This unknown presence...It's still expanding...?!

That was the most shocking part. Something gigantic had shaken the world, bent the numerous "layers" within it, and laid itself down in that space instead, seeming to blow out the laws of sorcery like a candle—and yet its pressure was still increasing as though that were only the beginning. Not even a Crossist "saint" could do this much. But then how should she interpret this?

This is...Academy City's final line...against the occult...

Was this the reason for Aleister sounding so relaxed?

This wasn't good, certainly. Vento had put almost 90 percent of the city's functions to rest, and this trick up his sleeve could turn those tables. But on the other hand, it seemed like it had been too easy thus far. If the city couldn't do at least this, nobody would be calling it a force to rival the sorcery side.

"...It doesn't...matter. Come what may, I will accomplish my goal."

Vento then said a brief word to herself.

It was the name of her younger brother.

With just that, much of the shivering tormenting her vanished. The fear of not knowing why she was coughing up blood relaxed as well. A sense of calmness washed over her, and her shocked and shaken mind focused.

I stole 90 percent of the city's functions—that's a fact. I still have the advantage here. This just means Aleister was so pressured he had to use his trump card.

Which meant she could win, she concluded, wiping the blood from her lips.

The aid from the shadows—I can't use it anymore. I don't know how important Touma Kamijou's position is to this city, but even Aleister can't stop him from dying...

The ones from Anti-Skill and Judgment, who protected the city, were annihilated. Because those kinds of people were easiest for her attack to affect directly. She'd almost forgotten due to the giant newcomer's appearance, but Vento was steadily progressing with her task.

She just had to kill.

Kill her target, Touma Kamijou.

Science...how I hate you.

Vento thought to herself, both hands gripping the railing.

Science...how I detest you.

She despised science for making her like this. For not saving her brother's life.

Wiping her mouth with her arm, she took a slow, deep breath.

She reinvigorated her damaged body.

Just as she thought to herself that she would go and kill her target, Touma Kamijou, and left the iron bridge…

…suddenly, there was a tremendous roar.

It seemed to be some kind of long-range attack. Several buildings near the discharge site collapsed, the "bullet" flying close to ten kilometers over and upward before appearing to collide with another building.

What was that…?

The act was unrelated to God's Right Seat and the Roman Orthodox Church. She thought that the invasion force should still be on the outskirts of the city.

Did that mean Academy City was in the middle of some trouble aside from her?

Vento frowned, but she didn't have the time to pursue the question deeply.

"…"

From out of thin air she produced a hammer wrapped in barbed wire and grabbed it.

The piercings in her face held an association of "piercing the body with metal" and possessed the attribute of "nails," symbolizing the stakes that nailed the Son of God to the cross. The hammer didn't need explanation—a hammer had been the execution tool.

What spurred her to prepare for combat was a particular sound: Footsteps.

11

Touma Kamijou, following the advice of the "voice on the phone," ran to the nighttime iron bridge.

But Last Order wasn't the one he found there.

God's Right Seat.

Vento of the Front.

"What…? You!!"

No sooner had Kamijou roared than Vento swung her giant hammer over her shoulder.

A wind club tore through the rain, and Kamijou flicked it away with his right hand.

An invisible tension dominated the space between them.

"Why the hell are you here? Where did you take Last Order?!" he shouted.

Vento frowned slightly, then answered. "You came all the way here to get killed?"

"I asked what the hell you did with the girl!!"

"Last Order? I don't have a damn clue what you're talking about!!"

Once again, their shouting clashed.

But the two of them didn't.

Bang!!

An incredible flash assaulted their eyes.

Kamijou's vision whited out. He guarded himself, thinking this was another of Vento's ploys, but then he heard Vento grind her teeth as well.

Before they knew what was happening, a lightning strike hit, the sound and impact coming a moment later.

His joints cried out in pain.

"Guahhh!!"

Kamijou fell to the ground. This large bridge was supposedly made of iron, but it rocked like a rope bridge. He heard several bolts bouncing out, unable to stand the movement.

…Argh. What was…? Kamijou shook his head, getting himself into a leaning position. If the light and sound arrived at different times, did that mean it happened far away?

Where's Vento…?!

The flash hadn't been bright enough to blind him for very long. Panicking, he stood up and looked around.

…What?

The woman wasn't even looking at him. She had her hands on the bridge's railing, her hammer set aside on the road, glaring into the distance at something with intense concentration.

"That bastard...Aleister!!"

Her wrathful scream rang out. It was clearly hundreds, thousands of times angrier than how she'd acted toward Kamijou.

Vento turned around to him. "I'll leave the small fry like you for later...I'll kill him. I see. This is the whole story—the Imaginary Number District—the Five Elements mechanism! Screw that—do you look down on me that much, you bastaaaaaaaaard?!"

She grabbed her hammer and smashed it into the ground at her feet.

Craaash!! Fragments of asphalt scattered everywhere.

"!!"

By the time Kamijou guarded his face with his hands, Vento was nowhere to be found.

...She disappeared? Did she—?!

He quickly ran over to the railing. But all he could see below was a flowing, roaring black river far underneath. The water level had risen quite a bit because of the rain. Had she fallen in? Or had she used some kind of sorcery?

What the hell...? What was she looking at before?

Vento had attacked Academy City to kill him, hadn't she?

She'd completely abandoned her biggest target.

Kamijou's eyes moved off the river and ahead of him...

...to see what it was Vento was staring at.

"...It can't be."

12

——Commencing partial deployment of Imaginary Number District Five Elements Mechanism.

——Suitable target found: Academy City, center of School District 7.

——Overwriting additional module using the theoretical model Hyouka Kazakiri as a base.

————Confirmed outer and inner transformation of theoretical model.

————Host individual Last Order, controller of the Sisters... additional code authenticated.

————Successful artificial induction of all involuntary diffusion fields in Academy City via takeover of Misaka network confirmed.

————First phase complete.

————Confirmed alteration of physical rules.

————Fuse Kazakiri will now appear in Academy City.

————To whom it may concern, please brace for sudden impact.

13

Rain enveloped nighttime Academy City.

There was extremely little traffic compared to normal times, and there wasn't much light, either. The buildings were the same. It was like everyone in the city had gone out, with some unlit and others left on as though forgotten, leaving behind something of a night-scape without any uniformity to it.

And one corner of the city overflowed with brilliant light.

Boom!! Feather-like objects blew violently around the light's central point. They were sharp like blades, and there were dozens of them. Each one ranged from ten to one hundred meters long, spreading higher and higher as if to oppose the heavens themselves.

Buildings were nearby, but they didn't seem to care.

They tore through one after another like wet paper. As they devoured the frail structures built by man, the wings flapped slowly—as if telling the world that their master was no human.

They were like the feathers of a giant crystalline peacock.

"Is that...?"

Touma Kamijou watched them from the bridge.

He knew.

He knew exactly what the completely and totally unscientific thing far in front of him was.

There was the same terrible presence he'd felt when *it* had appeared under the name Misha Kreutzev.

A being with a spell that could wipe out humanity without moving a fingertip, and one that had nearly killed a saint with one hand.

It was...

"...An angel?!"

Though he said the word, his head couldn't keep up with the sheer absurdity.

G-give me a break here! We're already in trouble up to our eyeballs!! What the hell's been going on in this city today?!

Vento had paled at the sight—did that mean it wasn't something the Roman Orthodox Church had brought along?

But how else could it be explained?

Why was *angel* even a word being spoken in Academy City?

Had an even more dangerous sorcerer's society than God's Right Seat or the Roman Orthodox Church snuck into the city?

Or...

Had Academy City called down that angel, despite being in the science faction?

The distant angelic wings paid no heed to the unknowing Kamijou as they moved slowly.

Between the remarkably large wings flashed a strange light, as if from an electrical discharge.

A moment later...

Boom!!

It unleashed destruction.

The magnificent lightning it created flew through the air, writhing like a snake, outside Academy City. Kamijou followed its afterimage. When the fierce light struck the ground, it sent forests, earth, trees, and people flying into the air like the entire place had just been

thoroughly carpet-bombed. The exit to the city was almost beyond the horizon, but even Kamijou saw something, something like a wave, moving up and down. That was how colossal the amount of matter sprayed into the air had been.

A few seconds later, the sound of an explosion rattled him.

It was just the shock wave at this point, but it packed an awful punch and almost sent Kamijou to the ground. The entire bridge started to sway and creak eerily again, just like it had when the angel first appeared. He could feel he was in danger here.

"...!!"

All sorts of problems were happening today, what with Last Order, Vento, and those guys in the black suits. But this was on another level. If something like that just started moving around, it would be enough to bring Academy City down to its foundations.

And the damage wouldn't be confined to within the city, either.

But what do I do about Last Order?!

He also needed to make sure she was safe. The "voice on the phone" said this iron bridge was their meeting point, but Last Order was nowhere in sight. Had she ever actually been here? Or had she run away upon seeing Vento?

Damn it!!

He took out the children's cell phone Last Order had been carrying and called the number registered in it. It connected immediately.

"Hey! I'm at the iron bridge, but Last Order's nowhere in sight! Did you find—?"

"Are you a fucking idiot? You actually believed me?!"

Before he could finish speaking, the voice yelled at him.

Surprised, Kamijou listened as the irritated voice continued.

"I've almost got a read on where the brat is. At least, she ain't anywhere you'd find her blindly running around the city. I'll handle the rest—now go home already!!"

"..." *Shit*, he swore to himself. The fact that he couldn't help was like a thorn in his chest. "Sorry. Did you see that thing before? I definitely saw, like, dozens of wings sprout up in a corner of the city and make this huge light show."

"…The one that shot at something outside Academy City, right?"

"I need to stop that angel. I really don't think I'll be able to help you out."

"I don't care," said the voice without hesitation.

"Sorry," said Kamijou. "Don't die."

"Same to you."

He ended the call, put the phone in his pocket, and looked up.

The angel that had mowed down numerous buildings had clearly shown its majestic appearance.

INTERLUDE EIGHT

He thought his eardrums would blow out.

Motoharu Tsuchimikado, covered in blood, lay in a puddle of muddy water. He'd been in the abandoned bus service facility in the forest, but not a trace of the building was left now. Everything was torn up, blown away, or otherwise smashed to atoms and poured onto the ground again. With syrupy, crumbled earth all around like the aftermath of a large-scale landslide, most of the trees had simply been buried.

Not a trace of any enemies now, either. Either they'd been buried in the dirt or smashed into atoms.

Tsuchimikado, personally, was thankful it was raining today.

His best spells were Black Style—which meant he specialized in water.

Motoharu Tsuchimikado boasted the pinnacle of an Onmyou expert's strength, and though he'd used the defensive spell reactively, he'd poured every fiber of his being into it for protection. It had allowed him to narrowly survive.

"Gh...*urgh*?!"

But chunks of blood still made their way out of his mouth.

His body wasn't supposed to be able to use sorcery, but that recoil wasn't the only thing at work. An outside impact had clearly ripped through his defensive spell and torn up his body.

Not a single wooden stake was left, either.

Rather than destroying the actual spell, he'd just taken out the entire plot of land they were on.

What...?

His own body half-buried by dirt, he thought hard.

What...the hell happened...?

A long-range attack seemed to have hit him, but he had absolutely no clue what kind of spell it actually was. On top of that, the blow had come from Academy City. The situation was clearly too unnatural to simply decide that a magical attack equated to the Roman Orthodox Church.

Unable to stand, he turned his head to look.

It...can't be...

Far in the distance, he saw innumerable unfurled wings inside Academy City.

It was only a tiny figure from here. He couldn't see where the wings came from due to the walls and tall buildings on the outskirts, but just catching sight of those wings made him stop breathing.

An angel.

Its appearance was similar to Misha Kreutzev, but its nature was completely different. The archangel, the POWER OF GOD, had a piercing coldness to it. But this was incredibly uncomfortable, like the thick smell of glue in a steaming-hot room.

Yes—that was an angel created by man.

The attack had been precisely aimed at the sorcerers opposing the city.

A...lei...ster..., Tsuchimikado thought, unconsciously moving his lips.

The Imaginary Number District's Five Elements Mechanism. It was a man-made "plane" of existence centered on Academy City, born of controlling the involuntary diffusion fields of the Sisters scattered all about the world.

"That bastard...He really used it..."

The angel's appearance must have let hell loose inside the city.

But by Tsuchimikado's prediction, the completion of this "plane" would destroy everything occult, cause sorcerers to die, and destroy all magical facilities. Tsuchimikado, though, was still alive—and didn't feel anything unnatural about the spell's construction.

That Imaginary Number District was likely incomplete.

If it were, Tsuchimikado would have been eliminated along with all the magic in the world.

If Aleister had needed to drag out something so imperfect…

God's Right Seat…So even Academy City is at a loss for what to do…

Or perhaps this was all just one of his "plans," too.

Unfortunately, this wasn't the time to think about it.

He had to stand up and get out of here before the next attack came. If Aleister brought out something this devastating, then he was actually planning on the enemy's total annihilation. It wasn't resistance—it was a counterattack, meant to wipe out every assassin the Roman Orthodox Church had sent. And Tsuchimikado was about to get caught in it.

"Guh…" Tsuchimikado willed his legs to move, but they didn't do what he wanted. With the previous shock wave, his body had accumulated damage to its very core.

"Gheh…aaagh…"

He gasped for breath, movements sluggish, trying somehow to stand up.

His body wasn't moving.

The angel in Academy City once again began to fire a devastating light.

The second shot was on its way.

Tsuchimikado knew that, but his legs wouldn't move according to his will.

He gritted his teeth.

Then he looked ahead.

There was a reason he couldn't die here—and so he still wouldn't give up.

CHAPTER 9
Difference of Obstacles
Two_Kinds_of_Enemies.

1

In a School District 7 garage, several giant automobiles were parked.

Their white chassis were as large as tourist buses but had no windows. And they weren't buses—but rather the world's biggest ambulances. The so-called hospital cars, in addition to packing life-support-equipped beds for ten, featured onboard equipment for performing simple surgery.

Around ten of these hospital cars were parked in the garage. Fully occupied, they provided accommodations for one hundred patients.

Several short figures stood behind those hospital cars.

They were the Sisters.

Assault rifles and anti-tank rifles hung from their bodies, not even slightly matching the Tokiwadai Middle School uniform blazers the girls wore. About ten of them stood there, on guard for the enemy group called the Hound Dogs, released by a man named Amata Kihara.

Amid them, a girl's voice rang out.

"Let me go! If you don't have a 'Misaka Network Connection Battery,' I don't think there's any point in me staying here! The city is acting weird, too, so I have to go check on it!!"

A group of nurses was restraining a girl dressed in a white nun's habit. Her calico's hair was on end, too, but a doctor had him clutched in her arms, so despite flailing his legs, the cat couldn't slip away.

Little Misaka was listening to the uproar as well, but she couldn't turn and look.

Her body wasn't moving the way it was supposed to.

"(———Confirmed signal from host individual #20001.)"

"(———Estimated danger level 5. Misaka #10032 suggests reject—)"

"(———Rejection refused. Accepting signals via routes R, V, and Y.)"

"(———Misa…large, heavy burd on thoughting process—)"

"(———Rejection refused.)"

Zzzz!! A certain signal spread like a giant wave through the Misaka network. It covered the world within moments.

It was an emergency code from Last Order.

Whatever the code actually contained, the individual node Sisters couldn't oppose it. With most of their working brain regions repurposed, the girls were reduced to breathing organisms. Each of them froze in place.

What now? they all thought.

Last Order had clearly fallen into someone's hands. However malicious the commands she sent were, they couldn't resist them. But twiddling their thumbs and watching was out of the question.

I must take…action…that doesn't oppose…the command…

#10032, Little Misaka, sent information to the Misaka network.

…If that…is able to resolve…this critical situation…as a result…

All the Sisters responded.

They would stop their futile resistance against the virus (or so the Sisters had redefined the emergency code from Last Order as). By doing so, they could once again secure the calculation regions of their brains that were, in the past, dedicated to resistance. From that they gained only a tiny bit of thinking ability, though; Little Misaka still couldn't move a finger.

But with ten thousand of them doing it, everything coalesced into a single power.

The Sisters didn't hoard the power for themselves.

They all knew someone who could use it more effectively.

2

Smooth sailing.

Those two words described Thomas Platinaberg's life.

· Born into an affluent household, he was allowed to live without restrictions. He attended higher education, then emerged victorious in bold business ventures, resulting in the acquisition of vast fortune and influence. He'd been selected for the Academy City General Board in his midthirties, an exceptionally young age, excluding Aleister. It was a trophy to cap his travels and career.

He had never failed at anything, nor would he walk any path in the future but success—he never had a doubt about that. He'd never spoken of it to anybody, but he considered gaining the title of chairperson and gaining control over all of Academy City a simple task. These weren't his ambitions saying so. He thought it was just the natural course of things. If he kept doing his best, the rest would fall into place on its own.

Indeed.

He probably hadn't even dreamed of this. His front door had opened, and a moment later a shotgun muzzle was pressed to his chest and its trigger was pulled, sending him flying five meters backward.

"…"

Bang!! Accelerator watched with icy eyes as the young upstart flew into the air and slammed into the floor without bouncing. He'd at least seemed to be aware that he was under constant threat; Thomas was wearing a bulletproof jacket underneath his clothes. It had prevented his body from separating into an upper half and a lower half, but his rib cage, without a doubt, had been shattered. The man's body trembled with convulsions as well. He was completely unconscious.

Accelerator felt somehow relieved.

It had probably begun when he launched the attack on the windowless building. It was no longer taboo who he made into an enemy. Now he understood what that shit doctor told him. Limit yourself to one goal. He was absolutely right. He should have rescued Last Order *even if he made her into his enemy.* If he was already willing to go so far, why should he have to hesitate against other people?

Why hadn't he thought of doing this in the first place?

He had to grin, mocking himself for how psychological blind spots had formed without his realizing.

"Piece of shit."

Without a thought to his soaking-wet clothes, he made his way into the house, rubbing deep black stains into the extravagant carpets. Despite how much consideration went into each item inside it, the estate itself was extremely small. It looked more like a cottage than a Western-style house. Each piece of furniture was the price of a small house.

He glanced around the rooms to see several men and women—housekeepers, by the looks of it—sleeping on the beds, sofas, and floors. Maybe that was the reason the upstart prick had answered the door in person.

Spotting an office, Accelerator walked in and went over to the big ebony desk within. It looked like an antique...but flipping a switch raised a part of the polished desk, revealing an LCD monitor and keyboard. The movement made no noise; its utility was similar to the black-suits' luxury cars.

It had several key locks, but it didn't take long for Accelerator to get through them. It didn't use any biometric authentication such as fingerprint or retina scanning. The man had probably done it that way so that someone couldn't get in by cutting off his wrist or head and using it. And that was, in fact, exactly what Accelerator had been planning to do.

On the thirty-inch display was a mountain of data no ordinary person would ever see.

It contained several documents summarizing political activity in Academy City. The bias in what data existed here probably meant politics was the man's field of study. The data looked meaningless, but skimming over them revealed some possibly important information there. Still, who knew how many days it would take to comb through every file one by one?

As Accelerator examined them, growing ever more impatient, he finally arrived at the data he needed.

"...Here it is."

Information regarding the Hound Dogs.

It said that Academy City was currently under attack by an unknown threat, and to eliminate it, they needed to recover Last Order quickly. It was almost like a joke—they were actually playing at being saviors of the city.

What a load of bullshit..., he said to himself.

If they were thinking in such an "upright" way, then the first thing they should have done was become shields themselves. Bringing a tiny little brat so much suffering, then asking to be praised? *You've gotta be kidding me.*

"This is...," he said as he stopped breathing, looking further into the data.

Apparently, to oppose the threat to the city, the guys on the General Board were trying to overwrite Last Order with a virus. That meant they couldn't have her die—at least not until that "threat" was gone.

Maybe it wasn't over yet. Maybe he could get something back from all this.

Accelerator typed on the keyboard, very slightly trembling in expectation.

Unfortunately, it didn't say exactly how they'd use Last Order and how they'd "eliminate the threat." It didn't touch upon details about either the threat or the virus, of course. It clearly lacked information. The file was just a strategic suggestion (though in practical terms, a written order), saying only what had been suggested. Any further data might exist only in Aleister's head.

The code name for the strategic direction document, however…

"ANGEL"?

It was the English word *angel*. It called to mind the giant feathers that had somehow appeared in one part of Academy City—and the one who said he was going to stop it.

Was Accelerator not the only one fighting in the darkness?

"…"

Whatever the case, he didn't have time to pay attention to that. Last Order was his top priority.

Accelerator had already gotten rid of the virus someone tried to write into Last Order's head on August 31. But that was only because he had information about the virus already and because he had been at full strength. In this situation, that didn't seem doable.

Above all, he didn't have enough battery power. He could activate ability usage mode for only another two minutes at most. He couldn't heal her like this.

No, I don't need to use my power to heal shit. Kihara would be using a Testament program to mess with the brat's brain. That's fine with me. The original script for the virus should be in his hands anyway.

After writing the virus to her, Kihara might destroy the Testament device…but Accelerator decided that wasn't very probable. If something happened to go wrong during the process, he wouldn't be able to redo it. Kihara would have some kind of insurance for that.

Which means I still gotta do the same thing.

The keyboard's keys clacked under his fingers.

Hah, bull's-eye!!

He immediately found where the Hound Dogs were standing by.

Just gotta kill Kihara and wrest the brat away. Ha-ha, now that I know what I'm gonna do, I really wanna do it!!

The residence contained several hunting rifles.

He searched out one with bullets whose shape matched his shotgun, then loaded up and left.

3

Index burst out of the parking garage into the rain.

She'd been shaking around in a big hospital-like car before, but she didn't have the time to be hiding out any longer. Voices yelling for her to stop came from behind her, but she didn't turn back.

I swear, what on earth was that "Misaka Network Connection Battery" thing, anyway?! Did he trick me? Anyway, a lost child is a problem, but I never thought something like that would appear in Academy City!

Just its wings were gigantic; she couldn't see its main body, hidden behind the buildings as it was. She could see dozens of layers of feathers moving slowly—about the speed a person walked.

An angel.

Index had no idea why something like an angel had appeared in Academy City. Plus, this angel wasn't in her 103,000 grimoires. That hadn't happened since Aureolus and his Ars Magna, which meant this rivaled that incident in importance.

*I have to stop it...*She glared at the hundred-meter-long wings far in the distance. *If I don't, it will do something terrible.*

Just the one attack from earlier had incredible destructive power, but if it really was an angel in the sense that Index knew them, that wouldn't have been its true value. It would have the strength to end all life on earth with a fingertip and even greatly affect the stars in space.

The archive of forbidden books.

Necessarius, the Church of Necessary Evils.

It was all created for situations like this, but they'd never felt so unreliable before. She was a professional sorcerer, and even she felt so much fear from it. She knew she couldn't let the angel strike that fear into others who had nothing to do with this.

Index ran through the eerily quiet streets. She passed by nobody, perhaps due to the downpour.

Then, the being far, far in the distance began to roar as though tearing apart the night sky with its cry. It sounded like a beast being pulled by a collar made of barbed wire.

Its layers of giant feathers rattled, squirming ominously, as though it was stirring, trying to endure pain.

And as the angel moved, it cried out.

Index focused in that direction, wanting to get as much information as possible.

"...Huh?"

But suddenly, she grunted, confused.

The sound, a simple vibration of the air, which humans could never understand.

But for some reason, when she heard that voice, *she felt a longing.*

"..."

The angel held her giant wings in front of her.

Wings of light, not meant to be in this world, divine yet spine-chilling. At times the wings would blur as though blown by the wind, then return to normal. Like waves on a beach—like mist swaying in a breeze.

The motions looked random, but they actually followed a fixed pattern.

Index had perfect recall, and that information gave her a match.

She'd seen those movements before.

September 1.

After defeating the sorcerer Sherry Cromwell in the underground mall, when she and Touma Kamijou had gone to the hospital with the doctor with the frog face.

It was...

The reserved air, cowering in the face of everything...Its owner was...

"...Hyouka?"

4

"What on earth is that?" Mikoto wondered aloud.

She stood dumbly in the middle of a rain-pelted street under the umbrella she'd bought at the convenience store. A street on which—whether because the final school closing time was past, the weather was bad, or some other reason—nobody could be seen.

She'd been looking for Touma Kamijou, but it was late, the passing shower had turned into something a lot more serious, and she was on the verge of throwing her hands up, when suddenly, a group of buildings elsewhere in the city crumbled into dust and dozens of giant, sharp, wing-looking things had appeared.

Even for a supernatural ability, they were enormous. Could any ability even do that in the first place?

Plus, a moment later the wings had done something like an electrical discharge, which had obliterated part of the area just outside the city.

It was only "like" an electrical discharge—it wasn't actually one. Mikoto was the most talented electromaster in Academy City. By her estimation, the power hadn't used electricity.

But then, what was it?

The more it resembled electricity, the more trouble she found herself having identifying it. Gradually, she started to realize that the scientific rules she'd always believed in didn't apply here.

She tried to call Kuroko Shirai but didn't get an answer.

Calling the Judgment station and even Anti-Skill yielded the same result.

She felt like she'd been left behind in a terrible place. And she didn't know why, but Academy City's peacekeeping functions had completely shut down. Now there was this big monster. She found herself in a completely unexpected, unreal situation, and now she stood stock-still, her umbrella open.

Then.

Someone, footsteps splashing through the puddles, passed by

Mikoto from behind. They were headed straight toward the distant monster. The girl was soaking wet, running without any rain gear. Mikoto remembered her. She was the sister always with Kamijou, the one with the pure-white habit.

"W-wait! What the heck are you doing here?! Can't you tell it's dangerous?!" Mikoto reactively went after her and grabbed her arm.

"Get off of me!!" shouted Index without turning back. "I have to go. Hyouka's there. I don't know why, but I have to stop it. That's my friend over there!!"

Her explanation didn't make sense—maybe the situation was too overwhelming. Mikoto began to wonder if she was hysterical because of it, but then another figure appeared to her.

"Touma!!"

Yes, it was Touma Kamijou.

He came around a bend about a hundred meters away and onto the main road they were on. He didn't seem to notice them. His eyes, too, focused only on the cluster of giant wings.

Having found the one she was looking for, Mikoto opened her mouth, but no words came out.

Because despite finding someone she knew, Mikoto felt Index's resistance to her turn explosive. She wrenched her arm away from Mikoto and shouted into the heavy rain.

"No, don't, Touma! Please don't kill Hyouka!!"

5

Touma Kamijou was on the run.

He was just about to return to the main city to stop the angel, which was his top priority, after losing sight of Vento at the iron bridge. And just like he had when going after Last Order, he'd managed to bump into the black-suits.

He fled into a narrow alley too small for a car to easily enter, then tried to throw off their pursuit by following a complex pattern of roads. But despite his home-field advantage, he couldn't lead trained professionals around by the nose. It was a miracle he hadn't been shot by now.

"No, don't, Touma! Please don't kill Hyouka!!"

So when he heard the yell, he thought his heart would stop. It wasn't so much what she said as the fact that he simply conflated the "loud noise" with a gunshot and thought he'd been shot.

"!!" He froze in place and then took two seconds to turn around. Finally, when he saw Index and Mikoto running toward him, he relaxed a little. Right away he changed his mind—this wasn't the time to relax—and grabbed their arms and dove onto another back road.

Several splashing footsteps rang out on the main street.

It was the black-suits.

They were looking here and there, but they'd eventually find where they were hiding. But Index—and Mikoto, of course—didn't care a wink about the black-suits. Index looked up at him with frightened eyes for some reason.

She didn't ask what had happened or why he was on the run. She only stated the more important things. "Please, Touma, don't go over there. I don't know how or why, but I'm pretty sure that angel is Hyouka. I have to stop what's happening no matter what, but you can't get involved! If you touch her, she'll disappear, even if you don't mean for that to happen!!"

Index urgently pleaded with him, grabbing his shirt, which had absorbed water. She must have been agitated, because her words didn't link together. But he knew the name "Hyouka," at least.

Hyouka Kazakiri. An aggregation of involuntary diffusion fields. One with a human mind but not a human body.

Seriously...?

The girl Kamijou knew had nothing to do with such destructive behavior. But if someone outside were to interfere with the composition of the fields, maybe it could cause that sort of change. If they were completely in control of them, then maybe they could even control everything, from her form to her actions.

It seemed like a natural phenomenon, somehow incomplete.

But then who made her like that?

Is it because Vento took down all the students in the city...? No, it's not...

As Kamijou thought desperately to himself, Index continued in earnest. "Touma, I'll do something about Hyouka, so please, don't get involved!"

Hyouka Kazakiri was the first friend Index had ever made. She wouldn't want to make Kazakiri her enemy, even if she did waver due to her position as the archive of forbidden books.

Kamijou mulled it over. Hyouka Kazakiri was a good person. But if she was out of control, all bets were off. Someone's usual personality didn't matter if they were dead drunk, either.

So he said this: "That won't work."

"Touma!!"

"I'll be the one to stop her. And *she's not the only problem here*. I can't leave everything to you."

"But if you use your right hand, Hyouka will die!!"

"I won't let her die!!" Kamijou yelled back, forgetting that they were hiding from the black-suits. He grabbed the complaining Index by the nape of her neck and pulled her to him. When she froze in surprise, he continued. "I'm not doing this to kill her! I'm doing this to *rescue* her! Does that look like how Kazakiri's supposed to be to you?! Of course it doesn't. Something happened to make her like that! I need to go save her, damn it!! Don't get involved? Screw that. I don't need your permission to save her!!"

Index's mouth opened and closed.

Kamijou continued anyway. "I don't know exactly how she's built magically or what an angel is supposed to be here. I need your knowledge for that. But the involuntary diffusion fields are involved in all this, so you won't know everything, either. I'll tell you about that part of it. Together, we can save Hyouka Kazakiri!"

The sounds of rain started to grow distant.

Eventually only the boy's words dominated their surroundings.

"A ton has been happening in the city today. I honestly don't even know the half of it, and I don't have any clues how to solve it, either. But I know that I've gotta do this! We're going to rescue Kazakiri! Am I wrong?!" he demanded.

He had to wake up the girl going on about misdirected things regarding her friend, like kill or don't kill.

"Let's go, Index. Help me out so we can save her!!"

Index heard his voice and nodded.
Kamijou let go of her neck.
Then he scanned the exit of the alley again. First, they had to shake off the black-suits on the main road somehow. The bullets were really just normal bullets, without any sorcery or powers behind them. They were the worst kind of problem for Kamijou. His right hand worked only on unnatural powers.
Then…
"Haaah…" Mikoto, who'd just been pulled into here with them, heaved a sigh and tossed her umbrella aside. She examined Kamijou and Index with a tired expression for some reason. "I don't get what's going on, but I can tell you're up to your necks in some ridiculous problem."
"W-well, you're not wrong."
"And that an acquaintance of yours is at the center of all this."
"Not an acquaintance, a friend," corrected Index.
Mikoto's face grew even more exasperated as she stared out of the alley. "Just to make sure, she's not a bad person, right?"
"Definitely not," said Kamijou immediately and without hesitation. "Index says so, too. That person's our friend."
"Your friend…"
Mikoto looked at the angel spraying around electrical discharge–like phenomena between its wings as it moved in the distance, then back at Kamijou and Index one more time. "You mean, um, that person, right?"
Index and Kamijou answered at almost the same time.
"Of course, who else?"

"Quit asking the obvious."

"Ha-ha-ha. Anyway, those people in black before were bad guys, right?"

"Can't figure out why they're after me, though. They're not good guys, at least."

Then they heard several sets of footsteps enter the alley. The black-suits, who had been examining the entrance, had stormed in. Not simply entered but stormed in. There was no time.

Mikoto grinned anyway. "Oh, whatever. If that's your friend, who cares? I won't ask again, so go save her already. I'll make do here."

"You idiot, you'll…!!" Kamijou tried to grab Mikoto's shoulder.

"Sorry, sorry. No time to stop. Starting now!"

Mikoto had already launched an arcade coin toward the alley's exit.

The Railgun.

Her Mach-three strike gouged out the walls on either side, thundering and spraying flashes as it darted toward the main street. She probably picked a trajectory that wouldn't hit the black-suits, but the shock wave alone flipped over several of them.

A gray dust cloud danced into the air.

Before the raindrops could push it back down, Mikoto stomped on one of the grounded black-suit's stomachs to knock him out, then leaped onto the main street, which had no cover.

"Misaka!!" shouted Kamijou.

Unfortunately, the black-suits who had been waiting on the main street were returning fire, so he couldn't go any farther. Meanwhile, Mikoto, who had incredible strength in terms of "normal combat force," shouted back to him from the battlefield of bullets.

"The punishment game!!"

"What?!"

"Where you have to do anything I say! It's effective all day, so you have to save your friend and come back, got it?!"

Kamijou tried to shout something back, but the sounds of crackling electricity and gunshots cut him off. *Shit*, he swore to himself. "I'll protect her! Don't you die either!!"

He let Index pull him along, and he ran farther into the alley as though shaking free of something. They had one destination. If Index was right, it was where Hyouka Kazakiri was waiting.

After hearing the wet splashing of footsteps, Mikoto sighed on the battlefield.

She'd totally drawn the short lot.

The punishment game...Ended up using it for something like this, huh?

But she figured there was no helping it.

He said he'd risk his life to save a friend. She couldn't put a damper on that. But if these black-suits (was that what they were?) hadn't caused this issue in the first place, maybe she'd have gotten to continue the punishment game in a better way.

When she thought of that, she got a little mad.

"I am in a really bad mood right now."

Several muzzles openly pointed at her.

But right before they could squeeze the triggers, a bunch of manhole covers, water pipes, and signboards in front of her gathered to her to form a shield. It was magnetism. The bullets all bounced off the shield of steel.

"If you're not going to run, come at me like your life depends on it."

Right on the heels of her shield, she fired lances of lightning out at random.

She didn't plan to lose.

6

Kamijou and Index ran through the streets in the downpour.

Kamijou was worried about Mikoto behind them, but he would probably only hold her back. He forced his mind from her and looked ahead.

As he did, Index, running beside him, asked him, "Hey, Touma, why is the city so quiet? Besides Hyouka, I kind of feel a flow of mana!"

"Yeah, it's quiet because everyone's probably unconscious. Because of the sorcerer who got into the city! I'd like to know how her attack works, too. And if there's a way to heal them!!"

He summed up the occurrences in Academy City. Index fell silent after hearing it and looked down in thought.

As her feet plodded over the rain-pelted road, she looked back up. "I think…it's probably divine punishment."

"What?"

"It's using a certain emotion as the key. It takes down anyone who has that emotion, no matter how far away they are! That's why it's divine punishment, like from God. Basically, no matter who or where they are, they won't be forgiven for spitting on the Lord!" Index continued. "Touma, did you see the sorcerer acting in a certain way? Like trying to guide you to a specific emotion more than she had to?!"

A specific emotion. Kamijou thought back to his confrontations with Vento of the Front.

———Her words and actions, purposely provoking.

———Her makeup and body piercings, purposely creating a sense of revulsion.

———Her many attacks, purposely fired at civilians with nothing to do with this.

Vento could have had her own reasons—or more likely, there was a magical meaning to them—but it was possible her role aside from that was to make him feel a certain way. Which meant the emotion had to be…

"Disgust…No, *hostility or malice*? Could that be the trigger for the divine punishment spell?!"

If she had an attack like that, Vento would be nearly invincible. Nobody would be able to stand in her way. Just considering the thought would trigger the spell.

As Vento had tried to go through the gate to Academy City without permission, Anti-Skill, who protected the city's peace, had tried to stop her. The other officers had been informed via radio they'd been taken out—and then the whole city saw it on the news after that.

"I think there are stages of the divine punishment spell depending on their hostility! Like making them unconscious, binding their flesh, or blocking outside interference. But whatever stage you get, it's over by then. Until the sorcerer decides they don't need it anymore, I don't think those people will ever get better!!"

That's why everyone collapsed.

Not even just in Academy City anymore. It could be happening outside the city—and with news broadcast to Japan or the rest of the world, the damage could be spreading. Aside from them, in groups and agencies cooperating with Academy City, they could have automatically gotten notice of it and seen victims.

But…

"Is that even possible? Is sorcery really just that convenient to use?!"

"Not normally! There's nothing about it in my 103,000 grimoires. But this is the only way to explain what's happening! …I know it sounds crazy. Divine punishment is just that—punishment meted out by the heavens. There's no way regular people could do it!!"

But Vento had. Was that simply the power of God's Right Seat?

"That bastard—so that's how she…!!"

"Wait, Touma! If this is all true, don't tell me about the sorcerer at all! My Walking Church doesn't have its papal-class defenses right now. Unlike you, the spell could affect me, too!!"

"Oh," said Kamijou, quickly shutting his mouth.

Not even Index could defend against Vento's divine judgment spell. As long as there wasn't an exception like Imagine Breaker, Vento could crush anyone if that condition was met. And Index was someone who specifically fought sorcerers who hurt people.

Either way, if there was no way to heal them, there was no point sticking to the topic. Kazakiri came first right now.

Maybe Index knew about that, too—she'd even exposed Vento's divine judgment spell. "What about Kazakiri...the angel? She'll be all right, won't she?! We can still save her, right?!"

"Well..."

"Shit, why did that thing show up *now*?! Is it related to the divine judgment in the city?! Why is it clearly an angel and not just a simple phenomenon going out of control?!"

"I don't know!!" shouted Index in denial, which was unusual given that she had memorized 103,000 grimoires by rote. And yet that had to be an angel, something from the magic side, out there in the distance.

"...It looks and works a lot like the ones from the grimoires in my head, at least. But the parts it's using are all over the place, and I've never seen any of it before! It's like looking at a mural with letters you don't know on it. The picture shows basically what's happening, but you can't figure out the culture or mental state of the person with it!!"

"..."

The most frustrated was probably Index. She was the "index" of forbidden books meant to solve these problems, after all.

"At the very least, I can tell that the core commanding the angel is somewhere else, but..."

"So even you can't figure it out..."

Hyouka Kazakiri was made out of involuntary diffusion fields.

That very foundation contained supernatural ability research and cutting-edge scientific technology. And if Index couldn't deal with those, then she couldn't take any countermeasures against this angel.

As Kamijou and Index ran, they continued their conversation, driven by impatience enough that they didn't worry about the downpour.

"What about you, Touma? Do you know anything about how Hyouka's angel works?"

"Not really..."

It was easy to say *it uses involuntary diffusion fields*. But he couldn't explain how that worked. Everyone knew cars ran on gasoline, but very few could actually draw up a blueprint for one.

...Isn't there anyone who knows more about this than me? Someone on a college-professor level who could draw a "blueprint" like that while humming to themselves...?

But Kamijou didn't have any adult or scientist contacts like that. He was about to curse when a single person came up in his mind.

"Miss Komoe!!"

Back at the beginning of September when Sherry attacked the underground mall, she'd figured out Kazakiri's identity just by his story. She would know a lot about involuntary diffusion fields.

Her phone number was still in his cell phone from when he called her back then. As he ran through the rainy streets, he immediately contacted his homeroom teacher on his phone.

But...

"What's the matter, Touma?"

"Shit!!"

She wasn't picking up. Maybe she'd fallen victim to Vento's attack, or maybe there was some other reason she couldn't use her cell phone right now. No matter how long he waited, she didn't pick up.

Out of options...!! Kamijou clenched his teeth and started scrolling through his contacts list. But all the entries were students. Nobody here would know more than Miss Komoe about—

"!!"

Kamijou immediately called the bottom number in his list. It was the newest number he'd added.

And the name was...

"Misaka!!"

"Gah!! Wh-what? I'm really freaking busy! Don't give me more work to do!!"

Bang-bang-bang!! With all the gunshots in the background, Mikoto's voice was mixed with static. Maybe the connection was particularly poor because she was using electric attacks.

Kamijou didn't have any time, either. He got right to the point without asking about her trouble. "Tokiwadai has totally different lesson plans than regular middle schools, right?! They teach you all so you guys can be at the forefront when you graduate, so *you take college-level courses, too, right*?!"

"What?! What are you—? Yikes! What the heck are you talking about?!"

"I need information to stop that angel! I need an adviser who knows a lot about involuntary diffusion fields!! You're my only hope! Can you do it?!"

He heard a weird sputter come across the cell phone. After taking it away from his ear for a moment, he shouted, "H-hey, Misaka! Did you get shot?! Hey!!"

"I did not!!"

Buzz-spark-crack!! came a series of lightning attack noises.

Misaka's voice followed in their wake. "N-not like I have a choice!! No mercy, huh? Asking me to fight while thinking about something else!!"

"Okay, then Index, you take my phone. Anything you don't understand, ask her!"

"Huh?" Index looked at him blankly as Kamijou tried to give her the cell phone.

Meanwhile, for Mikoto's part…"What?!"

"??? What's the problem, Misaka?"

"Well, no, er, it's fine, but, whaaat?!"

"I'll leave it to you!!"

He wasn't sure what she was talking about, but he didn't have time to worry about it right now.

"I've got my right hand, and I don't think I can help you with anything sorcery-related," said Kamijou, pushing his phone at the sister in white. "Sorry, Index, but can you do this by yourself?"

"What will you do, Touma?"

"You said the angel and the core commanding it are in different places, right? You go to where the core is and solve the problem. Meanwhile I'll do the angel job myself."

He continued, saying, "Like I said before, there's a sorcerer using the divine judgment spell. A sorcerer named Vento from a group called God's Right Seat is after this angel version of Kazakiri. I'll have to stop Vento first if we want to free Kazakiri. I want you to handle the core causing the problem. While you're at it, I'll protect Kazakiri from Vento's attacks!!"

When she heard that, Index frowned a little bit in worry. She was probably thinking about the sorcery involved. But she didn't verbalize it. Instead, she replied, "Okay. I'll leave Hyouka to you, Touma!!"

"Yeah, I'll be relying on you, too, Index!!"

The two separated and ran down different paths...

...both with the same objective: rescue Hyouka Kazakiri.

7

"Ha-ha, that's fuckin' crazy! What the hell is it?!" cheered Amata Kihara in the obsolescent office room.

Tons of these "feathers" had suddenly appeared hundreds of meters in front of him, leveling buildings all around. He could see only the "feathers" from his window, but for some reason, the term *angel* came to mind at a mere glance.

After inserting the virus into the mind of Last Order, sleeping on the desk right now, no sooner had he rebooted her than that being appeared. The name of the virus the higher-ups had given him was, in a stroke of unoriginality, the English word *ANGEL*. It couldn't possibly be unrelated. Something unconnected to science had manifested through science.

But Kihara didn't reject this unscientific state of affairs. No, he was astonished science had actually set foot into this territory at last.

Aleister, Academy City General Board chairperson...Kihara thought of himself as a mad scientist, but this guy was something else.

"Damn, now I'm jealous! You're fucking insane, Aleister!! Don't you even know the meaning of the word *theory*?! A scientist rejecting science? What kind of scientist does that make you?!"

Unlike Kihara, his five subordinates nearby were bewildered. They didn't know how to deal with what they were seeing as something real, and they looked like they were perplexed as to whether it *was* even real.

"Your goal was to use that thing to crush Academy City's enemies?! Yeah, I guess if you had somethin' like that, most assholes would be helpless. Dunno who was sticking to the outside walls, but too bad for them! Check it out, you bastards! He brought out a fucking *angel*! Forget the three antinuclear principles!! Since when was the Bible a freaking *pop-up picture book*, anyway?!"

His Hound Dog subordinates, their minds unable to process the information, sluggishly followed Kihara's command and looked out the dust-covered glass window.

But none of them was looking at the distant angel.

Because Accelerator was flying through the air and about to smash through the window.

Craaaassssshhhh!! The glass exploded.

He'd already unlocked his ability usage mode.

One of the black-suits near the window took the brunt of Accelerator's flying kick and careened back to the opposite wall. The man struck the thin inner wall without bouncing, his combat armor pulverized as he crumpled to the floor.

Accelerator didn't bother to check if he was alive. His blood-red eyes rolled to and fro, then locked onto his target.

"Kiiihaaaaaaaraaaaaa!!" he screamed, leveling his shotgun and pulling the trigger without hesitation.

He aimed for everything from the chest to the waist. He wanted to kill him with perfect certainty.

Kihara thrust one of his nearby lackeys in front of him. The man gave a stupid-sounding grunt and danced right out to where he'd block it.

Countless shots ripped into him, spraying his Hound Dog blood everywhere and sending him to the floor. Kihara didn't care. He started laughing so hard, it looked like pieces of his face would break.

"You gotta actually aim that thing! You'll be a bother to everyone if you don't!!"

Accelerator ignored the clear provocation. Instead, his gaze shifted to glance over the flustered black-suits hastily readying their weapons. *Annoying fucking shields...*He ground his teeth. *Fine! Hope the bunch of you don't start pleading with "please forgive me, I was only doing what he ordered me to"!!*

He changed the vector of his leg strength, set his sights on the Hound Dogs instead of Kihara, and lunged up to one of them. Rather than use his shotgun, he extended four fingers and his thumb. A knife and a pistol were fixed on the man's combat armor, and four whole grenades were equipped near his shoulders.

Those were what he was after. He used his four fingers to remove all their pins.

Not a moment later, he kicked the man in the gut, sending him flying into the other Hound Dogs before they all went down like bowling pins. The man on top quickly reached for the grenades still attached to him...

...and then the human bomb exploded.

The shrapnel grenades sent blood and flesh spraying everywhere.

Now there was only one Hound Dog left besides Kihara.

"Ahh?!" squealed the last man as Accelerator's eyes rolled around to look at him. He immediately grabbed something lying on the desk. It was Last Order, limp and unconscious as though they'd done excessive processing on her with the Testament.

Right now, Accelerator was holding a shotgun that couldn't aim very precisely. The man must have thought Accelerator wouldn't be able to attack with his shield.

Unfortunately for him...

"_____"

Accelerator's eyes changed. There was a *grr-crash!!* After altering the vector of his leg strength, he closed the distance to the Hound Dog in an instant, arriving right beside the man.

The man had been right—Accelerator didn't fire his shotgun.

Instead, he brought the meter-long metal gun barrel around in a full swing and smashed it into the Hound Dog's face. The impact shattered the shotgun, spraying tiny springs and cylindrical bullets from the magazines into the air. With a muffled sound, the man spun around four times in midair like a flying top before slamming into the floor, and then he stopped moving.

Last Order ended up released and in the air; Accelerator caught her with one hand and gently put her on the desk.

Then he looked at Amata Kihara, the culprit of all this.

But Kihara cackled, as if to say Accelerator had just made it easier for him. "That was so cool!! Now that you're showing your true colors, I think I'm in love, Accelerator!!"

"Time to turn you to scrap, you shithead!!"

The two villains' shouts shook the air.

Kihara opened his fists, then clenched them again, licking his lips. He ran for Accelerator.

His "reflection" wouldn't work on Kihara, but Accelerator wasn't shy about it anymore.

He opened his own fingers and began to run.

Remaining time for ability usage mode: sixty seconds.

8

Touma Kamijou had reached ground zero.

It was a corner of School District 7 he was familiar with. The tall buildings were rather high-grade, famous department stores and corporation sites, for the place to be called student-oriented. You could always find restaurants and such inside the department stores in magazine columns. He didn't visit the place every day, since it was out of the way of his school commute, but Kamijou had come here several times to eat with Index (with absolutely no "mood" of any kind involved).

School District 7 had both a high-quality feel like the Garden of Learning and the more civilian smell like his own student dorm, and this corner was in one of the more high-quality areas. Normally, during the day, many girls in Tokiwadai Middle School and Kirigaoka Girls' Academy school uniforms would have been walking around here.

It was a uniquely adult atmosphere that needed more than children to exist.

And now...

...like a collapsed sand castle, it was a pile of wreckage and debris.

"..."

Every single building about a hundred meters out from here had been destroyed, mowed down. Not that it was a complete crater without even any broken pieces remaining—no, it was a more disorderly disaster, like a giant had used its arm to wrench each individual building free. On the other hand, though, the buildings tilted diagonally and department stores with only their first floors remaining were strangely vivid scars, and they shook Kamijou's heart.

Vento of the Front.

There must have been a ton of people her special attack immobilized. And in that situation, all these buildings had collapsed around them. He couldn't even imagine how many people were buried in this mountain of wreckage. Rescue teams were running late, but even if they got here, how many would they be able to save?

His nerves felt numb.

With floaty movements, he stared at the center of ground zero.

There was an angel.

Her main body was the same size as a normal person. Her wings, however, were enormous—so gargantuan they looked like they'd swallow up the person inside them.

They gave off a dazzling light, seemingly enough to ward away all the gray dust clouds and heavy rain. They ranged from ten to a hundred meters long. They had no uniformity; they looked like sharply edged weeds sprouting every which way. Each of the dozens of giant wings connected to the back of the small-statured girl.

The angel was about a hundred meters off, slowly moving to the size relative to him. She was simply walking with her two slender legs, but every time her foot hit the ground, there was a dull *thump*.

The girl.

Hyouka Kazakiri.

Her hair was long and pretty, with a little bit of brown mixed into its black. It mostly reached down to her waist, but one tuft of it was tied to the side and hung down. Her skirt, part of her blue school-designated uniform, looked timid, its length unchanged. Atop her blue blazer was an accenting red necktie.

It should have been a girl Touma Kamijou knew. It should have been a fainthearted, blubbering girl, the kind who would hesitate to punch even a villain.

But…

Right now, what Kamijou was seeing was clearly different from that image of Hyouka Kazakiri. Her head hung low, lips half-open and tongue hanging out. Her eyes were wide open, and they shook irregularly, like a mechanical lens reading tiny letters. The rainwater on her face mixed with her drool, dampening the top of her uniform. But even the slimy light and feel didn't move her an inch.

Dozens of giant wings. An inhuman atmosphere. A wall-like presence. It was a lot like Misha Kreutzev. But the huge angel before him now was even more unnatural, more twisted.

Her face held no emotion. Her uncannily wandering eyeballs shed no tears.

Something wasn't letting them shed any.

A kind of restriction.

Above her head was a ring, about fifteen centimeters across. The ring's rotational speed changed in time with her footsteps, and its

diameter kept growing and shrinking. On the outer edge of the ring were several pencil-shaped sticks pointing outward, which were quickly retracting and extending, making *click-click-clack-clack* noises.

Touma Kamijou remembered something. Inside Hyouka Kazakiri's head, there was an object that looked like a triangular prism. Her hands and feet moved to match that prism.

That's what he felt like he was watching now. It was even more chilling than seeing a person controlled by a bunch of electrodes in his head.

Kaza...kiri...

Kamijou averted his eyes from her terrible face right away. It would have been easier to look at a corpse. He knew deep in his heart that he had to stop this. He didn't need a reason.

"Kazakiriiiiiiiiiiiiiiiiiiiiiiiiiiiii!!"

He shouted despite himself.

Kazakiri's feet, on their way somewhere, stopped suddenly. Her neck slowly turned toward Kamijou.

However...

With the loud *scritch* of metal against metal, the angel halo above her head spun around quickly. All the pencil-sized rods surrounding its outer edge went *shh-ghh* at the same time and stabbed inward, into the halo.

He heard something like a scream.

It forced Kazakiri's neck to stop moving and shake madly. Then, like something got inside the gears, her neck shifted back to its original position. She resumed her slow pace forward, her neck unnaturally twisted.

Spark!! An electric sound rang out.

Far overhead, as each of the giant feathers got close to another, they sparkled with a pale-blue light. They almost looked like they were checking themselves before firing.

Crack-crack. Strange lights sparked around Kazakiri, timed as if aligned with her angel halo. Then, as though guided by those lights, her body moved.

It looked like she was afraid—she didn't want to do anything, but something that way was worrying her too much, and she wouldn't be satisfied until she went over there.

Just like someone worried about whether they'd left the gas on. Just like thinking the dirt on your hands wasn't coming off despite washing them numerous times.

...Like a severe case of obsessional neurosis?

He had a vague idea—it wasn't based on any rules, but it was that feeling of just having to make sure. The lights he saw were the same. They were mentally guiding Kazakiri's movements by appearing in one "important spot" after another.

However...

If she went on too long in that state, it would have to wear down her nerves. It was the same as pressing a burning iron plate to the back of someone blindfolded, as leading a lost person to the exit of a labyrinth.

And the act completely ignored Kazakiri's human mind.

Damn it...This is bullshit!!

Kamijou almost ran up to her, but his feet stopped. What was he planning to do? He couldn't touch her. The Imagine Breaker would destroy the illusion called Hyouka Kazakiri, no questions asked.

"Damn it...!!"

Kamijou clenched his teeth and pounded his useless right hand into a wall of wreckage. He couldn't save the people buried here. He couldn't save Kazakiri, attacked by this strange phenomenon. He felt so incredibly small and hopelessly wretched.

Then, as though the misfortune in front of him had called forth more misfortune, he heard a new set of footsteps.

"Oh my. Were the mortal sinners busy licking each other's wounds?"

Kamijou turned around.

It was the woman adorned in the archetypical dress from an age long past with piercings all over her face. A member of the group called God's Right Seat, who had robbed the city of almost all its functions and now strolled leisurely through it, come to kill Kamijou.

Vento of the Front.

Her hands gripped a giant hammer covered in barbed wire.

Whether due to sickness or some other reason, red blood trickled from the corner of her mouth, and it had dyed her rain-pelted clothing here and there, too. And yet her expression was the same.

All the piercings ruining the balance of her face, Vento, weapon in one hand, grinned at him. A grin filled with scorn and disdain, the kind you wouldn't think anyone would direct at another person.

"I went through all that trouble to save you for later, and now you come to me to be slaughtered. Were you so sick of seeing tragedy that you wanted me to crush you first?"

"I won't let you kill Kazakiri."

"Really, now. You feel things for something like that? What an awful philanthropist. That thing is a symbol of blasphemy, even more hideously corrupt than the great pregnancy in Revelation. Even perverts would never accept something like that."

"Bastard!! Take that back!!"

"Take what back? Oh, are you trying to tell me she's not normally like that? How absurd. This may be the first time I've seen it, but do you really think the head of Academy City would use the entire city to make something harmless, useless? It has such vast power and worth. Maybe what you saw before now was just an incomplete, imperfect irregularity."

The head of Academy City.

The one with half the world, the science side, under his absolute control.

If using all the involuntary diffusion fields in the city had made Hyouka Kazakiri, the leader of the one who was (or might have been) controlling her had to be him. If she hadn't spontaneously appeared, if there was some kind of goal behind her creation, then the terms *incomplete* and *imperfect* did indeed sound credible.

"As one of God's Right Seat, I can't overlook that monster. I mean, we're not exactly organized, but none of us can approve of something like this. A lump of blasphemy, scorning everything we offer to Crossism—she must be purged."

Craaack!! A loud roar hit Kamijou's ears.

…?! Again?!

He turned around to see lightning-like flares flickering out of the giant wings connected to Kazakiri's back. The sparks formed bridges between feathers, and the sound's pitch was steadily growing higher. It could all rush out of it at any moment.

Kamijou fell silent for a moment and thought about everything.

And then he said this.

"Can I just say this again?"

"What is it?"

"Take it back, you shithead."

"Oh?" Vento said with an amused smile. "So you do have a cute side to you. All right, fine. I'll sympathize with your feelings. Either way, you're both set to be killed in turn, so I'll be nice and kill you together."

For her, that was probably the biggest concession she could make. Though from Kamijou's standpoint, it was such a meaningless condition he wanted to spit.

"Oh, did you want to save that monster? That won't work. Not even the two of you together can defeat me," said Vento in an entertained tone of voice.

"Did you know that angels don't actually have their own wills? They're nothing but God's tools," she said with a scornful laugh. "If it malfunctions or gets confused with other chains of command or something, it turns into what we call a *fallen angel*. The most famous would be the rebellion of Lucifer, or Bearer of Light. A single 'bug' in the program dragged a third of all the angels assigned in Heaven into confusion, and then into war.

"But anyway," she said, scraping her hammer along the asphalt. She looked at Kamijou.

"Is that monster there sacred? Or is it corrupt?"

"!"

"It isn't even worth asking! That thing is just a goddamned fallen angel!! And it's not even the kind God made before it went out of control. It's a man-made doll with misshapen wings, then further corrupted with sin after sin! A miserable pile of unholy guilt!!"

Vento lifted her hammer off the ground with one hand and pointed it at Kamijou.

"I don't know what Academy City has in mind! Did he fail to make a perfect angel, or was he trying to make a fallen one to begin with?! It doesn't matter—I will never agree to anything you bastards do!!"

Just the emotion in her voice was enough to overwhelm most people. Her words were a perfect rejection of the being known as Hyouka Kazakiri.

"I don't think my 'real spell' will work against that thing now. I don't even know whether it has the same mental structure as a person in the first place. But I'll kill it! Even if I lack the power, that fallen angel is incomplete! I'll make a spell to interfere with its complete mess of an internal control system and have it destroy itself!! I'm telling you I'll blow the damn monster away with its own strength!!"

Kamijou listened to her speak. He clenched his teeth, glared straight at her, and moved his lips.

"…Not happening."

He was struck by how unreasonable the combat conditions were. He didn't even know if he could beat Vento in the first place, and now he had to protect Kazakiri while he fought. To add to that, Kazakiri might not be harmless, either. The insane sparks jolting from those wings would kill him in one shot if they hit him in the back.

But Touma Kamijou clenched his right fist hard anyway.

And he spoke.

"…She's already been put in this situation by the higher-ups in

Academy City, controlling her limbs, staining them with blood, and even sealing away her ability to ask for help or shed tears…And you think I'll let someone who just waltzed on in here treat her like a monster and kill her?"

It didn't matter whether his words reached "her" or not. Kamijou had decided to protect her. To make good on that decision, he now stood before Vento. With the downpour soaking him and the giant angel behind him, continuing to accept as many of the disadvantageous conditions as he could.

"Don't screw with me. The hell do you think a person's friends are?!"

CHAPTER 10

Their Respective Battlefields
The_Way_of_Light_and_Darkness.

1

His time was limited to sixty seconds.

Killing Kihara was the only thing he could do. If he had even ten seconds left at the end of the battle, he wouldn't have any problems. The battery consumption levels of ability usage mode and normal mode were wildly different. Even a few remaining seconds of battle mode would provide dozens of minutes of movement if he switched to normal mode.

In one corner of the abandoned office lay a modified, portable Testament.

With it, though it would be only the bare minimum, one could say the stage was set to heal Last Order's brain.

If Kihara really had injected her with the virus here, he'd probably still have the original script. Writing a vaccine program shouldn't be too hard.

Then kill him. Just kill him!! Kill him and it's all over! Don't think about other shit. You can't return to the path of light anyway, so focus on dragging Kihara to hell with you!!

His mind focused on that single thought, Accelerator shot through the wide office space at Kihara like a bullet. He opened his right hand. His demonic hand, able to reflect vectors by merely touching the skin, could reverse the man's blood flow and rupture his veins and organs as a result. Considering Last Order was on the same floor, he couldn't do anything too flashy. But he could still easily kill a man.

He shoved it sharply from below, aiming for Kihara's face.

Kihara swung his head over and easily dodged it. Accelerator couldn't sense any fear or nervousness from him, who could sense death from a mere touch away. The man's face actually seemed confident, like he'd never get hit in the first place anyway.

As Accelerator's swing missed, Kihara came in with a cross counter.

A punch ten times more precise than a boxing jab, which he brought back immediately after swinging.

It slipped by Accelerator's "reflection" and crashed mercilessly into his nose.

"Ah…!!"

There was a dull, grinding *gshhh*.

The strike was by no means a flashy, heavy hit like with a hammer. His vision swayed—he'd been hit in the nose, after all—but it wasn't enough to knock him out.

However…

Just for a moment, the pain stopped Accelerator from moving, and a series of additional light attacks came at him. Face, chest, shoulder, abdomen, face again, face, face. When Accelerator swung his arm, Kihara moved back, and when Accelerator tried to follow, Kihara closed in and attacked.

"Gyah-ha-ha!! You shithead!" shouted Kihara. "How dare you stand up to me!"

Another dull impact rattled his head.

His "reflection" still wasn't working. The power that should have blocked a direct blast from a nuclear weapon without singeing a single hair on his head. His impenetrable wall.

Accelerator tried to back off for the moment.

Kihara took a long step toward him and came in with another punch at his face.

"!!"

Accelerator's "reflection" wasn't like a thick bulletproof shield in front of his body. All it did was redirect the force coming toward him to the opposite direction. The reversal of energy approaching him was what protected him from all attacks.

Which meant…

If a force going backward hits my reflection, it'll deflect forward!!

Accelerator wiped the blood from his punched, cut lips. He was sure of it.

Amata Kihara was reversing the punches he was throwing at Accelerator just before they hit—at the last possible moment before hitting his protective layer of "reflection." By doing so, his punch, which was traveling back toward him, would go straight away from him.

In that case, altering the vector control applied to his body would work, but Kihara seemed to have predicted that, minutely adjusting the angle of his fist as needed. The brain directly responsible for developing *the power of Accelerator* wasn't for nothing.

"What's the matter, squirt?! I thought you came to save that brat!"

His timing was ruined, his rhythm deciphered, his initiative stolen. Kihara's blows, each of them, though light, steadily racked up damage to Accelerator's body like the effects of alcohol. Every time Accelerator's movements slowed, Kihara switched to more bold actions, accentuating his "drunken" state.

"Guh…ahhh…!!"

More time passed by ruthlessly.

The strongest ability in Academy City used to its fullest was already this far behind. Without the protection of his electrode, even standing upright would be difficult. If that happened, he'd never have the chance to turn this around.

His impatience lost time, and that lost time made him more impatient.

…Piece of shit!! I don't have time for the likes of Kihara to stop me! At this rate, I won't have any time to use the Testament and fix the br—!!

"Lookin' real relaxed there, you scrap murderer!! Already thinking about after you've won?!"

There was a loud *thud!!*

As Accelerator was thinking, his consciousness shook for sure this time.

Kihara's swings were getting pretty big. He must have judged that the damaged Accelerator couldn't deal with his speed anymore.

The interval between attacks lengthened, but each punch grew heavier.

"You think you're totally cool or somethin', kid?"

A shattering strike to the face made his legs totter. If he wasn't careful, he'd trip and fall.

"Standing up to the evil organization all by yourself, running about tryin' to save the poor captured brat...You think that'll erase everything you've done?"

Even while he was noting that, Kihara's fist came at him again. He tried to guard his vitals with his arms, but the punches landed every time, slipping through his defenses. His damage reached an extreme, and a chunk of blood burst from his closed lips.

"Gyah-ha-ha! Don't fuck with me! You'll be in the mud your whole life, kid! You can squirm and crawl all you want, but you'll always be covered in it!! Just sink already! A slimy shit like you walking around will just get everything else dirty!!"

Ga-thud!! An even harder impact sent Accelerator crashing into the floor. He came down on his knees, falling forward and almost slamming his head on the dust- and hair-covered carpet.

...God...damn...piece of shit...

Nevertheless, Accelerator grabbed the steel desk to prevent himself from falling all the way. Kihara had bored out all the stamina inside him. Every part of his body cried out for rest as though he'd just finished a marathon.

...I know I'll always be in the mud. You shitheads were the ones who reminded me of that. I don't have any regrets about that. That isn't what I'm after...

He clenched his teeth, desperately clamping down on the pain, and put energy into the hand on the desk he was using to hold himself up. Wobbling, he began to rise.

...Give me a break. Every single goddamn one of you is after that fucking brat. You and me, we're the only ones who need to go to hell. Don't get the brat involved there, you shithead...

However, his resolution ended in vain.

He heard a soft electronic *beep*.

A tiny, tiny final notice from the electrode choker around his neck. A mechanical signal to tell him one minute, sixty seconds were up. And its meaning: His battery was dead.

Ka-thud.

With all his strength gone, Accelerator collapsed to the dusty floor in front of Amata Kihara.

2

A thunderous *crack!!* boomed.

Sparks lit up in bridges between the "angel's" feathers, seeming ready to overflow at any moment.

"Ha-ha!!"

Vento of the Front charged straight at Kamijou, her giant hammer in one hand. As she did, Kamijou dashed forward to smash it, with all the force he could muster into his right fist.

Shoo!! came the sound of cutting wind.

Vento swinging her hammer hadn't created that sound.

The sound of Vento jumping three meters into the air.

Rather than ducking or dodging to either side, she'd gone up. Probably with a spell that used the air.

His fist missing, a counterattack in the form of a flying kick sailed mercilessly at his face. With a dull *bam!!* his body fell on the wet asphalt.

Gah, ah?! She...!!

He held his nose and quickly rose. Vento was barely an inch in front of him. She'd already brought her hammer up, and now she sent it crashing down at his body on the road.

Clink-clink-clink! went the scraping chains.

He looked to see her tongue chain, blood-soaked and dyed red, drawing a spiral lance toward Kamijou's face. A wind club appeared along the path of its shape.

"Guaahhh!!"

With a shout, Kamijou stuck out his right hand. It repelled Vento's attack, sending a storm of wind all around them. For just a few seconds, the wind completely diverted the path of the rain.

Neither of them watched.

"Ha!!" Vento inhaled then recklessly swung the hammer around again. Her tongue chain writhed like a living being. Kamijou gave up on blocking with his right hand and rolled backward to dodge. Relying on the Imagine Breaker wouldn't compensate for his disadvantages forever. Instead, he used the momentum of his roll to continue backward, then fluidly stood up.

The missed air club smashed into the asphalt. Its fragments flew into the air.

Kamijou used both arms to protect his face from the storm of stone as Vento's annoying voice came to him.

"Geh...Shit, my output really is down..."

She coughed a chunk of blood from her mouth and glared at the angel behind Kamijou.

Shaking her chain, which was dripping with blood, she raised her voice. "Ha-ha, you sure are being a pain!! Dangling that disgusting right arm of yours, protecting that vomit-worthy 'angel'...How much do you want to make me laugh before you're satisfied?!"

"Shut the hell up!! You think your viewpoint is the only one in the world?! Why don't you even try to accept other people?!"

Vento plunged through the storm of stone and ran up to Kamijou again. Mysteriously, the asphalt didn't hit her body. It was almost like the fragments themselves were dodging her. Kamijou guessed it was another air spell.

She swung the hammer around, shouting, red blood leaking from the gaps between her teeth.

"I hate science!! I detest science!!"

As Kamijou tried to use his right hand to smack down the hammer, it suddenly vanished into thin air. When Kamijou's fist swung through empty space, another hammer appeared in Vento's hands, perfectly timed.

There was a muffled *thump* as Vento drove the hammer's tip into Kamijou's defenseless abdomen—with her tongue chain coiling around the hammer's grip.

"I hate science for making me like this!"

A moment later, a wind club stormed out of the hammer's tip. Kamijou immediately twisted his body, but the blunt attack still scraped his side. That was all it took to send his body into a helicopter spin. And with no way to land safely, he crashed into a collapsed wall.

"I despise science for letting my brother die!!"

Heaping unintelligible, one-sided abuse on him, Vento swung her hammer horizontally. The chain, which had been tightly wrapped around it, had come off at some point. A wind club formed, then sailed at Kamijou. His body pressed against the wall, he burst out to the side to dodge it.

The building wall smashed apart like a plastic toy. The raw power left Kamijou in shock, but he abruptly froze.

On the other side of the crushed wall, there was an unconscious college-age man.

"Wai—!!"

Kamijou tried to stop her, but…

A thunderous *slam!!* overlapped Kamijou's words. It was sparks from the "angel's" feathers. The sound was no longer just a roar—now it was more like a shock wave.

"!!" The immense tremor made Kamijou cover his ears and wince. He looked away from Vento and turned around to see. The sparks arcing like bridges between Kazakiri's feathers had finally surpassed critical levels and unleashed themselves.

Boom!! Something surged past, something beyond the realm of sound.

It traced a snakelike, organic line behind it as it instantly shot out of Academy City. Despite it going so far away that the horizon hid it behind itself, he could definitely see soil exploding upward in a wave.

The angel had probably launched another attack to kill an "enemy."

*Shit...*His head was pounding. He knew that if he didn't stop Vento soon, she'd end up involving passed-out bystanders, but he couldn't move his body well.

Vento, on the other hand, didn't seem to care about the pain. "This is all science is!! And you're one of them! You mean to tell me you don't think this is disgusting?!"

Vento, from whose mouth blood continued to flow, swung around her hammer as hard as her strength would allow. Her tongue piercing determined the aim as an especially large air club shattered the concrete—as though intentionally dragging the civilians there into the disaster.

3

He couldn't tell front from back, left from right. He couldn't even "calculate" which direction to apply force to in order to stand up. He could see his outstretched arm, but when he tried to look at each of his fingers to see how many he had, he lost count.

The electrode choker around Accelerator's neck had died and lost its effect.

He couldn't use his ability now. He couldn't comprehend words now. He couldn't even do simple calculations that would involve only his fingers and thumbs. Far from clenching his fist and letting Kihara have it—he couldn't even manage his own body weight or center of gravity, so it would be hard just to get up properly.

The abandoned office floor was covered in dust, with the carpet's tips mingling with bits of fluff. Accelerator's cheek was pressed against it, and while he felt this situation was "unpleasant," he thought, *How...again...do I...get rid of this...unpleasant feeling?*

He could passively receive information, but he couldn't show an active reaction to it. The "calculations" in the middle were no longer available to him.

A voice came down to him from overhead.

"Little by little, coming after going to sleep, that's good, is it really that far from so many bad problems?!"

He had no idea what was being spoken to him.

What had he even wanted to do in the first place? He could ask himself questions but not answer them. He was pretty sure Last Order was here. He thought he needed to bring her out of here. He knew that. He didn't need to "calculate" that information, since it'd been input into his brain ahead of time, and Accelerator could still bring that information to the front of his mind.

But…

How exactly was he going to do that?

"……………………………………………………………………………………………………"

At that, Accelerator stopped moving.

Of course, arriving at that specific answer would have been impossible even if he still had his full ability to think. Even though he'd used the full power of Academy City's strongest ability, Amata Kihara had predicted it, confused him, and limited his power—and then he came in with scathing counterattacks. Contrary to Kihara, who was nonchalantly beating down the power capable of destroying the world, Accelerator, without the support of his electrode choker, only had the physical ability to cling to his cane and push himself to his feet. Like this, it was too harsh to tell him to calculate the odds of winning. Even if one had used the Tree Diagram, the result would be a resounding 0 percent.

However.

"…?"

At that moment, Kihara, who'd been pummeling Accelerator with insults, went quiet, and a bit of confusion entered his scorn-filled expression. He couldn't help it. Especially since he'd looked at the device on Accelerator's neck and almost perfectly predicted its function and weakness.

Grrk.

As the desk creaked, Accelerator, clinging to it, rose again.

*　　*　　*

He certainly wasn't in any condition to fight.

He couldn't even support his own weight. He had placed both hands on the desk, but if he let go, he'd fall straight back to the floor. His eyes weren't focused, either, and they shook around erratically. Only he knew what those black eyes of his were seeing.

Accelerator couldn't stand up against a powerful enemy. He couldn't even beat the earth's gravity.

As he stared at the unsightly display, Kihara laughed like he was an idiot.

"In the same way, what have you given the artillery company by their retreating?!"

He pelted Accelerator with abuse that would never get across. He was saying something along the lines of "what do you think you're doing now that your battery's dead," but Accelerator wouldn't understand it. And even if he had, it never would have changed his actions.

Accelerator, right now, could do no calculations of any sort. He understood the situation was hopeless, and he couldn't think of his chance of winning.

But...

On the other hand, Accelerator also couldn't calculate any way he could lose.

So he never flinched—no matter how he was cornered, even knowing the next strike would kill him.

Until the very last moment...

...without any calculations, he would earnestly decide to continue the fight.

4

Kamijou's eyes were wide open. His right hand, his Imagine Breaker, hadn't made it.

In the steady downpour, the attack Vento unleashed shattered the concrete wall like a bomb. Everything, including the person passed out there, disappeared into a cloud of ashen dust.

It was an act as cruel as attacking a field hospital on the battlefield, going through all the gravely injured people awaiting treatment one by one, pressing a gun to each of their heads and squeezing the trigger.

There was clearly no way anyone caught in that would have survived. Once the gray dust cloud cleared, there would be only a smattering of human flesh torn asunder.

Meanwhile, a series of electrical discharge–like attacks continued firing from Kazakiri with *bangs* and *booms*, as if to crush Kamijou's spirit even more.

"You…youuuuuuuu!!" The shout left Kamijou's mouth quite a few moments later. The sight before him was so hideous his mind had trouble keeping up.

Swhoo!! came a storm-like howl, suddenly blowing away the dust.

However.

Behind it all was a civilian—unconscious but without a single scratch on him.

"What…?"

"Uh…?"

Kamijou and Vento looked at the college student on the ground.

The attack had definitely hit him.

What is this…? Damn. Killing a civilian before his eyes should have at least rattled his emotions a little bit, thought Vento.

But then—something was floating.

Pale lights like cotton balls were slowly descending from the night sky.

Kamijou and Vento turned to look at them.

All around the unharmed college student were these dimly glowing scalelike things floating around. They were evidence of a weak power of some kind, so weak they really had to focus to see them. But they were floating around the college student, covering him up, as if to prevent impact. They must have been responsible for protecting him from Vento's attack.

Where are they coming from? wondered Kamijou, glancing around.

The glittering scales drifted lightly around, unaffected by the deluge.

Then, something completely different caught the attention of Kamijou and Vento, as much attention as the survivor had.

The light from the scales.

Touma Kamijou knew that glow.

He turned around to look behind him.

Hyouka Kazakiri was there, shedding countless scales from her wings.

"Ha-ha…"

He laughed. What else could he do now that he'd seen this?

The wreckage around them began to make noise. It started to break apart, and what appeared from it were many other civilians who had been buried alive like the college student. Men, women, children, adults—there were many.

The scales engulfed a hundred people—no, a thousand—simply protecting them.

None of them had a scratch on them.

Not a single one.

Ssshhh!! echoed the rain as the glowing scales illuminated the entire area.

Her feelings were wiping away the darkness!!

"Ha-ha-ha…"

He didn't know who had made Kazakiri like that, but whoever it was, Kamijou was willing to bet they didn't care about people surviving. The destructive blasts were one thing, but nobody behind the scenes had commanded her to create those glowing scales that saved the survivors.

And that meant she had done this of her own volition.

They'd altered her body and taken away her freedom, but she never stopped resisting. She had drawn a final line in the sand and given her all to defend it.

The pencil-sized rods attached to the angel halo above her head began to move rapidly with a *click-clack-click-clack!!* Lights guiding her path blinked in succession, probably commanding Kazakiri to stop her independent action.

Ghh-krr! A strange sound came from her right arm. Its outline began rapidly falling apart under an extreme binding force.

But the scales—they were still drifting around.

She would never stop protecting them.

With repeated thundering *ga-bam*s, the discharge attacks from Kazakiri's feathers continued, firing outside Academy City. However, countless scales floated in their paths to block them. The immense destructive force easily blew away the scales, but Kazakiri didn't stop resisting. No matter how much pain it caused her.

Destruction and protection—two conflicting actions. The presence of both described Hyouka Kazakiri's current state.

Even if she couldn't break free of whoever's control it was, even if she couldn't stop the attacks against others, she wouldn't let that make her give up.

She was resisting so much, her body was screeching…

…so that there were just a few less unfortunate people…

…as she rallied all her strength and bloody determination…

…*to fight alongside him.*

"You…you…hypocrite!!" shouted Vento, her face bright red. "What are you doing?!"

Kamijou didn't hear her. "Ha-ha…"

Thank goodness, he thought.

Touma Kamijou standing up to protect Hyouka Kazakiri had been the right choice.

That was all it was, but now it was clear to him.

"Ha-ha-ha-ha-ha!! This is crazy! This is great!! I ramble on about my rotten luck every day, but *this is really all you need to be happy*!! Right?!"

"What, what are you…? What the hell are you talking about?!"

Kamijou's unhinged laughing caused Vento, who had kept the initiative until now, to pull away. Her bloodstained tongue chain trailed her movement. He didn't feel like answering her, though; he was already fully satisfied. He didn't need any more answers for himself, so he wouldn't respond to Vento's words. Now that he had the answer, no matter what Vento said or did, his heart would never waver.

"Wait for me, Kazakiri."

This time, with the conviction that his voice was reaching her, he spoke.

To the girl who was still resisting, who was launching both attacks to destroy and scales to protect.

"Index is doing what she can to save you now. We can leave all the tough stuff to her—no problem. And I mean, she's your friend. She'll answer your hopes."

Kamijou clenched his right hand.

He clenched it far more tightly than before, creating a rock-hard fist.

"Don't worry. I'll hold this one back until she's done."

5

"You...fucking disabled bastard!!"

With a shout, Amata Kihara punched Accelerator for real this time, sending him flying from the office desk he was propping himself up against. Accelerator couldn't use his ability anymore. He wouldn't have a problem putting all his weight into his blows rather than the "fist pullback" method he'd been using.

The result was Accelerator's body dancing through the air like stardust.

But just before that, he'd grabbed Kihara's wrist. With a stronger grip than imagined and simple, instinctual movements on a dog or cat level of "catching something thrown at you," Kihara's body ended up stuck to Accelerator.

"Shit!"

Kihara tried to push Accelerator's hand away, but he had trouble. Meanwhile, Accelerator made a loose fist with his other hand and drove it into Kihara's face.

There was a dull *plop* but almost no pain.

That is, there wouldn't have been if Accelerator hadn't reached right above Kihara's ear—*then grabbed the hair on the side of his head and tore it as hard as he could.*

"Gwaaaaahhhhhhhhhhhhh?!"

With a scream, blood sprayed.

Accelerator had pulled the hair out in a clump like weeds, and he tore the skin underneath along with it. Just like soil underneath grass, the "clump of hair" Accelerator held had a thin layer of skin and pink flesh attached to it.

No sympathy.

No mercy.

Right in front of Kihara, whose expression had broken, Accelerator's lips opened into a grin.

He was attacking almost entirely on instinct, and his face displayed an incredibly primal exhilaration.

"You...little shit...!!"

Holding the side of his head, Kihara tried to back far away.

But Accelerator latched onto him like a zombie, pushing him down to the floor. Kihara shouted "bastard!!" but Accelerator had no ability to process language, so it was completely wasted.

Don't underest—

Kihara tried to shout, but at that moment, Accelerator grabbed his ear and tried to rip it off.

"Ooorgh?!"

He quickly shook his head to get the fingers off, then punched Accelerator in the face and escaped backward. He moved in a roll along the floor. *Don't screw with me! I'll kill you right now!!*

Still on the floor, Kihara spotted a handgun lying there. The weapon belonged to one of the Hound Dogs who Accelerator had killed.

He decided to use that and turn Accelerator into a beehive.

"_____"

But then Accelerator grabbed his hand.

Kihara tried to edge his hand closer to the pistol, but Accelerator had already shoved his other hand into Kihara's solar plexus. He did so a few more times, and Kihara gave up on the pistol for now, ramming a shoulder into Accelerator's face and trying to put distance between them.

Accelerator's actions were mostly instinctual, and yet he still fell between Kihara and the gun.

This little shit...The more ability to take action he loses, the crazier his movements get?!

Kihara glared at Accelerator as he squirmed across the floor and exhaled sharply. If Accelerator still had the faculty to think straight, maybe he would have realized something was wrong. About how strange it was for a monster who could easily deal with Academy City's strongest Level Five to be acting this nervously.

Kihara had a trick.

When all was said and done, Amata Kihara had been overpowering Accelerator only because *he'd personally developed him*. Kihara had all his data, from his personality profile to his supernatural ability to his physical prowess—all he'd done was learn a fatal tactic that would be effective only against Accelerator.

Of course, to make this tactic work, he needed much more than a normal person: a superb martial arts sense and a level of genius able to develop the vast amount of research data into a cohesive tactic. But even if he pulled it off, it wasn't enough to put down one of only seven Level Fives in the city in a fair fight.

If he really could kill a Level Five without any little tricks, Kihara wouldn't bother having the Hound Dogs as subordinates. He'd have dealt with the piercing-covered woman in a flash, too. But in reality, if he needed to kill anyone other than Accelerator during this operation, he *always* left it to his henchmen and never came to the forefront.

But his true character had been unmasked...

...by Accelerator switching from a Level Five to a completely impotent Level Zero.

Now that he'd abandoned all his tactics thus far, Kihara's "countermeasure" was meaningless.

Think you can fuck with me? I'll kill you. I'll kill you for sure. Shit! Why is this happening? I was supposed to have the upper hand at all times. I can't think of a single damn reason to be crawling on the floor like this...

As Kihara muttered abuse under his breath, he suddenly noticed something strange outside the window.

The "angel" was acting odd.

He couldn't figure out exactly what about it was wrong, but it still felt wrong. If expressed vaguely, the biting sense of ominousness was gone.

Something...wrong? thought Kihara, dumbfounded. *No...no. Could there be a problem...that not even Aleister...?* He wiped the sweat from his brow and tried to stand up, then saw Accelerator's face.

His lips were moving as if to speak words. But the sounds didn't reach Kihara's ears. Even if they had, Accelerator wasn't in a state where he could speak human words. It should have been impossible for Kihara to understand what he was saying.

And yet Kihara felt a blood vessel in his temple pulsate strangely. He could tell just by Accelerator's expression and the air around him that he was making fun of him.

*Don't...get cocky...*Kihara's eyes immediately became bloodshot. *Killing him isn't enough. Even if I just stop his heart, he'll have an easy death. Take more from him. Remove from him the very meaning of death. How do I do that?*

His mind raced. What was Accelerator's weakness? What were his vulnerabilities? What could Kihara do to cause him the most pain? Direction, writing, outcome—he took them all together and began constructing the worst possible scenario.

"Ah-ha!" He chuckled.

He swiftly reached into his lab coat, then took out a chip.

On it was the original script of the virus he'd injected into Last Order's brain.

The data would also be absolutely required to repair her mind with Testament.

Without it, he would never save Last Order.

He took the chip…

…and, before Accelerator's eyes, crushed it in the palm of his hand.

"Gya-ha-ha-ha-ha-ha-ha-ha-ha-ha-ha-ha!!"

A scornful laugh exploded, shaking the abandoned office.

The plastic fragments scattered and fell to the floor. Accelerator didn't move. He couldn't calculate anything and couldn't figure out what the chip's destruction meant. And yet Kihara was satisfied. It was unbelievably entertaining to destroy everything right in front of him like this.

"Take that! See what happens?! There's never just one victory condition! Now you'll regret it, you little shit!! I just destroyed everything you hold dear! You can't get any of it back!! Ah-ha-ha-ah-ha-gya-ha-ha!!"

This was the world Accelerator and Kihara lived in.

There was no moderation, no mercy, no sympathy.

Good and evil alike died. The weakest were served up as food for the strong. When someone like Last Order strayed into that world, there was no chance they would survive. It was obvious, not even worth mentioning: a fundamental truth of the underworld. Now another had lost her life for being caught up in it.

That was all.

That was supposed to be all it was.

As Kihara cackled, he kicked Accelerator in the side. Stealing his hope wasn't enough. Now he'd beat him to death. The joy of a plunderer was deeply engraved on his face.

"See? Next, it'll be you. Might want to start thinking about dumb shit, like whether heaven exists!!"

There was no more hope.

But salvation, on the other hand, hadn't forsaken Accelerator and Last Order just yet.

*   *   *

"There she is!! I found her!!"

Footsteps came into the abandoned office.

The girl's voice felt very nostalgic, despite him having heard it only a few hours ago.

The beaten and crumpled Accelerator's head turned toward the voice. And there…

…was Index, her soaked white habit dragging behind her.

6

With the giant angel scattering thunderous, crackling, discharge-like sounds behind him, Touma Kamijou dove for Vento.

He sped like an arrow. His earlier movements seemed like a lie. No, it was probably the opposite. Now he knew the people buried were alive, and that Kazakiri's mind was still there. She knew well that he wouldn't easily direct "hostility" at others. And now Vento's erratic attacks wouldn't continue to affect innocents nearby. Liberated from all his worry and concern, Kamijou's shackles were off, and he could fight at full strength.

He just needed to protect her.

He just needed to protect the friends important to him.

It was simple.

And because of that, Touma Kamijou was released from everything.

"Shit!!" swore Vento, swinging her hammer around. By that time, though, Kamijou had already gotten very close to her. *Ba-bam!!* He blew the air club away with one hit, then reached forward, forward with his right hand, wanting to grab the part of the hammer not wrapped in barbed wire.

"!!"

Right before he touched it, the hammer disappeared from Vento's right hand. It instantly switched to her left, and Kamijou's palm swiped through empty air.

Vento swung her hammer horizontally at him, aiming for his wide-open chest.

Kamijou ducked underneath. There was a loud *vwoosh!!* as it passed overhead before he came in at a sharp angle at Vento and rammed his elbow into her gut.

Wham!! exploded a dull sound.

"Geh?!"

Vento doubled over, and then the bottom of her foot slipped and she fell to the ground. Kamijou tried to stomp his heel into her like a nail, but before he could, she swung the hammer with all her might from her prone position.

An air club soared straight at Kamijou's face.

"!!"

Kamijou beat a hasty retreat, and with another *swoosh!!* the wind attack carved through the air right by him. It tore through the downpour, leaving a particle-like trail behind.

They were back to square one, but his face had a smile on it.

He could do this.

Vento didn't want me to grab her hammer with my right hand. He opened up his right hand's fingers, then closed them again. *That means it can be erased. And it doesn't seem like she can get her broken hammer back to normal very quickly, either. If I break it once, I can prevent her from using it!*

"I guess this doesn't do me much good if you get up close…" With a *swish*, she spun the long hammer in her hand and put it on her shoulders.

The red blood dripping from her lips trickled down the slender chain and onto the cross on the end.

Kamijou reaffirmed his grip on his fist, then gave a savage smile. "Now that I don't have to worry about what's around me, I can really go at it."

"Hah. It's almost like that monster behind you is helping."

"Not 'like.' She really is helping me!"

"Keep talking!!"

Vento swung her hammer down in one motion from her shoulders, and Kamijou dashed forward.

He repelled the air club flying at him with his right hand, and the second attack fell to his feet. The asphalt exploded underfoot, sending huge pieces sailing at him.

He ducked, reducing the number that hit as much as he could, and crossed his arms in front of his face to protect it. Then he started running forward again.

As he ran, he shouted, "You've hit your limit!! This is all you can do when you're not using other people as a shield!!"

"Don't...you...underestimate God's Right Seaaaaat!!"

Vento screamed, then swung her hammer around again to create an air club.

He'd already seen through her attack. She used the hammer to create a "weapon," then fired it along the path indicated by her tongue chain. That was her only pattern. Kamijou's right hand could deal with that.

No, Vento had more than this to begin with.

She had a spell that crushed everyone who directed hostility at her. With that and these air-manipulating attacks, most people probably couldn't stand up to her. *And even if she can't hit them, she can create "hostility" in the opponent just by aiming her weapon at them.*

But Kamijou's Imagine Breaker prevented Vento's big play, the divine judgment spell, from affecting him. Right now, all she could do was use her "clubs" meant for feints. *So I can win!! I'll end this now!!*

Kamijou clenched his right hand into a single balled-up fist and jumped at Vento.

Before his hand got to her, Vento swung her hammer sideways. An air club appeared. But before it fired off, she retracted her wrist, then swung her hammer again, this time in an upward path. With a booming noise, two air clubs appeared.

They didn't come at Kamijou separately. Instead, they carved into each other, forming a single mass, then exploded into a fan shape like water from a showerhead. Hundreds of sharp drills of air shot at him at once.

He couldn't block them all with his right hand.

"Ahhhhh!!"

As his foot reached forward for another step, he wrenched it away and rolled desperately to the side. With a dull *sh-bam!!* a dozen meters of asphalt behind him flipped up into the air. It ripped off the arm sleeve of his uniform and tore at his skin sharply.

Kamijou came out of his roll and immediately ducked, and then Vento swung the hammer up again. After a series of swings, both vertical and horizontal, she forced out *three* air clubs this time.

Kamijou tensed up. *Not good!* He hadn't gotten all the way up yet and couldn't make any nimble movements. If another one of those showers came at him, there was no assurance he could dodge this time.

"Shit, they're gonna hit…!!"

Kamijou immediately brought up his right hand.

Cough!!

But suddenly, Vento doubled over, and chunks of blood burst from her mouth. The three clubs, with nothing controlling them, exploded on the spot. With a thundering *boom*, they blasted her straight back.

"Vento!!"

Out of reflex, Kamijou shouted after his enemy. He'd seen her coughing up blood before, too.

"…What…nonsense are you babbling?"

As she spat puddles of blood out of her mouth, Vento shakily readied her hammer again. The explosion had torn parts of her yellow clothing, and blood was starting to seep from the openings.

"You…and the science side—you're the ones who put this together, aren't you? With the appearance of that 'angel,' you've put pressure on everything magical on this entire 'plane.' In a word, you've created a mana circulatory failure. Aleister, you bastard. How repulsive your tricks are…"

Vento was speaking vaguely, and Kamijou didn't really understand what she was saying. But it apparently meant Vento would cough up blood whenever she used sorcery right now. Maybe creating several air clubs was putting needless strain on her body.

But still…

…As she coughed up blood, she kept on swinging that hammer.

Kamijou paled. "You idiot!! What reason do you have to fight that hard?!"

"You're the one trying to beat me to death, you heap of excrement! I see through your shameless words!!"

Her hammer danced, first vertically then to the side, creating three air clubs, then creating a whirling wind to fuse them all into a single sharp spike that flew at Kamijou.

With a booming roar, the spike sailed straight past his ear.

Not because Kamijou had dodged right away. He couldn't react to it in time.

The reason it hadn't hit was that Vento's own aim was off.

Her stamina wouldn't hold out much longer.

Creating multiple air masses, multiplying their vectors, launching winds with completely different directions and strength…

"That attack…It uses the principles of fluid mechanics?!"

"You irritating little prick. Don't analyze someone's spells with that knowing face of yours…! Just the very usage of scientific words makes my skin crawl!!" she shouted, but she hadn't the stamina to back up her resolve.

The hammer, swung upward, pulled her arm down and fell to the ground with a *smash*. Her hands hung limp at her sides, but the glaring hostility in Vento's eyes never went away.

"Oooahhh!!" She clenched her bloody teeth and swung her hammer up. Its trajectory was wobbly, enough so that Kamijou could almost feel the limit of her endurance. The attack missed him and struck the road right next to him.

Kamijou watched on. "Hah, you need someone to rescue you now?"

"Don't…give me that…crap…"

"Sorry, but I've got my own shit to deal with. I'll send you straight to the hospital!!"

"Silence!!" roared Vento. "I will not give my body to the likes of science ever again!!"

Kamijou frowned slightly at that. "Again?" he said in spite of himself.

An even deeper level of fury appeared on Vento's face. She spat blood off to the side, wiped her lips with the back of her hands, and spoke. "...Science was responsible for killing my younger brother."

"What?"

She gritted her bloodred teeth, swung her hammer up with all her might, and continued. "Thanks to a theme park attraction's motor going haywire. Both my young brother and I ended up a total mess after that. They told us that scientifically, there wouldn't be a problem! Dozens of safety features, brand-new lightweight strengthening materials, fully automatic speed control programs! They rambled on and on, feeding us all those reliable-sounding words!! But in the end, they were of no use at all!!"

"You..."

"I don't believe science can save anyone. Your angel is no different. Protecting people? Hah! Meanwhile, it's still doing its real job—destruction!!"

Kamijou had no words.

Vento stuck out her tongue at him. "Surprised? That one of the God's Right Seat, which controls the world, would be fighting for a reason like this? I detest science so much that I'd even use God's Right Seat to obtain my revenge!!"

Though she was infuriated, no attack came immediately. Vento could probably feel the limit of her stamina clearly. She edged around to the side, trying to time an attack to kill him for sure.

She stuck out her reddened tongue again and said, "Type B, Rh negative. The blood I'm spitting out now? The doctors said it's incredibly rare. They couldn't even find much of it in their transfusion stock. What do you think happened to my brother and me once we were in the hospital?"

"..."

"*They couldn't get enough to transfuse for both of us.* They called everyone, but they could only get enough for one. We were waiting on the verge of death when the doctors told us the hopeless news—they could only save one of us. And only I lived! He told them to save his sister, so they just let him die!!"

Blood trickled from her teeth, but Vento still didn't attack—as if implicitly declaring she would wait until she could kill him for sure.

"Science stole our path, and on top of that, the Bible, which I took to be a means of salvation, is being sullied by that *thing*! This is what science really is. It's nothing but an obstacle!!"

She breathed deeply, her shoulders heaving, shaking the air sharply as if to multiply her own power level.

"That's why I hate science, why I detest science! If science is that cold and heartless, then I'll wreck all of it and fill the world with warmer rules. That's my duty as someone who tore apart her brother's future!!"

"_____"

So that's how it is, thought Kamijou. After everything was said and done, Vento had always regretted letting her brother die and thought it was her own fault. Her greatest enemy wasn't science—it was probably herself. It was Vento, who was still alive yet had let someone she personally protected die.

The divine judgment spell. A sorcery that defeated all who showed her hostility, no questions asked.

When he first heard about it, it sounded like a convenient power indeed. But if you looked at it the other way, *unless you created an environment in which a lot of people continued to be hostile toward you*, it was completely useless.

Vento had chosen to be hated by everyone in the world.

Without being on the receiving end of others' hostility, she couldn't create any value or results. To fight back, she had to plunge into the world's darkness. The way she lived her life—it was like she'd given up any possibility of someone showing her goodwill.

She believed that was fitting for her. She ran about, destroying, for her dead brother alone.

Kamijou could never do what she'd done.

But he still said this:

*   *   *

"Don't give me that crap."

"What?" Vento frowned.

He continued. "Science killed your brother? Those doctors didn't want to let him die from the start, you know. They obviously wanted to save both of you!! And the theme-park ride with the accident, too. They didn't make that thing so they could hurt people. They wanted to put smiles on their faces!!"

"Silence..."

"When your brother told them to save you right before he died, how do you think he felt?! He knew exactly what situation he was in, and he still wished for you to be saved!! You think he'd want you to get revenge on science?! The person who wanted more than anyone else for you to be happy?!"

"I said, shut your goddamn trap!!"

In her blind fury, Vento recklessly whipped her hammer around. It had none of the calculation behind it that it used to. The wind attack came flying at him in a disorderly fashion, and Kamijou easily blocked it with his right hand.

"He wasn't even ten years old! All he saw in his near-dead, hazy mind was a family member who had been hurt! Anyone in that situation would agree if you told them to make the choice!! It's a little kid's opinion. How is that valuable?! If they didn't have enough blood, they should have given it to my brother! They might as well have just used my blood for it!!"

Kamijou's expression didn't budge. As the rain fell, he leveled his gaze at Vento and looked into her eyes. "I say it's valuable," he spat. "Even if it's a little kid, you're only here because of his decision! It was valuable!! And you should understand that best of all!!"

"This is absurd!! Are you trying to comfort me?! I've shattered people's futures!!"

"Could you say that to someone in your exact situation?!"

"!!" Vento held her breath.

Kamijou continued, driving the point home. "I couldn't do it. That's why I'm arguing with you!! The way you live your life is wrong! I don't know what your brother was like. But he did something I could never do. He did the greatest thing anyone could possibly do!! And you're rubbing dirt in that?! If you died hating science your whole life, you'd be wasting his last words!!"

"——Don't make me laugh," said Vento of the Front, barely moving her lips. "You think I'll change my ways just for that? I'm committed to this path. Someone who just heard the story now won't be able to twist things around so easily!!"

She took only one step back, rallied what little strength remained within her, lifted her weighty hammer, and readied it. Blood slipped out of her mouth and trickled down her slender tongue chain, wetting the cross on the end.

In response, Kamijou clenched his right fist and faced Vento head-on.

Only five meters separated them.

Kamijou could get within punching range in two steps. With Vento in such a weakened state, one hit would be enough to knock her out.

But she would fire an attack of her own in the meantime. She'd use her killing move, where she combined several air clubs and used principles of fluid dynamics to change their shape and vector.

It was a straight-up duel, and they'd each have one attack.

With the sound of nearby wreckage breaking apart, hostilities began.

""!!""

Kamijou plunged forward.

Vento whipped around her hammer several times as she coughed up blood, creating seven wind clubs in one go. They all ate into one another, changed vectors, spun up into a whirlwind, and transformed into a single giant spike.

Kamijou couldn't even react to three of the bundled clubs.

With more than twice as many, he couldn't imagine how much force they had behind them.

But he didn't flinch.

He didn't take any evasive action. He put even more energy into his fist to meet it head-on. If his fist and the spike were even a few centimeters off, Kamijou's head would explode for certain. He understood, yet his eyes never wavered.

The danger Academy City and Hyouka Kazakiri are facing...

Or maybe he could predict Vento's attack by her eye movements and breathing. If he used the raindrops, he could also read where the wind attack was.

The hatred of science shackling Vento...

But Kamijou abandoned any such schemes.

This battle wouldn't be decided by petty tricks like that.

As he watched Vento pour everything she had into one grand, final attack, he thought.

I'll destroy all those stupid illusions at once!!

"Oooooaaaaahhhhhhhhhhhhhhhhh!!"

Kamijou and Vento shouted.

His fist and her spike flew at the same time.

With a thundering *boom*, the spike streaked through the space between them, breaking through raindrops, scattering them into particles. The rain exploded into a thin mist, and for a moment, it blocked their vision. It burst outward like steam.

Sounds ceased.

A moment later...

A primal *ga-gah!!* rang out as Kamijou's fist caught the tip of the spike, destroying it all in one hit.

"...!!" Vento tried to swing her hammer, but she couldn't muster the strength.

Kamijou stepped in deep.

"Compared to your brother, it might not be much..."

He clenched his fist as hard as he possibly could.

And he stared into Vento's eyes.

*   *   *

"…but I can save you a little. Come back after you've started over, you gigantic moron!!"

Wham!! Kamijou's fist plunged into the bridge of Vento's nose. She flew several meters back, then fell to the rain-soaked asphalt.

7

Index spotted the beat-up and collapsed Accelerator and a man in a white robe kicking him. By curious coincidence, it was the same scenario she'd first spotted them in, near the underground mall entrance.

He's from that time!! Are these people related to what's going on?!
Unfortunately, she didn't have the time to go to them.
The most important thing for her was the key to suppressing the big angel.
However…
?! Index's eyes went wide. The man in white walked in front of Accelerator and slammed his foot hard into his head. Accelerator rolled away helplessly. She began to run over there out of reflex.
"Ooohhhhaah!!"
But after producing a sound from his throat that wasn't quite a shout or a cry, Accelerator slapped a hand onto the office desk and got up. Right between the man and Index, like a shield.
For a moment, she vacillated, but she had too much to do. After grabbing a disconnected phone from off the desk, she threw it at the man in white. Seeing Accelerator charge at the same time, she turned her gaze to the ten-year-old girl sleeping on the desk.
Index had seen her once, in a cell phone picture. This was the one Accelerator had been searching for.
She was the key to everything.
I can't do it here. I need to get her somewhere safer to do any "work"…! Index picked up the limp girl. But as she was about to leave the abandoned office, she saw that Last Order had grown very

weak and decided any careless movement would be dangerous. Instead, Index lowered her from the desk to a spot in the shadows so she wouldn't be caught in the fighting.

"You little shit!! What the fuck do you think you're doing?!" shouted the man in white before Accelerator grappled onto him.

Index inspected the girl again, from head to toe—from a magical viewpoint.

Yes, she's the core of it all. The fundamentals are angel fabrication. It pours formless Telesma into a pocket in the shape of a human, then starts building the silhouette like a balloon doll. And this spell was used by the golden sorcerer's society, which Crowley was a part of.

Whoosh!! The information in her 103,000 grimoires elucidated the sorcery in the blink of an eye.

Unfortunately...I can't see any more than that. Index bit down on her teeth. *I understand the general composition, but I can't figure out what sort of things it's made of!!*

As an analogy, this was like telling a craftsman who carved violins out of wood to make an electric guitar out of electric parts. While both were musical instruments, they were so far apart that all the craftsman could do would be to hash out a very rough idea.

And a "rough idea" wasn't going to be enough for delicate work. On her own, Index had hit a wall.

Therefore, she didn't hesitate to ask for help.

"Short-hair, questions!!" shouted Index into the cell phone in her hand. There was a certain girl on the other end.

"That's *Miss Mikoto* to you!! Anyway, what did you—*zzzzttt! Kkkrrrkk*—want to ask?!"

Bam-bam-boom! came frequent explosions from the other end. None of them touched Mikoto—as though saying she didn't need to shoulder them.

Index decided to take her up on her friendliness. "What is a 'brain-wave-utilizing electronic network'?!"

Mikoto began to answer her questions using the full scope of the knowledge she'd gained at Tokiwadai Middle School.

After hearing the answer, Index threw another question at her.

"What does 'involuntary diffusion fields proliferating Academy City' mean?!"

The two girls each lacked knowledge: one ignorant of science, the other of magic. Neither of them could completely understand the answer they were both trying to arrive at.

"What is 'safety device for the electronic network using brain waves as a base'?!"

Yet the two girls pressed on—to solve the problem. They didn't need to understand the methodology as long as they got the right answer. In a way, they threw away their pride and accepted it was beyond their respective fields, hoping only to recover the situation little by little.

So basically, the city is filled with a special power, and that girl is all that bundled up. All they did was make an "angel" by restricting her mind and bending the special power to their will!! In that case...!!

"We have to untie the 'knot' in her head!!" Someone from the science side might have called it a "virus." *But how can I put this idea into practice?*

Index couldn't use sorcery. And sorcery couldn't be used to save Last Order. To untie the "knot," she decided to use "words." That may have sounded quite particular when it came to tinkering with a person's mind, but reading and studying a book were the same things. From the start, humans had their "windows" for that open.

She would choose words attuned to that "knot," and by saying them, she would "untie" it.

In concrete terms, that meant...

"...A song." That's what Index thought. "It's easier to get across than normal words. People can sit through hour-long lectures and not cry, but one-minute songs can do the trick. You can use rhythm and pitch to exchange emotions on multiple levels, so..."

But when Mikoto heard that, she argued, flustered. "Wait, wait. Are you sane?! The fundamental way to overwrite things in someone's brain is through repetitive learning. Plus, their memories and brain compatibility might not even be that good in the first place!!"

Besides, if you want to get into an electronic network, you need to input digital values into a specific device, like a Testament. Are you telling me you could make that happen with primitive, analog methods like voice and song?!"

Index didn't know the meaning of the scientific terms Mikoto mentioned, and she didn't have any proof her own method would work. She knew several ways to attack people through their minds, like Sheol Fear and Spell Interception, but this would be the first time she tried this.

"I can do it...," she answered, despite everything. "Prayer will reach. It will save people. I'm a nun, and that's how I've spread the teachings!" She looked only ahead. "We'll save them with our prayers—this girl, Hyouka, and Academy City!!"

8

Punched, beaten, and crushed by Kihara, Accelerator's body slid across the floor.

He wasn't in any condition to fight right now. And because of his brain injury, he couldn't stand on his own two feet to begin with. The way he'd fought until now—half falling into Kihara to prevent him from moving—would be rendered useless if Kihara took caution and kept his distance.

"Ah-ha-ha-gya-ha-ha-ah-ha-ha-ha!!"

Kihara's laughing continued, seeming to burst out of his throat. He certainly wasn't wearing the face of someone who'd just had skin torn off his head.

Kihara grabbed Accelerator's collar, dragged him up from the floor, smashed his back into the office desk, and then threw a punch to boot. Accelerator heard bad groans from his skull, and his face drew back in a pained grimace. The strength left his fingers thanks to the brain-rattling attack.

But if there was one thing he still had, it was consciousness.

That, and that alone, would never waver.

"_____"

He began to hear a girl's smooth melody.

With his speech functions gone, Accelerator could hear only her voice. He didn't know what she was saying. But there was emotion in her singing. It made him feel, beyond the barrier of language, her compassion toward Last Order.

What meaning lay in her voice was anyone's guess. Maybe she was just holding Last Order's hand, trying to ease her pain.

But that was a grand salvation in and of itself.

Last Order never had anyone do that for her.

"Oooooooooaaaaaahhhh!!"

With a scream, Kihara lashed out with a much heavier punch. Accelerator slid over the desk, scattering everything on it, and dropped to the filthy floor. Intense pain struck him in several places, almost too much to want to stand again.

But Accelerator smirked.

The nun's velvety song continued.

Her song was like standing in warm light. Her voice could have been produced only by a person who was from the same world Last Order belonged in. Accelerator simply listened, his mind bereft of calculation, to that voice he could never create on his own.

Last Order wasn't meant to be passed back and forth among shit-heads like Amata Kihara or Accelerator. The proper thing for a resident of the world of light was to be saved by the warmth of those from that same world.

But...

What did that matter?

Why did Accelerator have to feel inferior about that? Why did he have to decide that darkness like him should never touch such a dazzling radiance?

Could only just people perform just acts? Could only good people do good things? Yes, he saw, that was correct. It only made sense.

However...

Why did that "sense" have to be that way in the first place?

Accelerator wanted to save Last Order. From the clutches of unreasonable violence and abuse, he wanted to save her.

What was wrong with thinking like that?

Light, darkness—did it matter where you stood? He didn't want to protect her because she was part of the world of light. No matter what world she was in, he would feel moved to protect her with his own hands.

The distinction between worlds—it didn't mean anything.

Was there a problem with a bad person reaching out to a good person?

Would anyone complain about someone dark protecting the world of light?

After all this time, Academy City's strongest villain had always acted with ego and arrogance...

Why should he have to stay faithful to his past behavior at this point?

"…"

Bang! Accelerator, from his sitting position, reached out for the office desk.

There was a grinding sound as he slowly stood up.

He'd reached his conclusion.

Have pride, even if evil. Rescue the light, even while treading the path of darkness. Feel no shame because your road is different from others. Become so dark you could be proud.

Abandon all former rules.

Reset your ideas of what is and isn't possible.

Make a list of the conditions in front of you and demolish those walls.

"Ki…hara…"

From his mouth, without any ability to speak, dribbled words.

His feet creaked and groaned as he slowly used them to support himself.

"Kiiihaaaaaaraaaaaaaaaaaaaaaaaaaaaaaaaaaaaaaaaaaaaaaaaaaaa!!"

At that moment, Accelerator used his feet that by all rights couldn't move and began to run.

Straight for his mortal enemy, Amata Kihara.

Even if he had to fight against all the truth in the world, be hurt, and lose everything.

He would protect this one illusion.

9

Amata Kihara's smile began to savagely sink into his face on an even deeper level.

Accelerator was on his feet.

Despite all the pain, despite the beating he'd received, he still shouted Kihara's name and ran forward. As though trying to defend the space behind him.

Like he was trying to save the two girls hidden behind the office desk.

"...Cool," said Kihara, commenting on his enemy who wouldn't fall. His face was filled with a savage glee. "I know, I know!! You'd never go down that fuckin' easy! Glad you've got my interests in mind here, Accelerator! You've been doing nothing but driving me up the fuckin' wall lately. I won't use a gun. I'll beat you to a pulp, then kill youuuuuuuuu!!"

Kihara's mind raced. He howled like a beast, but that didn't stop the strange girl's song, much less Accelerator. She was intensely focused and couldn't see anything around her—she was probably in a state of meditation. Everything around him was shining full of enemies. It was the greatest stage.

A few corpses would make it perfect—but why the fuck are you still alive?!

Kihara met Accelerator's charge head-on. He clenched both fists and cracked his joints. Once his fist was hard as steel, he launched it into Accelerator's face without mercy.

There was a thunderous *wham!!*

The minute creaks and groans of physical stress traveled through Kihara's arm.

And yet...

Accelerator didn't even slow down.

"Oooooooooohhhhhhhhhh-aaaaaaaaaaaaaaaaaaaaaaahhhhhhh!!"

Ignoring his caved-in face, his counterpunch hit Kihara squarely in the face. Kihara's nose broke and he felt an explosion of pain. It went without saying, Accelerator had put everything into his assault.

...Gh...gr!! With a groan, Kihara brought his head back up to return the favor. He tightened his fingers even more. "Ooargh, that didn't do shit, little bastaaaard!!"

His fist slammed into Accelerator's slender face, sending him reeling to the floor. He managed to writhe around there, but Kihara came down with his foot—and the full weight of his body.

It was like being hammered by a huge nail. A booming *whack* resounded. Kihara continued his indecipherable screams, stomping down on Accelerator in one spot after the other. He heard something break, and red fluids scattered.

"Great, now I'm feeling it! My engine's all warmed up! What about you?! You're really something! Maybe you could actually, really save that little brat!"

His amused words didn't affect Accelerator at all. Despite being crumpled on the floor, he knew the glint in his eyes, if nothing else, never waned.

To rescue her. To save the girl from death.

His spirit would not break.

"Haaah!! Haaah!!"

It was such tenacity that Kihara was the one getting out of breath.

"Ha-ha-ha!" He laughed, looking around. Sprawled out on the floor nearby were the bodies of the incompetent Hound Dogs Accelerator had taken down. The guns and other weapons they'd had were on the floor, too. Now that things were getting annoying, he went over to them and stooped down.

"...I'm gonna make things more interesting. Come on, show me some more, will ya?"

He plucked a weapon from the floor and smiled thinly. His face looked like a runner finished with a marathon. Amata Kihara took the item in his hands, then looked at Accelerator, who was still collapsed, and tossed it at him.

It was an antipersonnel grenade with the pin removed.

With his brain function partially gone, the broken and beaten Accelerator didn't have the energy to dodge or bat it away.

With a soft *clunk*, the grenade hit Accelerator's forehead.

The small object didn't even have time to float through the air.

Ka-bam!! The grenade blew. A shock wave and a good amount of shrapnel exploded in all directions, whipping up a gray cloud of smoke. The close range meant one of the shards hit Kihara in the cheek. It dug into his skin sharply like a carving knife. But he was grinning. All he felt was exhilaration.

Silence fell.

Only the meditative sister's long verses echoed through the room.

"Hya…"

He'd won.

"Gya-ha-ha-ha-ha-ha-ha-ha-ha-ha-ha-ha-ha-ha-ha-ha-ha-ha-ha-ha!!"

Kihara roared with laughter from deep within.

Accelerator was dead. That killed him. After all, it exploded not two centimeters from his head. No unarmed person could ever withstand that. A smoky dust cloud was covering him right now, but when it cleared, he would see a mangled body destroyed so badly he wouldn't even be able to tell what had gone where.

The gray cloud the grenade created spread out, thinning as it did. Like a great wave, it flowed past Kihara, blocking the view. When the dust cleared, Accelerator's corpse would appear. The unsightly end would mark the last of Amata Kihara's fight.

Aleister told me not to kill the mass-produced brat, but that means I can do anything else. Guess I'll kill that nun singing the weird song, give the girl both corpses, and break her spirit, thought Kihara with a laugh—

—when there was a *crash!!*

Someone's hand grabbed his face.

"…!!"

They stood in front of him.

He couldn't see who because of all the smoke.

Gah…ah…?!

Thinking normally, it was most probable to be Accelerator. But that didn't make sense to Kihara. Without usage of his ability, he was weaker than most high school kids. Without any tricks up his sleeve, he could never endure a grenade blast at close range.

He didn't think something had brought his "reflection" back, either. Ash clung to the arm grabbing him. If his reflection was working, it would have repelled even the tiniest flecks of dirt.

"Why…?"

But still, there in front of him was Accelerator.

White hair, red eyes, sculpted face, firm skin, slender lines, neck choker, gray clothes, bony limbs, glaring black shoes...

He ignored all those things and screamed:

"What the fuck are those black wings coming out of your back?!"

They looked more like engines than wings.

Blacker than ink, they sucked in even light, those mysterious spurting feathers.

Kihara had seen what an "angel" was. He knew he had been a part in the creation of one. Despite that, unfolding before his eyes was something he couldn't properly identify.

Y-you little...

Accelerator's power was to place all vectors under his control, regardless of type. His ability to talk, his ability to walk, and this "new power"—it all had to be using something in this space for power.

From a scientific standpoint, Accelerator couldn't do any calculations based on natural laws, so he couldn't be controlling that power.

But what about other laws?

In the first place, was his preexisting ability to calculate necessary or even related to grasping unscientific theories?

The occult.

Only scientists of Kihara's caliber would have been aware. After thousands, tens of thousands of scientific experiments, they peeked out a tiny bit every now and again—irregular laws *or something resembling them.*

He gained a new clearance, expanding his zone of control? What the hell kind of values did he enter into his personal reality...? Who the hell did he establish communications with?!

If he had one idea...

If there was one representative of the power filling Academy City...

Involuntary diffusion fields... Wait. No... That angel or whatever... The power source, it's...?!

Unfortunately, he wasn't thinking about it at all.

With a *crack*, Accelerator tightened up his arm, which pressed down on Kihara's skull.

"_____"

And he laughed. Quietly.

"Hah, ha-ha…!" Amata Kihara laughed back despite himself, his arms and legs hanging.

Then he asked it.

"B-behind you…You see that, monster?"

"Ihbfkillwq."

Boom!! The black wings erupted.

An inexplicable, invisible power burst from his palm toward Kihara.

His body left Accelerator's hand, shot through the abandoned office like a bullet, flew out the broken window, and carved a line through the night sky at many times the speed of sound. The extreme speed caused an orange glow of plasma to trail behind him.

Nobody would need to check to see if he was alive.

10

In the middle of the downpour, Kamijou sat on the road. He was already soaking wet, so the rainwater-covered street didn't concern him. Eventually, he felt he'd rested enough, and he exhaled.

The angel's feathers had been silent. The enormous sparks they'd been firing all over were now totally quiet.

…What about Index?

Things must have gone well for her, too. Kazakiri's wings and angel halo hadn't disappeared completely yet, but their shapes were steadily beginning to flicker. *If it were really bad, they wouldn't be doing that. Last Order…I hope that guy on the phone saved her.*

That reminded him.

He took Last Order's cell phone out of his pocket. Despite the current state of Academy City, he should probably call for an ambulance. Using someone else's phone made him feel weird, but now wasn't the time for awkwardness.

As expected, the person who answered told him they might not be able to provide their usual care. That was still far better than doing nothing.

He returned the phone to his pocket and looked around. Kazakiri's appearance had ushered in destruction as far as the eye could see...but thanks to her power, she just barely managed to save the residents in those buildings. Glowing scales were still visible, drifting in the dark.

Maybe I should rescue some of them. On the other hand, his Imagine Breaker could cancel the scales' effect. For now, he couldn't do much but leave them alone.

"Still, though..."

Kamijou looked over at where Vento was lying, very clearly unconscious.

He wanted to ask for a way to wake up the people in Academy City she'd knocked out with her divine judgment spell, but after several slaps to the cheek, she showed no signs of waking.

What would happen to her now? She'd ground the city's functions almost completely to a halt; the city wouldn't let her run loose. And there was all that stuff about the power balance between science and magic. The magic side was the one who broke that, after all.

Maybe they'd crossed the line.

Academy City would try to wipe such dangerous capabilities from the world, even if it meant killing her. On the other hand, God's Right Seat and the Roman Orthodox Church wouldn't let go of such a high-powered spell so easily. Science and magic had held discussions in the past, but it didn't look like that would work this time. It was dangerous, and it might even be the trigger for universal destruction.

Shit...

It was important to look at what Vento had done in the past; he wasn't denying that. But as someone who knew about what had happened to her, he didn't agree with simply executing her or making her into a tool of war. It would be the worst kind of repentance.

Making both science and magic her enemy means she can't run away forever on this cramped planet. But I have to do something. I have to get her to hide, even if it's temporary, at least until the dust settles. Maybe I should ask Tsuchimikado. Whether it'll work, on the other hand...

He couldn't simply hand her over to the English Puritan Church. Vento was far too involved in everything for that. Besides, a mere high school kid couldn't solve a global-scale problem. But he still felt like he had to do something. If he abandoned Vento here, it would leave a bad aftertaste in his mouth.

"For now, guess I'll wait for her to wake up. I punched her pretty hard..."

As for Kazakiri...he looked away from Vento, but Kazakiri didn't react to him. She hadn't changed. Her eyes were kind of empty, and there were still lots of giant wings coming out of her back. As time passed, the wings began to blur, little by little. In fact, the shorter ones were on the verge of losing their form altogether. Index had probably done something to intervene.

But it looked like it would take a while longer for her wings to go away completely.

Kamijou looked at his right hand. If he used it, he could get rid of dozens of those wings just by touching them...maybe. But if Kazakiri herself was affected by it at the same time, it would be in vain. He felt a little bitter about his power not helping in times like these.

Still...

Vento had directed her hate at Kazakiri, which meant Academy City must have caused this. The upper echelons, probably—but what were they after? It didn't seem like they'd created her just to defend and intercept against the randomly appearing Vento. They had a different goal.

Problem after problem, Kamijou said to himself.

Then...

Crash!!

Suddenly, the mountain of concrete in front of him exploded, casting a veil of gray dust over his vision.

*   *   *

"?!"

Kamijou put a hand to his face and took a step back.

These weren't some random pieces of rubble losing their balance and crumbling. The entire pile of wreckage had exploded like somebody threw a bomb at it.

The deluge pushed away the dust in the air.

There, stuck in the ground where the blast had come from, was a wind turbine propeller. It was like someone casually threw it there. About half its pillar portion was buried in the middle of the crater that had blown away the debris. A pillar as big as a telephone pole.

What kind of ridiculous strength would you need to *do* that?

!! ...Where's Vento?! He quickly scanned his surroundings.

Vento, who had just been unconscious right next to him, was nowhere in sight.

Instead, Kamijou spotted something else—a single man, standing a short distance away.

"Who are you?!" Kamijou shouted aggressively, for the man was holding the limp Vento in one hand.

He wore a short-sleeve white shirt over a long-sleeve blue shirt. On his legs were breathable, thin slacks. It was a sporty look, but it lacked energy. It reminded him of the clothes middle-aged male golfers liked. With his chic black umbrella, he gave off a presence quieter and more unyielding than a high school student like Kamijou could muster.

But in the face of all this disaster, his distinct lack of tension was scary instead. His pale skin and brown hair—everything looked like a sharp blade.

"Excuse me," said the man in fluent Japanese. "I need something from this girl. I blinded you to avoid violence. Have I offended you?"

"I asked who you are!"

"Acqua of the Back. Like Vento, I'm with God's Right Seat."

The man didn't hesitate to name himself, and the one he gave put Kamijou even more on his guard.

He didn't know the hierarchy in God's Right Seat, but simply assuming he possessed equal strength to Vento meant this was really bad. Academy City was completely exhausted. If a second wave came, it wouldn't recover.

As Kamijou stood there, tense and trembling, Acqua smiled slightly. It was a very strange expression for a man who looked so stalwart.

"You needn't worry. Pointless troop losses are undesirable. I will retreat for today—it would clearly be reckless to fight that 'fallen angel' at your back. At least, not until we're ready."

On the other hand, once he was ready, he could fight it. That brought another level of harshness to Kamijou's stare, but it didn't cause the man to react.

"It seems to have already lost the sorcery-destroying effect that caused Vento this pain, but we have our own business to take care of." The man exhaled, casting a glance at Hyouka Kazakiri, standing still a distance away.

He knew one thing about angels: Even Kaori Kanzaki could only so much as equal it. It seemed like it was a gamble even for this God's Right Seat group.

Whatever the case, Kamijou wouldn't care one bit if Acqua shut up and went home.

But...

"Let Vento go."

Kamijou flung those words at Acqua.

"...You plan on getting from her a way to save the wounded in Academy City?"

"That too," Kamijou answered—meaning that wasn't all. "Her hostility toward science is just a misunderstanding. Deep down, she knows that, too. But she can't ever get away from those feelings because she's with your shitty God's Right Seat or whatever!"

"Vento's darkness is not that easily dispelled," answered Acqua, discontent. "God's Right Seat does not offer aid to simply misfortunate girls out of pity. We exist to affect the world. Vento has decided to stay true to her own way of life, even to the point of using such power. And do you know how much she's paid for it? Can you imagine how vast that power is?"

Now that he said something, the reasons Vento acted didn't involve bringing any results to her organization. Which meant in order to remain in that organization, she'd have needed to constantly prove her worth.

Kamijou thought for just a moment. Thinking, though, was too simple to let him understand her feelings.

"...Why does that matter?"

"What?"

"Just because you can't get someone to listen, you're not supposed to say anything?"

Kamijou looked Acqua straight in the eyes.

Of course, unlike Kamijou, Acqua seemed quite relaxed. He snorted. "If I were to release Vento, were the science side to capture her, she would certainly face execution."

"!!" Those words made Kamijou freeze.

Acqua smiled more deeply at him—the way an adult might look at someone after reading someone's wish tag for Tanabata, the July festival where people wrote their hopes on slips of paper decoration.

"This is for you."

With a flick of the wrist, something flew toward Kamijou. He took it. It was the chain and the cross accessory that had been attached to Vento's tongue.

"In any case, she doesn't need it—your right hand destroyed it. It's a piece of junk. Now that it's broken, Vento cannot use her 'divine judgment' anymore. Those affected should recover soon. Rest easy in the knowledge that you have protected Academy City."

"Wait!! You think that'll convince me?!"

Kamijou clenched his fist, but Acqua wasn't going to take him up on it.

"Allow me to tell you one thing."

Boldly, the man turned his back, then said this:

*   *   *

"I am a saint. Challenge me blindly, and you will pay with your life."

With a tremendous *bang*, the man kicked off the ground.

Kamijou blinked, and Acqua and Vento were both gone. He couldn't even tell what direction he'd run. Or maybe he flew up. All he knew was that this guy's speed was on a whole different level.

The battle was over, but the problems weren't solved.

In fact, he felt like they were inviting an even bigger battle.

...I'll stop them.

The Roman Orthodox Church.

Academy City.

Damn it. I'll stop where this is going, I swear...

Amid the torrential rainfall, Kamijou gazed at the night sky and made the oath to himself.

The dark clouds showed no signs of clearing.

EPILOGUE

To Our Paths of Positive and Negative

The_Branch_Road.

With Vento's body in his arms, Acqua left Academy City.

Her Soul Arm destroyed, the city residents would begin sequentially waking up. The spell left no aftereffects; it just neutralized enemies. In a way, it was the perfect spell for mass pacification, but now it was gone, too.

From this point on, they couldn't be so optimistic.

The next time there was a clash, great amounts of blood would be shed.

"What a sad state of world affairs," lamented Acqua, sounding gloomy indeed. He shifted his unconscious associate in his arms.

He looked down at his hands in exasperation—one held his umbrella, the other Vento herself—then threw the umbrella to the side. For one whose name implied the attribute of water, as soon as the downpour hit him in the face, he wore quite the grimace.

A familiar number had just come up on his cell phone screen.

"Terra?"

"Yes, this is Terra of the Left. Have you finished over there, Acqua?"

The voice was grating, like metal rubbing against metal. He spoke politely, even a little jovially.

Acqua glanced at the woman in his arm. "Vento's down. I've just picked her up and ordered the other units outside Academy City to withdraw. We suffered over seventy percent casualties; hence, we will temporarily suspend our pursuit of Touma Kamijou and our attack on Academy City. It's all according to the list you designated beforehand of possible methods of resistance." He paused. "Though we didn't expect to be beaten this badly, especially considering the 'angel' being incomplete."

"Good work out there."

"No reprimand?"

"What would come of acting hostile to you, not to mention Vento? Of course, if she fell, it's highly possible her Soul Arm is done for, too."

"You don't sound frustrated."

"Well, her 'divine judgment' does spring from her property, Uriel. Frankly, losing a single Soul Arm doesn't frustrate me. We are, after all, quite different from ordinary sorcerers. We can't use any that aren't individually tuned for us. I am of Raphael; the tool would mean nothing in my hands, so what value does it have? You must understand that as well, being of Gabriel."

That made Acqua sigh. Everyone in God's Right Seat was so self-centered. "I've recovered Vento. What about the other forces I couldn't contact?"

"The fallen angel in question—its attack wiped them out."

"Though not up to our level, they were strong, were they not? And there were many of them. Were they really—?"

"Annihilated? Yep," came the smooth answer. "Of course, Academy City appears to have picked up the ones fanned out inside Academy City for local interception."

Acqua paused for a moment. "Then our pawns have died."

"They are badly wounded physically, of course, but also quite so mentally. They're barely alive. It would be simpler to supply more people rather than regroup with them."

Which meant he was considering taking advantage of the Roman Orthodox Church's most unique trait—its two billion followers. Acqua adjusted Vento at his side and said, "Then I'll gather up the wreckage."

"You? A member of the God's Right Seat, assigned to corpse collection duty?"

"I'm already carrying the defeated. It isn't much extra work. Even if there was significantly more wreckage, I could tolerate it. And if there is any chance they still live, it would be a nice bonus."

"How kind of you."

"I'll recover them alive or dead. I only mean to have those who can walk do so. It's less work for me that way," said Acqua with a disinterested sniff. Then, pelted by rain, he continued. "What comes next? I could always return now and take the head of our target."

"No, let's stop here. You saw it too, right, Acqua? Rumor has it some interesting information is flying around. I think we should find out the details and rethink how we're going to bring down Academy City."

"…To bring down Academy City…"

"Does that not suit your liking?"

"I've withdrawn in deference to your viewpoint, but I still feel it would be faster if I went back into the city alone, right now, and slayed Touma Kamijou and Aleister. I don't like parlor tricks. It's obviously easier to strike down those who must be defeated in a fair fight. I would be able to keep civilian casualties to a minimum, too."

"Well, well. Now I wonder. Crushing them would be a simple matter, but don't you think we can use them to our advantage? That fallen angel, for example. Isn't that a factor made specifically with God's Right Seat in mind?"

"…"

"I'd like to keep the enemies we need to defeat and those we should let remain in separate piles. Doing this now would be like starting a battle in a museum, wouldn't it?"

"I cannot agree with acts of plundering on the battlefield."

"Yes, right. How very much like a former knight. The tongues of nobles are ever silver. They say such different things than the rest of us."

"I am no knight. I am a has-been mercenary, a crook."

"A crook who cares about morals on the battlefield. In any case, please bring Vento back here at once, all right? This order comes from Fiamma of the Right, as well."

"Understood."

Acqua ended the call, then took one last look behind him at Academy City.

———*Crushing them would be a simple matter.*

———*I'd like to keep the enemies we need to defeat and those we should let remain in separate piles.*

After ruminating on Terra's words, he remembered something another person had said:

"Let Vento go."

Words from the young man he'd met a short while ago.

"Her hostility toward science is just a misunderstanding. Deep down, she knows that, too. But she can't ever get away from those feelings because she's with your shitty God's Right Seat or whatever!"

The thoughts of an enemy. One he would undoubtedly aim his sword at in the future.

"I must wonder...," Acqua said to himself, picking up the discarded umbrella—and remembering the face of his target, who even worried over his enemies' circumstances. "Is Academy City really as weak as you seem to think, Terra of the Left?"

"!!"

Touma Kamijou watched the great angel.

Had Index finished? The dozens of wings connected to Kazakiri's back were beginning to disappear into thin air, one after another. The ten-meter ones and the hundred-meter ones—everything vanished at the same speed. The angel lost her wings with even intervals between, like a countdown. And finally, the last one disappeared.

"She did it...Index really did it!!"

Tap.

Hyouka Kazakiri fell to her knees, limp, and then to the side. Her long hair traced after her slow movements.

"Kazakiri!!" shouted Kamijou, running over to her. Unfortunately, thanks to his right hand's Imagine Breaker, picking her up would be dangerous. As he stood trapped by impatience, Kazakiri put a hand to the wet ground and, wobbling, sat up.

"Thank goodness you're safe...," said Kamijou, all the more relieved for his lack of ability to help. He didn't know what he would have done if she couldn't get up on her own. "Does it hurt anywhere? You went through a lot. Index handled things, so you should be fine, but check yourself anyway. She was really worried, too, so if you're all good, we should finish what we need to, check on everyone else, and then go see Index."

Kamijou finally seemed to relax, but Kazakiri made a mystified face and said, "No..."

"Huh?"

"This isn't...good at all..." Her lips trembled as they moved.

She wasn't looking at him, but he knew what she was gazing at—the utterly devastated cityscape around them. And she was ignoring the rest: her losing control and being sucked into the utterly inexplicable situation with the "angel."

"...How...did this happen...?"

This was the city she always longed for. Now it had been smashed into oblivion—right before her eyes.

"It's all...my fault. If I hadn't been here, at least nobody nearby would have been hurt. Why am I the only one unharmed? This is... This is crazy, isn't it?"

"..."

"What the hell am I supposed to be?! I can't be with everyone else, and if I even try, everything breaks like this! Why was I even born?! I'm just being held together by involuntary diffusion fields! I'm a monster that only exists because of the espers' power!!"

Her own thoughts were probably too scattered to know what she was saying or what she was trying to say. That's how much pain this disastrous scene made her feel.

But she still felt it.

"She finally called me a friend, and I thought that made me more human. Then those wings grew, those violent sparks flew, and I crushed everything! I really am nothing but a monster, aren't I?! I hate this. Please, punch me and make this all end!!"

Kazakiri knew exactly what would happen if Kamijou's right hand touched her—a conglomeration of involuntary diffusion fields. She said it anyway.

What do you mean, monster? thought Kamijou.

Trembling so hard but not pleading for her life, instead worrying about everyone. What part of that was monstrous? All Kamijou could do was make a fist and get into fights with people. She was far more "human" than he was.

When he thought that, he couldn't help but grin a little.

"...Wh-why...why are you making that face?"

"I'm relieved," he said curtly. "I can't accept your request. I don't know why I have this kind of power. But I do know I can't use it for that. If it's meant for erasing my friends, then I'd rather cut the damn thing off right now."

Those words opened Kazakiri's eyes—he had called her a friend.

"But...why...?"

"I don't really know, either. You made those glowing scale things, right? Didn't you just protect everyone? You didn't know what was happening to you, didn't know what would happen after this, but you still did your best to protect them. Is that different somehow from what you think 'humans' are? Do you still not have enough 'human' in you after all that?"

Kazakiri couldn't say anything.

As the rain came down, only Kamijou's words continued. "You're a way better 'human' than a failure of a high school student like me. That's something you can be proud of, so stick out your chest. Look forward. You fought for people you've never even met, and you protected them all. You don't have a reason to look down right now."

But Hyouka Kazakiri still couldn't look up.

He heard a sniffle.

Smiling a little, he looked away from her and into the distance. They'd solved the problem, so he wanted to get back to Index. Unfortunately, she still had his cell phone. He didn't have a way to contact her. Before, he'd used Last Order's, but that was for a rescue, not personal conversation.

"Well, anyway. I think things will be fine thanks to your scales, but let's check around to see if anyone needs first aid. From what I heard, the city's functions should come back up soon, and then they'll start rescue operations, so it's not a big deal, but still." He spoke optimistically. "Once we're done, let's go home. Index will probably go back to the dorm in the meantime. I don't know when you'll disappear, and if I don't get you to her quickly, she'll probably get really mad." He paused. "Oh, this is the first time you'd be coming to my dorm. I hope you can put up with a little mess."

"Uh, ah…?" Kazakiri tried to ask a question, but between her sobs and hiccups, she couldn't get it out.

Kamijou smiled anyway and answered. "Don't start asking why now. It's because we're friends, obviously."

Accelerator leaned against the desk in the abandoned office.

"Are…are you okay?"

Scampering up to him was Index, who had come out of her meditative trance for the song. Of course, Accelerator couldn't understand anyone right now. All he could grasp, from her expression and voice volume, was that she was worried.

Index checked over his wounds, then stared hard at Accelerator's back, patting him with her pale hands a few times. "??? …Nothing here…?"

She knew she'd seen demonic wings coming out of him, but there was no sign it ever happened. No tears in his clothing, either.

She began to mutter. "…The field closely resembled Telesma but with a completely different substance. Applications of demonology are treated differently than normal Telesma anyway…I'm not sure if even a saint could muster up that volume of power…"

"Hey! So what the heck happened?! You haven't said anything since you were singing! Those gigantic feathers are gone, I think. Does that mean everything's okay now?! I took care of all the black-suits, so I can come over there if you need help with something!!"

At the voice from the cell phone, her face jerked up. She must have been prioritizing Accelerator's and Last Order's physical problems.

"W-wait just a little while. I'm going to call a doctor!! She'll be fine, so you can't die, either!!"

"H-hey, are you even listening to me?!"

Index burst out of the abandoned office. Accelerator lazily watched her go.

...Aahh, uhh...urgh...

He couldn't make out an ounce of what she'd said, but something was more important right now.

He turned his head.

On the filthy floor under the desk lay Last Order's limp body. He couldn't tell if she'd been saved or not. The angel havoc out the window had quieted for now, but without any calculation ability, he couldn't link the angel's disappearance with changes in Last Order's situation.

Was she all right? What happened to the virus? Should he call a doctor? These were the things a normal person would have thought. But without any battery left in his electrode, he couldn't organize even simple thoughts. His body was a wreck from the battle, too, and he couldn't get it to move much.

Then he heard a new set of footsteps.

They weren't Index's. There were several of them.

"Accelerator. We have something to discuss. Is that acceptable?"

Even in his current state, Accelerator could understand the voice. It wasn't coming through his ears. It was some kind of ability, communicating directly with his brain.

He looked that way just as several people entered the abandoned office. Each figure was two sizes larger than a normal adult male. They seemed to have nonmetal material on them, reaching from their crowns to their soles. The material had cracks in it for turning all the joints. The lines of the head, neck, and shoulders connected smoothly as one object. Those thin backpack-looking things on their backs must have been batteries. Every time they moved a limb, he heard soft motor sounds.

They were powered suits.

In their armor, short and stout, they were watching Accelerator with countless cameras, their domed heads swiveled at him. He heard high-pitched squeals, as though they were autofocusing.

After having "thought" that far, Accelerator frowned.

...My...calculation ability...?

It had returned, to an extent. It was far from what he needed for his power, but it was enough to compose normal thoughts for daily life.

Now that Accelerator had regained the ability to process "questions," for the first time in a long time, one of the people spoke. That person was the only one not in a powered suit. Instead, it was a slender figure, clad in slim black clothing. The face was hidden, though, so Accelerator couldn't tell the person's gender.

"We are using several techniques of telepathy right now. By linking our language and calculation abilities with you, we can sustain a very temporary state that makes dialogue possible. We should be able to understand any words from your end, too. Oh, but your supernatural ability is out of the question. We can't compensate for your personal reality."

"...An esper?" said Accelerator, his expression one of gloom.

"We, too, have jobs 'outside,' you see. Our recovery team is currently rescuing Motoharu Tsuchimikado and others, but we returned 'inside' as soon as we could."

Accelerator sucked his teeth in irritation.

Leaving aside the exception of the Sisters, he'd never heard of any special forces using both firearms and abilities. He thought Judgment only ever touched them once in a while for training. They were probably more dangerous than the Hound Dogs led by Amata Kihara. On top of that, they'd accurately tracked both Accelerator and Kihara. If not, they couldn't have walked in exactly when the battle ended.

They, more than likely, were an even deeper part of Academy City—darkness within the darkness.

Accelerator had finally made contact with them.

"What do you want?"

"We have something important to discuss."

"Guess I'll listen, but I've got a question. Answer it first."

"What is it?" answered the man lightly.

He spoke. "What happened to Last Order? The virus?"

"It's stopped temporarily but not in an orderly fashion. As an analogy, one of the gears has been taken out, so nothing can work. In the end, that was all they were able to do. We've stopped the virus's rate of progress, though, so with a Testament it is possible to readjust her..."

"Don't you fucking dare! I know a good doctor and scientist already!!"

"I see. There is no problem leaving things to them."

Accelerator spat on the ground. It looked like he already knew all about his combat potential, pawns, and personal relationships.

"...What do you really want?"

"Thank you for being cooperative," answered the man politely. "We wanted to talk about the string of occurrences you've caused as of late, as well as the damages Academy City sustained."

"..."

"Allow me to continue. First, the financial problem. Physical damages to buildings and facilities, medical care and replenishment of wounded Hound Dog personnel, information control expenses for the public—all said and done, we must request from you approximately eight trillion yen. Next, with regards to your assault on one of the General Board members, Thomas Platinaberg..."

The man went on to explain at length, but his tone was one of levity. Accelerator returned his stare with a look of annoyance. "You gonna cut me up and make me a test subject as payment?"

"That is an option, but we'd like to propose a different path." The man raised his index finger. "Would you be interested in joining us?"

"What?"

"I believe this is a realistic proposition, as your power can easily be used for military purposes. After all, the value of the war industry has been inflating. How much do you think a single jet, a single ship costs? Well, if you do the work of, say, a fleet, eight trillion yen is within the realm of payment. It will take some time, though."

Accelerator clicked his tongue again. "What the hell's Academy City so impatient for? They want to start swinging around a guy like me, after I did all this? The idea's insane. You tryin' to start a war or something?"

"We cannot answer that."

"Right. Whatever the answer is, I already know mine."

He leveled a glare at the man.

"...Don't fuck with me."

"I see."

"Reparations for losses? Damages to Academy City? The real reason for all that is shitheads like you getting together into your shitty little groups!!" roared Accelerator, still sitting with his back against the office desk. "After everything you've done to us, why the hell should we do anything you say?! You want me to fucking kill you?! This is the part where you should be apologizing to me! I don't know what you've been scrambling around behind the scenes doing, but don't get me or that brat mixed up in it!!"

It was a sound argument.

One from the mouth of someone who shouldn't have been able to make it.

"This is Academy City's moment of truth."

"...Are you even listening to me?"

"What I mean is, if things go poorly, *it could fall.* We want to oppose that, and we'd like you to help us. We won't force you, but it's something to think over. If Academy City disappeared completely, would there be a place for espers like us? Or *its other technology,* for that matter?"

"_____"

Ten thousand mass-produced espers for military purposes, forbidden by international law, disallowed even within Academy City. They didn't have a place "outside." If things went sour, they could wind up at even crueler military research establishments. After all, Last Order and the rest of them were valuable enough that some kind of huge plan revolved around them.

For the sake of the girl he had to protect and the scenery she loved, Academy City needed to exist. He didn't know who the enemy was, but he couldn't let them destroy this place before his eyes. However ugly it was, Academy City was the world of such small, young children.

The "teachers," the General Board, were dirty, but without them, the "school" of Academy City couldn't continue running. And no matter how much a certain student rampaged, he wouldn't be able to solve that problem.

In the end, there was only one path to take.

He clicked his tongue and made up his mind, then looked at the man before him.

"Tell me one thing."

"What is it?"

"The name of the one behind all this. I've got an idea but no proof. So tell me. Whoever controlled that brat like his puppet—I'll rip off his head. That sound good for the contract's terms?"

"I could answer you, but they are no more than a scapegoat."

Accelerator fell silent for a moment. "…I get it. Somebody valuable enough to refrain from answering, eh?"

"Anyway, *what will you do*?"

"Do whatever you want, I don't care."

"A good response."

The man removed the pistol at his waist, then put its muzzle up against the sitting Accelerator's chest.

"I look forward to working with you, newcomer."

Bang!! Boom!! A series of gunshots rang out.

Rubber riot-suppression bullets pumped into him, and he fell to the floor. As the man returned the pistol to its holster, he gave instructions to those around him.

"We're pulling out. Get rid of all traces of the battle. Carry the wounded via route B and Accelerator via route G."

Two men grabbed the unconscious Accelerator's hands and began to drag him away.

After finally having found a tiny light, he plunged into the darkness once again.

This time, so deep he would never be able to crawl back out.

The frog-faced doctor had returned to the hospital.

Doing so had required a lot of advance preparation, of course. Having the Sisters be the first ones into the building and checking for any good-bye presents, like enemy ambushes or bombs, had taken over an hour.

Never thought I'd be making my patients do work. He sighed, actually a little disgusted. In the future, maybe he should properly employ people to be his hands and feet.

He'd finished administering to the most important wounded people in the unique, tourist-bus-sized ambulances, or hospital cars. After checking on the empty beds, they'd returned each patient to their room...and he'd finally gotten to a point where he could take a break.

He now sat in the chair in his clinic, mindlessly staring at the ceiling for a while.

Eventually, he reached for a phone on his desk.

After pushing the external call button, he pressed the pound key a number of times. The act seemed random, but there was actually a certain rhythm to it. After that, he began punching in a special number.

When he put the receiver to his ear, he didn't hear the normal call tone. It had put him through almost immediately.

"Good morning, Aleister. How do you feel after letting yourself loose for a while?"

"Oh, no, no. I've just shifted to phase two at last. It's too early to call this 'letting loose.'"

The sound quality was surprisingly clear, to the point where it was dubious he was using the same phone lines. It would have been more convincing if someone had told the doctor it used completely separate cables.

But the frog-faced doctor was used to it. He'd mentioned this to Accelerator, too—how he was more experienced in the world of darkness.

"Too early, hmm? How long do you plan on ordering Accelerator and Last Order about?"

"Who knows? More worrying is whether they'll last until the end. I've finally just finished the work of putting involuntary diffusion field value settings into the vector control device, but the other is not...quite complete. There is a way to combine the Accelerator, the Last Order, and the Fuse Kazakiri into one, but that is too optimistic. I must go beyond that."

"To something beyond Level Six..."

"If not, the trouble of inviting the Imagine Breaker in from outside would be worthless."

"Aleister. I have something I need to say to you, hmm?"

"And what's that?"

"I'd appreciate it if you didn't use my patients as toys."

"Heh," came the laugh in response. The doctor remained silent, and the General Board chairperson spoke. "What will you do if I say no? Or rather, what could you do?"

"I know," said the frog-faced doctor quietly in his clinic, pitch-black, no lights on. Nobody could see his expression. "What could I do to you, now that you have this much power...? I know that, too.

"But, you see," spoke the doctor, "those children are still my patients."

"..."

"And I am a doctor. Aleister, whoever you may be, you cannot twist that fact. You understand my resolve, right?"

The frog-faced doctor gripped the receiver more tightly.

Then, in a low, quiet voice, he said:

*　　*　　*

"Your life—I saved it, after all."

Silence filled the dark clinic.

Both the frog-faced doctor and Aleister stayed silent for a short while.

Eventually, Aleister spoke up. "...I truly was on the verge of death back then."

The doctor frowned at that—as though the very situation of demanding gratitude pained him.

"It was a remote place in England. I was on the run from a sorcerer-hunting group sponsored by the state religion, lying on the ground like a torn-up old bag. You stitched me together, protected me from that nation, gave me a life-support device, introduced me to this place called Japan, and helped me create this institution called Academy City. *All of it was thanks to you.*"

"..."

"Do you regret it?"

"Are you asking seriously?"

"Now is your only chance to stop my life-support device from a distance."

"If you're trying to make fun of me, I'd appreciate it if you'd stop that."

"I see." Aleister sounded like he'd smiled. "I must make even you an enemy, even after your kind words."

"..."

"I've made many enemies—one of the most stringent factions of Crossism, the golden sorcerer's society said to be highest in the world, and many others, from states to families...To think after all this time, there was still something I could lose."

"Is your intent still the same?"

"You know my reasons."

"...I do."

"I cannot stop. The time for that has passed."

A distinct farewell.

It was a sad thing. All the more so because he hadn't been an enemy to start with.

Last of all, Aleister said this:

"This is good-bye, my kind, gentle enemy."

The call ended.

The final slender line of connection went away, leaving only a simple electronic tone.

The frog-faced doctor sat still for a good ten seconds.

Then, slowly, he lowered the receiver.

In his clinic, dark with no illumination, he sighed to himself.

You haven't forgotten, have you, Aleister?

The doctor glanced out the window. He couldn't see it from here, but a windowless building was in that direction.

His back was so small.

It had no presence, that tiny back of his, as he thought silently.

You, too, are one of my patients.

On that day, Academy City officially acknowledged the existence of sorcery-related groups.

Their reports described that outside Academy City, the Roman Orthodox Church *possessed a scientific supernatural-ability development facility under the code name of "sorcery,"* and it had attacked them. Within the day, the topic was all over the news in every country in the world.

Meanwhile, the Roman Orthodox Church confirmed the presence of an angel inside Academy City. The Roman pope himself criticized the city for conducting inhumane research violating Crossist religious precepts.

Each dismissed the other's allegations as absurd, using only their own to attack the enemy with. Not a gram of negotiation or compromise could be seen, and it even looked to some as though each wished for this conflict to escalate.

*   *   *

The war was about to begin.

An all-out confrontation between Academy City and the Roman Orthodox Church.

A vast, all-encompassing war—one that could become the third of its kind.

AFTERWORD

To those of you reading one volume at a time, thank you very much.

To those of you who read all thirteen in one go, seriously, thank you very much.

I'm Kazuma Kamachi.

And so, the uniform changing is over! This one was full of battles, wasn't it? Not a single heartwarming scene to be found. Fighting this way, fighting that way—but once in a while, a sanguine atmosphere like this is all right, I think.

I wanted to write about the protagonists and enemy characters, each with two organizations, going in completely different directions from each other. But if the protagonist had been swapped, then maybe the enemies would have been treated differently. Of course, maybe it wouldn't even have been a contest at all.

The occult keyword for this book was "angel." However, that doesn't mean it was a clear "sorcery story" or "science story" like it has been until now. Rather than simply having two viewpoints or two separate incidents, I wanted to blur the walls separating them.

If you have the chance and some time, you may find it interesting to look into where and how big those walls were and how many of those walls have, in fact, been blurred. One can express the number of those walls in terms of the defensive "walls" between organizations, as well. You should be able to glean some info about the larger, worldwide movements that I haven't actually touched on very much in this work.

* * *

I'd like to thank my illustrator, Mr. Haimura, and my editor, Mr. Miki. The series composition of sometimes-totally-comedy and sometimes-totally-battle has been quite an adventure, so thank you very much for sticking with me.

And a thanks to all my readers. I can't do much but apologize to those of you wanting comedy this time, but thank you so much for coming this far on the adventure anyway.

Now then, as I close the pages on this book,

and as I think to myself how nice it would be to have your support for the next pages as soon as possible,

today, at this hour, I lay down my pen.

When will their paths intersect once more?

Kazuma Kamachi

Discover the other side of Magic High School—read the light novel!

The Irregular at Magic High School

VOLUMES 1-5 AVAILABLE NOW!

Explore the world from Tatsuya's perspective as he and Miyuki navigate the perils of First High and more! Read about adventures only hinted at in *The Honor Student at Magic High School*, and learn more about all your favorite characters. This is the original story that spawned a franchise!

HAVE YOU BEEN TURNED ON TO LIGHT NOVELS YET?

SWORD ART ONLINE, VOL. 1–11
SWORD ART ONLINE, PROGRESSIVE 1–4

The chart-topping light novel series that spawned the explosively popular anime and manga adaptations!

MANGA ADAPTATION AVAILABLE NOW!

SWORD ART ONLINE © Reki Kawahara ILLUSTRATION: abec
KADOKAWA CORPORATION ASCII MEDIA WORKS

ACCEL WORLD, VOL. 1–11

Prepare to accelerate with an action-packed cyber-thriller from the bestselling author of *Sword Art Online*.

MANGA ADAPTATION AVAILABLE NOW!

ACCEL WORLD © Reki Kawahara ILLUSTRATION: HIMA
KADOKAWA CORPORATION ASCII MEDIA WORKS

SPICE AND WOLF, VOL. 1–18

A disgruntled goddess joins a traveling merchant in this light novel series that inspired the *New York Times* bestselling manga.

MANGA ADAPTATION AVAILABLE NOW!

SPICE AND WOLF © Isuna Hasekura ILLUSTRATION: Jyuu Ayakura
KADOKAWA CORPORATION ASCII MEDIA WORKS